More praise for *Patty Jane's House of Curl*

"Lorna Landvik stands by her characters...embracing their eccentricities, delighting in their accomplishments, forgiving them their failings. She knows these people and loves them—and gives us their story with uncommon wit and charm and, best of all, a wonderful sense of mischief."

—Steven Zaillian
Oscar-winning writer of
the screenplay for *Schindler's List*

"*Patty Jane's House of Curl* is the story of women 'who were lucky enough to find a place where they could not only talk, but be heard.' Like Ione's famous coffee cakes, the frosting may be treacle-sweet, but underneath there's something substatial."

—*The Dallas Morning News*

"Perky and life-affirming describe this well-done first novel."

—*The Free Lance-Star*

"Funny and romantic...Peopled with characters so real, so warm, so funny, the book could be a *Northern Exposure* in print....Readers will be reminded that this is what it is like to live."

—*The Stuart News*

"Landvik portrays the vicissitudes of life, the bonding of women, and the ties of family....Always amusing."

—*Library Journal*

"A very funny and often poignant reading experience."

—*Star Tribune*

"Elaborately crafted...Satisfying."

—*Kirkus Reviews*

Patty Jane's
House of Curl

◆

A Novel

Lorna Landvik

Fawcett Columbine
New York

A Fawcett Columbine Book
Published by Ballantine Books

This book is a work of fiction. Names, characters, places, and incidents are either
products of the author's imagination or are used fictitiously.

Acknowledgment is made to the following for permission to reprint song titles
and/or lines:

Cromwell Music, Inc., New York, NY, for "Mockin' Bird Hill," words and music by
Vaughn Horton, TRO–, copyright © 1949, used by permission.
Hanover Music Corp., Beverly Hills, CA, and Howard Music, Northampton, MA, for
"Shrimp Boats," copyright © 1951, used by permission.
Range Road Music, Inc., New York, NY, and Quartet Music, Inc., Los Angeles, CA, for
"What a Wonderful World," by George David Weiss, Bob Thiele, copyright ©
1967, used by permission.

Cover photograph © Jim Boeder/Tony Stone Images

http://www.randomhouse.com

Library of Congress Catalog Card Number: 96-96506

ISBN: 449-91100-4

Patty Jane's House of Curl was originally published by Bridge Works Publishing
Company.

Manufactured in the United States of America

First Ballantine Books Edition: September 1996

10 9 8

To Charles Gabrielson
My lucky stars were shining the night I met you.
and
To the memory of My Father
Glen Wallace Landvik
Who laughed at my jokes and always waited up for me.

Acknowledgments

Tusen takk to the many who have helped along the way; to those who read this book in manuscript form: Greg Triggs, Tom and EmiJo Winner, Renee Albert, Ginny Eckstein, Patricia Weaver Francisco, Roger Larson, Kimberly Hoffer and Susan Rolandelli; to Shelly Haagenson and her son Tim for the nice childcare arrangement we shared during the writing of this book; to the public libraries of Minneapolis, particularly the Nokomis branch and its helpful staff: Mary, Lucy, Pat and Mary; to my cosmic twin, Lori Naslund, and pal, Betty Lou Henson for the years of friendship and laughter; to Diane Sasaki for her belief; to Mike Sobota for his generosity; to Alexandra Shelley for her editorial assistance; to Betsy Nolan, my friend and agent for long-distance handholding; and to Warren and Barbara Phillips, for taking my dream to the printer. Finally, to my mother, The Amazing Ollie, to Evie, my mother-in-law, to my daughters Harleigh and Kinga, and to my husband Chuck — thanks for everything.

Patty Jane's House of Curl

Prologue

Patty Jane kept a drawer full of cotton bandanas spritzed with dimestore perfume — Tabu and Evening in Paris and, occasionally, My Sin, which I thought was as chic as chic could get. I helped out at the House of Curl after school and on Saturdays. Whenever anyone stank up the place with a permanent wave, I would be called upon to distribute the bandanas and tie them carefully, the way a nurse ties a doctor's surgical mask, over the nose and mouth of our customers. Everyone in the shop wore them (except for Clyde Chuka, the manicurist, who said Tabu gave him a worse headache than permanent-wave solution) so that the room looked overtaken by a bunch of Old West bandits assembled for a Dippety-Doo heist.

"Scented kerchiefs are just one of the nice touches that separates our establishment from the others," Patty Jane often said. Other nice touches included homemade banana bread served with coffee to women basting under hair dryers; pale green smocks monogrammed with the initials of our regulars (we kept a supply of less personalized smocks — "V.I.P." and "First Lady" — on hand for walk-ins); and harp concerts courtesy of my Aunt Harriet, whose accompaniment to my bandana distribution was always the *William Tell Overture*.

Patty Jane, my mother, was big on nice touches.

"For cripes' sake," she said, "if you can't be a class act, why bother?"

She studied what society news was to be found in the *Minneapolis Star* as if she were a candidate for a PhD in High Living; she drove her rattly old DeSoto around Lake of the Isles, picking out mansions she would live in were her inheritance more sizable than a pair of turquoise cuff links and an incomplete set of 1947 *World Books*; she tried on designer dresses at Dayton's Oval Room and Powers and then had my grandmother sew up copies on her heavy black Pfaff sewing machine.

"Just because my life began in the bargain basement," she said, "doesn't mean I can't take the escalator up to Fine Crystals."

Truth be told, if my mother were to spend any time in Fine Crystals, it was guaranteed something would break.

Once we were eating hot dogs downtown at Kresges and she suddenly nudged me so violently that the chocolate phosphate I was drinking took a nosedive down the front of my poor-boy sweater. She reached over, tugged a few napkins out of the dispenser and handed them to me, never taking her eyes off the object of her interest — some guy standing at the record bin, flipping through the 45s. Patty Jane made a sound like someone who had just gone off a diet and now stood at the head of a smorgasbord line.

"Put a handsome man in a well-cut suit and can you doubt that God's in his heavens?"

I sighed. "Remember, Mom. I'm just a child."

"We all are, hon. Some of us are just taller."

I got back to swabbing my deck. I was a follower of the seventh-grade credo advising, "What nature's forgotten, stuff with cotton," and now I gave my mother a dirty look for sabotaging my dimensions. She was too busy winking at the guy by the records to notice.

A flush rose to my cheeks as the man strolled over to the counter. He rapped his knuckles on the formica top and lifted his hand with a magician's flourish, leaving behind a business card.

"I'm married," he said to my mother, tipping his head to admire the scenery her miniskirt offered, "but I always enjoy the appreciation of a pretty woman."

He gave a little growl and wiggled his eyebrows, then swaggered out the revolving door.

"What a sap," said Patty Jane. Without reading it, she tore the card into little white squares and sprinkled them into the ashtray. "His wife'll catch him one day," she said. "And when she does . . . well, you'd be surprised how loud men can cry." Her eyes focused on the fuchsia liquid sloshing back and forth in the tank of the Tropical Punch machine. When she turned to me, she looked surprised.

"Well, you've really gone and soaked yourself, haven't you?" She tilted her head and appraised an area unused to much appraisal. "Pilot to copilot," she said, making a megaphone out of her hands, "You're losing altitude."

"Gee, Mother, tell me something I don't know," I said with all the dignity a damp twelve-year-old could muster. I had a brief fantasy of flinging the remaining phosphate at my mother's own slightly padded chest, but instead I picked up the check and paid for it with the five-dollar bill Grandma had slipped into my coat pocket.

I was my Grandma Ione's pet and, for years, the only one happy to listen to any conversation concerning her son, my father.

"Thor grew up to be more handsome than any man had use for," she said in her lilting Norwegian accent. "Ja, girls would send flowers and notes with the sealing wax shaped like hearts and one young lady knit him cashmere socks! I tell you, Thor must have dated half the women in Minneapolis and a third of them in St. Paul, but when your mother came along, he couldn't buy an engagement ring fast enough. 'Ma,' he said, 'love has finally got a hold on me.'"

"Some hold!" was all Patty Jane said when she heard that story.

I wondered how Grandma could take the abuse heaped upon her son by Patty Jane and Aunt Harriet. "Stinker" and "Creep" might be words Harriet chose to describe Thor; Patty Jane was partial to names less mild but more evocative: "That Blond Asshole" was a particular favorite. But Ione was stoic. When she heard the epithets her son inspired, her small neat bosom rose under the white cotton of her apron and she would tell me everyone has burdens to bear and how could she blame Patty Jane for thinking that way? — all the while patting my hand until the knuckles stung.

Sometimes late at night when they thought I was sleeping I would hear my mother and Aunt Harriet speculate on the whereabouts of my father, who had abandoned the family a few days before I was born. Once or twice a year, he sent a fifty-dollar bill wrapped in a terse typewritten note, but the small tourist-town postmarks suggested vacation places rather than residencies. Harriet guessed he was in Los Angeles or Chicago — "somewhere you go to disappear" — but Patty Jane thought no, he wasn't cut out for a big city; he was probably up north, working as a fishing guide in the Boundary Waters, or maybe he'd made it up to Alaska and was panning for gold.

The House of Curl staff and customers had their own ideas. Crabby Bultram was certain he was "dead as dust." Dixie Anderson, who trimmed my bangs throughout my youth, thought maybe he had married and started another family like "those Mormon guys." Inky Kolstat wondered where he was that Hollywood never found him. "With looks like his, he could have given Rock Hudson a run for his money."

This wasn't hyperbole; I had seen the Mighty Bites boxes.

"He had no plans to become a product model," Grandma Ione told me, showing me the stacks of flattened cereal containers she kept under her bed, "but a grocery clerk told me Mighty Bites practically flew off the shelves. It seems everyone wanted to have my son at their breakfast table."

When I finally met my father, I didn't want him at my breakfast table, or anywhere near me. As I teenager, I looked to *Tiger Beat* and *Seventeen* for answers to big issues but these contained no articles to help me learn how to love the man who used to be Thor Rolvaag.

Eventually I took my cue from Clyde Chuka, Grandma Ione, Aunt Harriet and most especially from Patty Jane. They had, after all, been knocked down more times and with harder punches than I and still found strength to stagger to their feet.

"Honey, life can be a ballroom dance," my mother counseled me, "and it can be full of shit. Your job in both cases is to watch where you step."

Patty Jane's got a store of "words to live by" and some of them aren't even profane.

Her personal favorite, "Expect the Unexpected," has long been the House of Curl slogan, with the addendum, "and a good haircut too."

Part One

---◆---

One

PATTY JANE DOBBIN'S wedding dress was shell pink and of such a high-quality rayon that in the right light it looked like satin. She had made it herself and although the hem wandered as if it had a mind of its own and one sleeve was a good inch shorter than the other, the amateur tailoring took nothing away from the radiance of the bride. Under her straw hat, her brown hair, styled in a short Italian cut, curled from the humidity. Her face was bare except for pink lipstick, most of which was chewed off by the time the nuptials were over. She was twenty-one years old and life bubbled inside her like a mineral spring.

She and her betrothed, Thor Rolvaag, stood on that July day in 1953 in the sanctuary of Faithful Shepherd's Lutheran Church and as Pastor Schulberg quizzed Thor on the many obligations he would undertake as a husband, Patty Jane wiped a line of sweat from under her nose and hoped that her dress shields would hold up.

Outside, the sun was a fireball, its heat blanching the color from the sky, softening the street tar so that shoe heels sank into it, and sending mailmen under shade trees and onto front porches for glasses of lemonade offered by sympathetic house-wives.

The church windows were open and Patty Jane could hear the aural Morse code of bees, short cantankerous dots, long low drones. Humidity clung to the skin like heavy silk and Patty Jane had stopped counting the number of times Pastor Schulberg had pulled at his clerical collar.

Her sister, Harriet, stood at her side, holding a limp bouquet of zinnias, blue phlox, amaryllis and daisies. She and Patty Jane had picked them on their way to church, sneaking up to front lawns and snipping the stems with manicure scissors brought especially for their larcenous purposes. They were gasping for breath when they reached the church and ran downstairs, giggling, to the ladies' room.

"Stealing the bridal bouquet," said Patty Jane, widening her eyes in the mirror to put on her eyebrow pencil. "Is that typical of the Dobbins or what?"

"If you were a flower," said Harriet, winding her long hair into a knot, "wouldn't you want to be in a wedding bouquet? Besides, we saved ourselves a mint. Try feathering it."

"What?"

"Your eyebrow pencil. The line's too harsh. You look like the bride of Frankenstein."

Patty Jane stuck out her tongue and erased the pencil marks with her thumb.

Harriet looked at her sister's feet. "At least I got you out of your old clodhoppers."

Patty Jane preferred homely, "sensible" shoes to flattering ones and Harriet had commandeered her into a shoe store to buy the low-heeled pumps she now wore.

"Yeah," said Patty Jane, admiring her legs in the mirror, "but when I'm up at the altar, all I'll be able to think is how much my feet hurt."

Harriet laughed and then her voice swerved into a musical

scale, three octaves of mi, mi, mi, mi, mi, mi, mi. Satisfied, she lit a cigarette and blew the smoke toward the ceiling.

Harriet could have been as pretty as Patty Jane but she was thin, so thin that things that should have curved became angles; and there was a brittleness about her, as if she could snap a bone by yawning.

Patty Jane blotted her lipstick with a scratchy square of toilet paper and straightened the ribbon around her hat.

"Well," said Harriet, surveying their images in the mirror.

"Well," said Patty Jane, "on with the show." She offered her elbow to her sister and they took the stairs, two at a time, singing, "Here Comes the Bride."

Ione Rolvaag stood next to her son, trying to stanch the flow of tears that filled her eyes. She considered herself an unsentimental woman and was surprised at the depth of her emotions. Her silent prayer was, "God, don't make me squeak." She seldom cried, but when she did, it was not with soulful sobs but little monkey sounds that embarrassed her, lessening the import of whatever had made her cry in the first place. She sniffed discreetly into her hanky and thought of her own wedding to Olaf Rolvaag in 1929. Held in the coastal town of Stavanger, Norway, it had been a perfect ceremony, except for when the organist, who liked to soothe her performance jitters with a liberal dose of schnapps, misjudged the size of the piano bench and fell off it, revealing to the congregation more than she had intended.

In 1930 she and Olaf had moved to Minneapolis and Thor was born a year later. Ione thought the good luck troll her mother made her take to "the new country" was doing its job until suddenly, at age 33, she was widowed, Olaf having been struck by a streetcar while playing softball. His teammates, all fellow employees of the Fresh 'N Pure Dairy, told Ione that he had been tracking a ball hit by Migs "Iron Arm" Coughlin, and with his glove held high in the air, he had run backwards across the street and right into a westbound car. The ball was found near his glove and was given to six-year-old Thor as a keepsake. Later, Olaf was posthumously named MVP of the Fresh 'N Pure Sluggers, and Ione received an invitation to the awards banquet but enough, she said, was enough.

Ione sniffed, willing herself to concentrate on the wedding couple in front of her. Thor and Patty Jane were a handsome pair. Ione didn't wish to toot her own horn, but she couldn't deny that Scandinavians seemed gifted with beauty — more so the Norwegians and Swedes of course; go south to Denmark and that odd strain of crooked teeth and pale red eyebrows began to appear.

"Italy," Olaf had told her, "now Italy's where you'll find God's angels. Italians could charge admission just for giving tourists the privilege of looking at them."

Olaf had sailed with the Norwegian Navy in his late teens and had seen every continent. Ione had been jealous of his tales of travel and vowed that one day she too would see the world, and not while wearing bellbottoms and a little white hat, either.

"Maybe now," she thought, watching her son answer, "I do." "Maybe now it's my turn. Maybe I'll get my passport picture taken tomorrow."

Thor slipped the ring — paid for in cash at Zimmerman's Jewelers — onto Patty Jane's finger. It stuck on the lower knuckle and there was a brief moment of tugging and pushing before it finally came to rest at the base of her finger.

Patty Jane giggled and whispered aloud, "Whew."

Ione thought the service was over after the rings were exchanged and was surprised when Harriet began singing. Her voice was clear and strong, its fullness rising to the church rafters:

"Then sings my soul,
My Savior God to thee,

How great thou art,

How great thou art."

Ione stared at Patty Jane's sister and after a moment, embarrassed, she drew up her lower lip which was hanging open. Harriet, the few times she had met her, had always struck Ione as a coarse, cheap woman, the kind men left crying in roadside motel rooms, the kind who sat in saloons in the middle of the afternoon drinking beer out of bottles. But Ione believed that talent was a gift from God and that anyone who made use of it held a ray of light within. Ione was certain, as she listened to Harriet's voice take flight, that this woman's innards must be positively luminescent.

Pastor Schulberg wondered if he should give a final personal blessing before pronouncing the couple man and wife. This hadn't been his best marriage ceremony; he liked a big audience filling up the pews and found it hard to warm up to a group of four, especially when the groom was so offputting. Pastor Schulberg thought it was gauche for a man to be so handsome; this Thor fellow's face had the devil's work in it; it served pride and vanity and sex. That Pastor Schulberg had a chinless profile and a weight problem that settled oddly in his hips and rear had nothing to do with his views on proper Christian looks, of course. The couple weren't even members of his church — how was he expected to deliver a rousing wedding service to virtual strangers? They had all spoken on the telephone and had a short meeting a week ago, but the couple had resisted Pastor Schulberg's invitation to join the flock.

"You couldn't find a finer parish," he had said when they were seated in his office.

"Oh, I'm sure of that," said Thor, "but with all due respect, we're not really looking."

Even though they had already made their payment for services, Pastor Schulberg wanted to dismiss them then and there. And now here was this hussy wearing a neckline that was risqué for a nightclub let alone a church, singing one of his favorite hymns.

"How great thou art,
How great thou art."

There was a moment's silence as the last traces of Harriet's voice faded into the summer air. Pastor Schulberg cleared this throat.

"Well, then," he said, with a short cough, "by the powers vested in me, I now pronounce you man and wife."

Later that night, lying in bed in their room at the Leamington Hotel, Thor poured Patty Jane her fourth glass of champagne. Patty Jane had never had champagne, and found that the bubbles more than made up for the sour taste.

"To us," she said and stood on the bed with wobbly legs, her glass raised in a salute.

"We already drank to us," said Thor, dodging some champagne that spilled from Patty Jane's glass.

"Oh, excuse me. To the desk clerk then." She put a hand on her hip and finished the glass in one draw. Then with a well-muscled arm, she threw the glass against the far wall where, instead of shattering, it bounced onto the dark green carpet.

"Hell's bells," she said, "it didn't break." She dropped to the bed beside Thor, the ruffled hem of her sheer black negligée floating around her knees like the petals of a flower. She looked into Thor's eyes, her own hazel ones wide.

"Can you believe that goddamn glass didn't even goddamn chip?"

Thor blinked. He had known a lot of women, but none who talked like this. In Ione's house, swearing was as nonexistent as dust and Thor still found it hard to say anything stronger than the Norwegian all-purpose epithet, "Uff-da." He found Patty Jane's swearing exciting; she cussed with no self-consciousness, often forming nonsensical phrases out of swear words. She gave no more thought to saying these words than she did to saying words like "bus" or "hotdish." Thor's taste in women leaned toward pretty, wholesome-looking types and although Patty Jane fit the physical mold, when it came to her vocabulary, she broke it into smithereens.

Staring at his bride now, her shiny brown hair curling over the edges of her ears, her lashes dark against her pink skin, he felt both his heart and erection swell, but when he reached for her, she sat up with a lurch.

"Oh, Thor," she said, pushing him aside, "I think I'm going to puke."

Their daughter Nora was conceived the next morning, after coffee had popped all residue of champagne bubbles in Patty Jane's skull.

"I knew it right away," she told Harriet later on the phone. "As soon as he rolled off me. I said, 'Thor, you're going to be a daddy.'"

"Oh, no," said Harriet. She and Patty Jane had decided neither of them would have children until they were older women — at least twenty-five. "Maybe it's just your imagination."

"You'll know in nine months," said Patty Jane. "I know it now."

She had read the instructions that came with her diaphragm until she had memorized them; she had used over a tablespoon more jelly than needed and yet still, somehow, she knew that one of her eggs and one of Thor's sperm had slipped through the heavy security and run off with each other.

Thor thought Patty Jane was a bit of a partypooper. He wanted to lie entwined with her in the morning sun, smelling her sweet skin and running his hand down her damp back until she was ready to do it again. Now he felt his desire blow out of the open window like a loose curtain. He stuffed a pillow under his chest and looked at her.

"But you're wearing that . . . thing, aren't you?"

"Diaphragm, Thor. It's called a diaphragm." Her face was close to his; looking into his eyes made her cross-eyed. She moved her head back against the pillow. "Yes, I'm wearing it. But I'm still pregnant."

"We'll see, hon," he said, "we'll see."

At twenty-three, he wasn't ready to start a family, but he was sensitive enough to know that Patty Jane didn't want him to dispute her. He believed in women's intuition, but he also believed in their tendency to get hysterical for no apparent reason.

Thor looked at Patty Jane's breasts; the right one was slightly bigger than the left and neither one could fill his cupped hand, but they were beautifully shaped and sat high on her chest. Her figure was better than a store model's, a small waist and slightly flared hips and legs so shapely they were almost voluptuous. Thor rubbed his hand over Patty Jane's stomach, an even plane between the sharp ranges of her hip bones. His breath was deep and filled with relief; her stomach was too flat for her to be pregnant, even if the pregnancy was only minutes old.

"Really, Thor, making a baby was not on my honeymoon agenda."

Thor pressed himself against her and kissed her under her ribs. "Shhh," he said.

The newlyweds moved into an apartment on top of a bakery on 38th Street and Minnehaha Avenue and every morning they were awakened at five-thirty by the smell of fresh bread and donuts. This olfactory alarm clock suited Thor; he was studying architecture at the University of Minnesota on the GI Bill (he had maintained jeeps at Fort Ord during the Korean Conflict) and he liked to study before his drafting class began at eight. He brewed a pot of coffee, using Ione's recipe (one egg and a teaspoon of cinnamon to each pot), set himself at the small kitchen table and reviewed his assignments.

Sometimes Patty Jane, who loved sleeping in as much as she loved staying up late, would wrap the quilt around her and go out to the kitchen, squinting against the light, to greet her husband. She was so proud of him; she had never expected to marry a college man, one who got blueprints back with notations that read "graceful lines" and "bold use of space." Patty Jane left his papers on the coffee table, displaying them like magazines, but Thor took them off, embarrassed.

On those mornings when she could rouse herself, she would sneak up behind Thor's chair, wrap her arms around his neck and slide her hands down his chest. He always groaned (Patty Jane knew his erogenous zones years before she knew what erogenous zones were) and slapped his notebook shut, saying something like, "But I've got a test in Electrical Engineering this morning."

His excuses didn't hold up under the weight of their passion and inevitably they would wind up on the kitchen floor or against the sink. When they were spent, Thor would suddenly remember his day's schedule, pull on his clothes, grab his books, kiss his wife and run out the door, his shirt tails flying behind him.

Patty Jane, humming something tuneless, would climb back into bed, enjoying the smell of her husband — moments ago an aphrodisiac and now a soporific — on her body.

At nine or so she would get up and run a bath and make coffee for Harriet, who usually stopped by on her way to work at Donaldson's Department Store.

One day Harriet, who indulged in a flirtation with old Mr. Vogstad, the bakery owner, brought up a bag of warm caramel rolls.

"Oooh, let me at 'em," said Patty Jane, tearing open the white bag.

"A half dozen for a nickel," said Harriet. "I think the old man likes me."

Patty Jane dumped out the grounds from Thor's earlier coffee. Her mother, to save money, had used the grounds over and over until the beverage that bubbled in the percolator had been like dishwater. Now the sisters were extravagant in their coffee habits and recycling grounds or reheating was prohibited.

The sisters sat together, inhaling the smells of the bakery and the perking coffee as the August sun fell in block patterns along the floor.

"Damn, Sam — I mean, dang-a-rang, these are good," said Patty Jane, sinking her teeth into a thickly iced roll.

"Dang-a-rang?" said Harriet, laughing. She tore open a roll and buttered it. "Is this part of your clean language campaign?"

A few nights earlier, Patty Jane had invited Ione over for macaroni salad and had been in the middle of what she thought was a very funny story.

". . . So the bus driver looks at the farmer and says, 'And take your damn chickens off my bus too.' And the farmer says —"

Ione set her fork and knife alongside her plate and excused herself.

"What's her problem?" asked Patty Jane, as she watched her mother-in-law walk briskly down the hallway to the bathroom. She sniffed at the bowl of macaroni salad. "I hope I didn't leave the mayonnaise out too long."

"The mayonnaise is fine, Patty Jane," said Thor. He made a criss-cross pattern on the tablecloth with the tines of his fork. "It's just that she . . . well, she doesn't like off-color stories and she can't stand swearing."

"Shit," said Patty Jane, genuinely confused, "was I telling an off-color story?" She pushed her brown curls off her forehead. "And I was swearing, too?"

Thor nodded glumly. He hated the hurt and confusion on his bride's face.

"Well, why didn't she say something?" asked Patty Jane.

Thor shrugged. "It's not her way. When something bothers her she doesn't say anything; she just leaves."

When Ione came back to the table, helping herself to some slices of fresh tomato as if nothing had happened, Thor wanted to shake her and scream, "Don't ever embarrass my wife again!" But Ione had taught him well; he had been brought up practicing the Norwegian's Eleventh Commandment, "Avoid Confrontation." With Patty Jane as inspiration, he had begun, with great effort, to break it. He cleared his throat. "Ma, Patty Jane would like to know why you —"

"Why you're such a nice mother-in-law!" said Patty Jane, pushing herself out of her chair. She rushed to Ione and knelt next to her. "Ione, what I mean to say, I mean, not that I don't think you're a nice mother-in-law, because I do." She looked at Thor helplessly. "But what I want to say is I'm sorry if my story offended you."

Thor watched his mother's face color — blushing was such a curse for people who preferred to hide their feelings — and found himself enjoying her discomfort.

"I really will try to watch myself," said Patty Jane and her brow crinkled as she thought hard. She tapped her fingers against her cheek and then snapped them. "I know! I'll pay you a quarter everytime a 'shit' or 'damn' passes my lips!"

Ione cringed and Thor laughed.

"Oops," said Patty Jane, "I guess that's fifty cents right there." She went to the cupboard and dug in the change jar until she found two quarters. She placed them triumphantly next to Ione's plate.

"No, keep it," said Ione, wishing she were anywhere but at her daughter-in-law's table. "I don't need it."

Patty Jane, happy about her resolution, sat down and sawed off a thick slice of rye bread. "I know you don't need it," she said, "but it's the principle of the thing. I'll pay you everytime I swear" — here she winked at her husband — "and either we'll go broke or I'll wind up talking like Mamie Eisenhower."

"Well, there goes your savings account," said Harriet, stirring cream into her coffee.

"Thanks, chum," said Patty Jane, hurt creeping into her voice.

"Face facts, Patty Jane, you have a mouth and it's foul and it's part of you. It's like a birthmark or a widow's peak or something." She lit a cigarette and Patty Jane felt a surprising, abrupt wave of nausea.

"I can change," said Patty Jane, swallowing hard.

Harriet sipped her coffee, peering at Patty Jane from over the rim of her cup. "Famous last words."

"I can change," was an oft-heard refrain/plea/threat in the Dobbin household, repeated by the sisters' father, Elmo, and by their mother, Anna. Involved in a race to see who could out-drink the other, most often the parents ended in a dead heat with both of them passed out on the shabby furniture in the living room. Neither of them changed — at least not for the better. Elmo died from liver disease and Anna would have too, but her heart gave out first, four months after Elmo's death. Patty Jane had been sixteen, Harriet fifteen, and they spent the year until Patty Jane graduated from high school living with their Aunt Louise, Elmo's sister. She offered the girls a roof over their heads, three meals a day and all the *WatchTower* pamphlets they could ever hope to read. Patty Jane and Harriet shared a fold-out couch in Louise's small, dark apartment and tried to stay out of their aunt's way as much as possible. While doing her darning or boiling water for her bitter black tea, Louise was apt to mutter things like, "God gave me a drunk for a brother and then he give me the drunk's two kids."

The day after commencement exercises, Patty Jane got a job

typing invoices at the Grain Exchange and by the end of the summer she had enough money to move herself and Harriet out of Aunt Louise's apartment and into one of their own. They lived there together three years, until Patty Jane married.

But in Patty Jane's kitchen on that warm August morning, their troubles seemed far behind them. They felt they had depleted their allotment of bad times, that their rough childhoods would now be balanced by splendid adult lives.

The only fly in the gravy, as far as Harriet could see, was Patty Jane's insistence that she was pregnant.

"What does Thor's mother think of this baby idea?" she asked.

"It's not an idea, Harriet. But Thor doesn't want me to tell her for awhile."

"Sure, why raise false hopes?" Harriet shook her head. Her sister was usually so rational. "Look at you," she said, trying another tack, "You're almost as skinny as me!"

Patty Jane peeled apart a spiral of caramel roll and stuffed it into her mouth. Harriet watched her sister with displeasure; as a rebellion against their parents and meals eaten on counter tops or in the car, both she and Patty Jane had tried to cultivate table manners.

"I've got this huge appetite," said Patty Jane, still chewing, "but I lost four pounds."

"Well, then, see?" said Harriet. "You gain weight if you're going to have a baby."

"Maybe not at first. Pass me the sugar, will you?"

Harriet watched her sister dump a fourth of the sugar bowl into her coffee cup. "What about your friend?"

"Harriet," said Patty Jane, smiling wide, "I haven't seen my friend since a week before the wedding."

Harriet felt her heart speed up. She took a deep breath. "Well, we're always skipping periods. Remember my senior year when I only had three? And the school nurse said it was nothing to worry about?"

"Harriet, I know the difference. Why won't anyone believe I'm going to have a baby?"

"Why don't you go to a doctor and find out?"

Patty Jane shrugged. Why should she pay someone to tell her something she already knew? She sipped her sugary brew and shuddered. She usually drank her coffee black.

Two

LOVE BLOOMED in bunches for both Dobbin sisters that year. In October, while walking out of Vogstad's Bakery with a bag of sugared donuts, Harriet met a man her dreams never dared conjure, Mr. Right times ten: Avel Ames III.

He was driving down Minnehaha Avenue in his brand new oyster-colored Packard Patrician when he saw Harriet and within a millisecond, his brain sent signals to his hands on the steering wheel and his foot on the accelerator to "Pull over! Pull over!" In the maneuvering, his bumper was almost sliced off by a passing diaper-service truck and amid beeps and honks, he swerved to the curb, scraping his right tires against it and skinning off a nice section of tread.

Harriet shook her head. She was all too familiar with erratic driving, having watched her father lurch his dented Studebaker into the driveway after the bars had closed, knocking over trashcans and woodpiles and once, a corner of the garage.

"There ought to be a law to keep them off the road," she thought. She flicked her long brown hair over her shoulders and walked past the gleaming Packard without bothering to look at its inebriated driver. When he honked the horn, the muscles in her back jumped, but she ignored him and increased her pace, her high heels making quick stabs at the sidewalk.

Out of the corner of her eye, she saw that the car was cruising along the curbside. Harriet was used to men following her. To her, they were like dogs or orphans: they'd do anything for attention.

Harriet turned right at the corner and saw the car make the same turn. "The creep," she thought, "he's on my tail." At the alley, she suddenly turned around and began to run back toward Minnehaha Avenue. The car lurched into reverse, its gears grinding, and Harriet was astonished to see it keeping up with her, traveling backward. She stopped and spun to face the driver.

"What, are you trying to kill somebody?" She swung at the air with the white bakery bag. "Why don't you go home, sober up and quit bothering people?"

For the first time, Harriet saw the man in the driver's seat. He smiled and shrugged and motioned her forward. Harriet marched over to him and opened the passenger door.

"You know, mister," she said, "there's gall and then there's *your* gall. Now beat it before I call the cops."

The man patted the grey leather seat, inviting her in. A wreath of black hair encircled his bald pate, his pudgy cheeks were rose pink and his smile was so engaging that Harriet's anger began to deflate. With a slight rotation of her head, she sniffed, smelling not liquor but leather upholstery and sandalwood cologne. She climbed into the front seat, pulling the door shut behind her.

"So you're not drunk," she said.

"Just with love," he answered.

"Oh, brother," said Harriet. She touched the edge of the dashboard with one finger. "Well, you sure drive like a maniac."

"Not usually. Only when my line of vision is obstructed by a thing of beauty." He held out a small, manicured hand. "I'm Avel Ames," he said. "Your paramour-to-be."

"Why didn't you get out of the car then and there?" Patty Jane asked later.

Harriet's eyes sparkled. "Well, Patty Jane, I just knew he was right."

As Avel and Harriet passed the bag of donuts back and forth, they drove with no destination in mind and little conversation; up side streets, alongside the Mississippi and into St. Paul, back over the Lake Street Bridge and toward uptown. The blue sky and warm sun and hundreds of trees, like official greeters waving red and gold leaves, conspired to make a glorious day.

"How do you feel about Chinese food?" asked Avel as they slowed to a red light on Hennepin Avenue.

Harriet shrugged. "I've never had any."

"Holy Toledo," said Avel, turning left. "Let's right that injustice pronto."

When he pulled over to a meter, grabbed his light overcoat and got out of the car, Harriet was surprised to see the coat had hidden a hard leather cushion, a hand-tooled booster chair upon which he sat. He dashed around the front of the car, looking like a twelve-year-old boy with premature baldness. He knocked on the window glass and Harriet rolled it down.

"Short little bugger, aren't I?"

"Why, yes," said Harriet.

"I'm 5'2" with lifts," he said, "but I never wear them."

He came back with two bags from the Port Arthur Cafe and Harriet held them on her lap, feeling the warmth and smelling the exotic aroma. They drove west to Lake Calhoun.

"A picnic by the lake?" asked Avel. "Do you think there's ever been a better idea in the history of our relationship?"

"Oh, I doubt it," said Harriet.

A thin, grey man stopped his gutter search for cigarette butts to admire the car from which Avel and Harriet emerged. He gave a long whistle and Harriet was about to tell him to mind his manners until she realized he was whistling at the car.

"Like it, do you?" asked Avel, running his hand along the side of the hood.

"It's a beaut," said the man, nodding his head, and Harriet saw in his eyes the look of rapture women have for babies and men for fine machinery. "I had me a Model T once upon a time ago." His wide mouth was toothless.

"Is that so," said Avel. "Ford's a good car. What's your name, friend?"

"Joe," said the man.

Avel dipped his hand in his pocket and took out his keys. "Here, Joe. Take it for a spin."

The keys glittered as they fell in an arc into the man's open palm.

Harriet stifled an impulse to touch Avel's forehead; surely he was delirious.

"Go on," said Avel. "My ladyfriend and I are going to have a little picnic. We'll all rendezvous here in an hour and a half."

The man's stupor broke and he raced toward the Packard like a kid seeing a Flexible Flyer under the Christmas tree. Harriet held the bags of food tightly to her chest, watching what she was sure was a big mistake.

"Hot diggedy," said Joe, jumping into the front seat. He fired up the engine and backed it up smoothly. "Thanks, mister." His two-fingered wave was jaunty. "In an hour and a half then."

They watched the Packard ease into traffic on Lake Street.

"Avel," said Harriet softly, "Say goodbye to your car."

Avel looked at her and smiled. "I'm not giving that man my car, Harriet. I'm giving that man my trust. He'll be back."

"Sure he will."

Avel took a bag from her and pulled her gently toward the grassy lake shore. "Oh, Harriet, that gentleman is so full of gratitude for me right now, he was crazy about cars, could you see that? Why, I'll bet he brings the car back with a new wax job, paid for with nickels he was saving for his next bottle of Mogen David."

Remembering the euphoria that transformed the bum's features into the face of a man who owned the world, Harriet tried to drown her cynicism under the wave of Avel's trust, but like a buoy, it kept bobbing up.

"Twenty bucks says that's the last you'll see of that car."

"You're on," said Avel and they shook hands. Ducks paraded the grassy lakeshore, looking for handouts. Harriet and Avel sat watching them, cartons of chicken chow mein and fried rice scattered beside them. Their backs were pressed against the wide trunk of a massive oak, which, when a breeze blew, littered them with the confetti of its falling leaves.

"I thought destiny had a blonde woman in mind for me," said Avel. He held Harriet's hand, bigger than his own. "My perfect woman was supposed to be small and plump. Southern probably, but schooled in the east, with a voice that trailed off at the end of a sentence. Like this-s-s-s." His voice faded in a drawl. "But then I see you through my windshield — a tall, skinny brunette with a ponytail sprouting out of the top of her head like a fountain, wearing a skirt that shows more knee than it should — and, kaboom, I say to myself, 'Pay severe attention, Avel, this is the one.'"

Harriet tugged at the hem of her skirt. "I'm not showing any more leg than any other gal my age."

Avel laughed. "You tickle me, Harriet."

There was a fan of wings as a dog ran away from its master toward the ducks. Harriet threw off Avel's hand and stood up.

"Hey!" she yelled, "get away from those ducks!"

The golden retriever stopped at the water's edge and turned toward Harriet, his upper lip caught above his teeth in a sneer, as if to say, "Who's the spoiler?"

His master blew a shrill whistle and the dog loped to him.

"You should keep that dog on a leash, mister," Harriet called after him.

The man waved her off without turning around.

"Oh yeah?" said Harriet, hands on her hips. "Come here and say that."

"Sit," said Avel, pulling her hand. "I'm pouring my heart out to you and you're trying to pick a fight."

Harriet sat.

"Not that I don't like spunk," said Avel, "for I truly do. The moment I saw you coming out of that bakery, swinging your arms as if you were the bantamweight champion of the world, I knew that you and I were going to have a very colorful life together."

"Why haven't I punched you in the nose a long time ago?"

Avel touched the bridge of his nose thoughtfully. "Because you don't want to ruin a pretty profile and because you know I'm right."

Harriet looked across the lake at the sinking sun and the trail of golden light it left shimmering on the water's surface.

"You *are* right," she said, shaking her head at the speed and circumstance in which she had not only met, but fallen in love with this man seven inches shorter and who knew how many years older. "I don't know why, but you're absolutely right."

When they got back to the street, the man who had borrowed Avel's Packard and his trust had not returned either. Avel looked at his round gold watch and dropped it into his pocket. Nothing changed on his face.

"What time is it?" asked Harriet.

"Five thirty-eight," said Avel with a bright cheeriness.

"Hmmmm," said Harriet. She rocked back on the heels of her feet, keeping her mouth in a straight line. Her ponytail slapped against her back.

"The man's only fifteen minutes late," said Avel, digging the toe of one of his shiny black shoes into wet leaves plastered alongside the curb. "He was probably punctual but decided on one more spin around the lake when we were tardy."

"Probably," said Harriet.

They walked the length of the block until the sky had purpled with dusk. Everytime a car approached, they exchanged hopeful expressions, only to have them dissolve when they saw it was not the oyster-colored Packard.

When Harriet began shivering, Avel gave her his overcoat. The sleeves were too short and the shoulders too narrow; Harriet thought she'd rip the underseam if she lifted an arm.

"Holy cow, you're an Amazon," said Avel.

"Holy cow, you're a shrimp," said Harriet.

They laughed, tight little snickers at first, then full-bodied shrieks that left them gasping for air.

"My booster chair," said Avel finally, wiping his eyes with a monogrammed handkerchief. "Couldn't he have left behind my booster chair? I had it custom-made. Did you read the words that were tooled on the front?"

Harriet shook her head.

"It said, 'Napoleon sat here.'"

"Aw, you can always get a new one," said Harriet. "It can read, 'Property of Munchkin Land.'"

By seven-thirty their jokes had dwindled and Avel finally seemed willing to accept that he was going to have to find other transportation. He called a cab from a gas station on Lake Street and when it arrived, he stood on his tiptoes and pulled Harriet's head to his, kissing her fiercely on the lips.

"Arrivederci, my pet. You'll hear from me soon."

"You're not coming with me?"

He opened the cab door for her. "I've got to take care of this car business with the police." He took a money clip from his pocket and from a thick wad of bills pulled out a twenty and gave it to Harriet. "This was a hard bet to lose," he said, "but the real loser's driving around in my car." He petted the top of her head. "Have a safe trip and know that you are loved."

Harriet settled into the back seat, pulling the wide lapels of Avel's narrow coat closer together. She didn't realize she was humming until the cabby, in a mellow baritone, joined in, and together they sang "Glow Worm," agreeing that outside of the cab, the Mills Brothers had just about the smoothest harmony anywhere.

"He sounds like a kook," said Thor, standing in front of a small mirror above the kitchen sink, a towel wrapped around his waist. His face was half lathered, half clean-shaven and Patty Jane sat at the kitchen table, finishing Thor's breakfast now that she was finished with her own.

"He does to me too, but talk to Harriet. She's gone ape over this guy." Patty Jane wiped a drip of egg off her lip. "Course Harriet's taste in men has never been what you'd call good." She grimaced, remembering Big Gene, Harriet's last boyfriend, who had a dragon tattoo that oozed from his scalp like a wound.

"At least the guy's not on the dole," said Thor. "I mean, he's got a new Packard, after all."

"*Had* a new Packard."

They shared a long laugh, trying to imagine the sap Harriet had attracted who would let a complete stranger, a hobo no less, take his brand new Packard for a drive.

Their laughter then triggered desire — an emotion that swarmed through their apartment like a persistent virus — and Patty Jane unfastened the white cotton towel around Thor's waist and let it drop to the floor.

It was hard for a man who barely measured five feet and whose hairline receded to the back of his head to look dashing, but Avel Ames did. He knew it, Harriet knew it, and so did the women who managed to steer their dance partners near them, fluttering their fingers and asking Avel to save them a dance.

"I'm booked for the evening, ladies," said Avel, dipping Harriet backward and holding her there for a dramatic moment.

When they returned to their table for cocktails and hors d'oeuvres offered by waiters in red boleros, clusters of people stopped to say hello.

A woman whose earlobes strained under the weight of chandelier earrings invited them to see her new Manet and after she left, Harriet said, "Avel, I get the impression that you're something of a big shot."

"In some circles," he said. "Yours, I hope."

The Harvest Ball to Benefit the Preservation of Courtney Manor was Harriet and Avel's first date. He had telephoned her at Donaldson's Department Store that morning. In response to her greeting, "Notions," he said, "Boy, have I got some" and invited her to "this dance thing, I'll pick you up at seven."

"Oh," said Harriet, cradling the receiver under her chin as she tore a receipt from the cash register, "You got your car back."

"Not yet," said Avel, "Although the police seem to think it will show up any day."

"Where are the hot-water bottles?" asked a fat woman holding the small of her back.

Harriet said into the phone. "See you at seven."

Avel Ames didn't ring the doorbell empty handed. He balanced a pyramid of boxes: a dress box on the bottom, a hat box in the middle and shoe and corsage boxes on top. He could barely be seen over the jumble of striped and glossy cardboard as he wedged himself through the door past Harriet. He dumped the boxes on the narrow sofa in the middle of the room. The hatbox fell off the pile and its lid tipped, exposing a glimpse of tissue paper and blue velvet.

Avel stood in a black tuxedo, his fringe of hair brilliantined and shiny as the satin lapels of his cutaway jacket.

"Why, Harriet," he said, "You're a glass of water to a man in the Mojave."

"I thought you said we were going dancing," she said. She was wearing a challis dress, printed with explosions of pink cabbage roses. It was the dress she always wore to VFW dances because its skirt flared so nicely when she twirled.

"Oh, I did," said Avel and he went to her and took her hand. "You'll be the belle of the ball. Let's go."

"As if I'm going to ignore this, Avel Ames," she said, throwing off the lid of the dressbox. She drew in a sharp breath and lifted out the dress as carefully as if it were a baby. It was a floor-length gown of blue velvet. Its neckline was cut deep and square and the long sleeves ended in points at the wrist.

"Oh, Avel," said Harriet.

"Oh, Harriet," said Avel, blinking back tears.

While Avel blew his nose, Harriet gathered up the finery and rushed into her bedroom feeling that, like Cinderella, she must get everything on before the clock struck and she found herself back in the challis dress, dancing the polka with Big Gene.

Harriet's hair streamed out from under the small veiled hat. Her new navy pumps gave her even more inches over Avel, but he stood as proud and confident as if he were six feet tall.

"You're rich, aren't you Avel?" asked Harriet as they left for the dance, Avel opening the door of a new black Cadillac.

"Very," he said, helping her tuck the yards of blue velvet inside the car door. When he had situated himself on top of a brocade pillow ("my booster chair's on order," he told her), he added, "Extremely rich," and they caught each other's eye and giggled.

Except for the time Harriet had to go to the bathroom, they danced every song the orchestra played. Avel refused to let anyone cut in, explaining, "She's allergic to stuffed shirts."

"What do you do, anyway?" Patty Jane asked Avel when Harriet brought him over to the apartment for inspection.

Avel smiled happily. "For one thing, I love your sister."

Harriet blew out the match that lit her cigarette and winked at him. Annoyed, Patty Jane filled his and Harriet's coffee cups, not caring that she sloshed into their saucers.

"I mean, what do you do for a living?"

Avel straightened his back and rolled his shoulders, understanding that Harriet's sister wanted some straight answers.

"I assist in the family business, Patty Jane," he said, and when he saw that the crease between her eyebrows didn't smooth, he added, "Ames Grains? Friendly rival to Peavy and Pillsbury? Makers of three-quarters of the breakfast cereal tucked away in your cupboard?"

"Ames Grains," said Patty Jane, sitting down. "Holy shit."

Harriet's hand, holding her cigarette, froze on its way to her mouth and she whistled low. In her three-week courtship, in spite of champagne, steak dinners, presents and long drives in luxurious cars, Harriet had neglected to inquire as to the source of Avel's benevolence. She had wanted to protect herself from the possibility that he was a gangster — a favorite speculation of Patty Jane's and Thor's. As for Avel, he had never known a woman who didn't know about his family business and he delighted in the novelty of being liked just for himself.

"I'm on the board, of course," he said, "but the company's run by individuals who care — or seem to care — about grains far more than I do." He tugged at the snow-white cuff that peeked out from his suit sleeve. "I prefer travel to wheat; philanthropy to oats" — he reached for Harriet's hand — "and love to barley."

He kissed Harriet's hand and she kissed his back.

"Thank goodness," said Patty Jane. "Thor and I thought you were with the Cosa Nostra or something."

Avel tugged at his tie. "Really? I'm flattered."

Patty Jane pushed a plate of cookies toward him. "You know, Avel, and I'm not saying this because of who you are, but Ames Grains Toasty Bites is my husband's favorite cereal."

Avel made a note in a small leather book. "There'll be a case on your landing by tomorrow morning."

Patty Jane was singing "Zip-A-Dee-Doo-Dah" when Thor got home that evening.

"Oh, honey, Harriet's snared herself a millionaire!" She grabbed his hands and before he had taken his coat off, she led him around the kitchen floor in a dance of hops and jumps.

"What?" said Thor, laughing as they knocked over a kitchen chair.

"Harriet's beau is Avel Ames!" Patty Jane paused for a moment, waiting for Thor's expression to change, but when it didn't, she added, "Avel *Ames*. Ames Grains?"

"The people who make Toasty Bites?"

Patty Jane nodded. "He's sending over a case tomorrow."

Thor's mouth split open in a wide grin. "Well, let's celebrate," he said and he kissed her, his fingers working at the buttons of her dress.

At winter solstice, in the warming house that offered shelter to those skating on Lake Calhoun, Avel proposed to Harriet.

"Oh, my beloved," he said, kneeling in front of her, "oh, my rarest flower, will you bring some light into this, the darkest day of the calendar year, and say that you'll be mine throughout eternity?"

A small child, tottering on her first pair of skates, fell against Avel.

"You are a dear thing," said Avel, propping the girl back up, "but you've interrupted the most important question of my life."

"Bally lally fally," said the child.

"Easy for you to say," said Avel, "but I'm not asking you, I'm asking her." He turned to Harriet and the child zigzagged across the rough wooden floor to the door.

Harriet sat motionless, certain that her heart had swelled so large her breath couldn't get past it.

"Say 'yes' or I'll tie the laces of your skates together."

Harriet broke her silence with a "yes" that filled the small warming house, making those who weren't already watching them look up from their business of putting on extra socks or wiping off their skate blades.

"That was an affirmative?" asked Avel.

They hugged for such a prolonged moment that the others in the warming house felt duty-bound to applaud.

The couple took a bow and Avel held Harriet's hand as she led him out of the warming house, down the wooden ramp and to the ice rink, where Avel learned at age thirty-five to skate backwards.

Avel's first engagement present to his future wife (beside a ring with a diamond the size of a raisin) was enrollment in the McKern School of Music. He had cried the first time he heard her sing "Come On-A My House" after a necking session in his Cadillac.

"Your voice is like a mixture of Billie Holiday and Miliza Korjus," he told her.

"Billie Holiday and who?"

"Miliza Korjus. She's an opera singer. I heard her in Vienna once and I was struck dumb." Avel pressed his fingertips together and looked out the car window, sighing. "What a performance." He turned to her. "Honestly, Harriet. You could have an outstanding career in music."

Harriet laughed and lit a cigarette. "How you carry on." They both studied the glowing tip of her cigarette.

"Harriet," said Avel finally, "my mission is going to be to make you believe in yourself."

A low laugh erupted from Harriet's throat. "I believe in my-self, Avel; I just don't make a religion of it."

"I've seen religions built on less worthy icons." He kissed her lightly. "But surely I'm not the only one who's found your voice rapturous."

"Well, the only A's I could count on were the ones I got in choir. I always sang solos in our spring programs, too." She laughed shyly, but when she stubbed out her cigarette in the ashtray, her laugh turned bitter. "I always wanted to play an in-strument, but Ma and Dad never let me. When the band teacher let me take home a school trumpet, Dad grabbed it as I was playing 'Three Blind Mice' and threw it out the window. 'Aren't things bad enough around here already without me hav-ing to listen to this racket?' he said." Harriet's eyebrows lifted as she sighed. "The mouthpiece was lost and the whole thing was all dented up. Mr. Deckom, the band teacher, told me not to worry; the school board had just voted to increase the funding of the music department. He told me I could practice in the band room on another trumpet, but I was too embarrassed to take him up on the offer."

"Then, you're going to learn now," said Avel. He petted her long, shiny ponytail. "You'll start trumpet and voice lessons im-mediately."

"Harp, too?" Harriet asked softly.

"Beg your pardon?"

"I've always wanted to play the harp." She snuggled close to Avel, putting her head against the small ridge of his shoulder.

"The harp and the trumpet," he said. "Instruments of angels and Louis Armstrong."

"One and the same," said Harriet.

With Avel bankrolling her, Harriet quit the notions depart-ment of Donaldson's and began music school.

After her first trumpet lesson and her first harp lesson on the following day, both teachers were giddy with the discovery of a gifted pupil. Ed Donavan, the trumpet teacher, began the lesson expecting his new student to spend at least a half hour trying to get a sound out of the mouthpiece, and the second half hour trying to vary the sound of the resultant duck call; but by the end of the lesson they were playing "Danny Boy" in harmony.

Mr. Donavan had sat back in his metal chair, holding his own trumpet upright on his knee, shaking his head at the tone and clarity of this new student.

"You say you never played trumpet?" he asked.

"Oh," said Harriet, "I did as a child," and after Mr. Donavan's knowing nod, Harriet added, "once."

When Harriet confessed she had never laid her hands on a harp, Evelyn Bright looked up at the wall clock in the small, acoustically-tiled room and thought the next hour was going to be slow-moving. Sixty minutes later she was asking Harriet to stay on an extra hour — after all, she had no further students until after lunch and wouldn't Harriet like to take a peek at Lesson III? Harriet had positioned the harp with none of the beginning student's awkwardness and right away she let the strings know who was boss, plucking them with a sure vigor.

Stella Amundsen, Harriet's voice teacher, thought her pupil was not merely gifted but the singer who could get Stella out of teaching and into managing; she envisioned business lunches at the Russian Tea Room discussing Harriet's contract with the Carnegie Hall booking agent.

And so when Ed Donavan and Evelyn Bright and Stella Amundsen dominated that week's faculty meeting with tales of their amazing student, each felt cheated upon discovering they were all talking about the same woman.

Three

DESPITE PATTY JANE'S pronouncements from the beginning, it had been easy for Thor to ignore what seemed a nonexistent pregnancy. Finally, in her sixth month, when her belly began to swell like a ripening melon, Thor, twenty-three years old and with two and a half more years of school, was forced to realize he was to be a father. There were things in his life he had been more excited about.

He was, for example, thrilled that one day he was going to be an architect. At five, he had built a birdhouse with his father and his love of building was sparked that Saturday afternoon when Olaf taught him about leveling and planing and roof pitch.

"My little builder," his father had said, ruffling Thor's white blond hair, "maybe someday you build American houses, ja?"

In his head, Thor had built dozens of them. A fan of the Prairie School, he loved beautiful buildings with clean lines and unexpected spaces, and he was anxious for the day when he would see them rise from the ground.

A winter ago, Bing Norling, one of the top scorers in the

NHL, had come into Bill Blaine's Sporting Goods, where Thor worked part-time. He came in for a hockey stick and wound up in a half-hour conversation with Thor about who the chippiest players in the league were. That had been exciting. Almost going to war ("We need you installing mufflers more than we need you in Seoul," his commanding officer told him) had been exciting. But fatherhood was not a prospect that had Thor waving banners. He was not ready to shoulder the responsibility of some kid loving him the way he had loved his father. Not yet. Maybe, when he had forgiven his father for dying on him, but not yet.

Nor was Harriet thrilled. Patty Jane had tended to people all her life; Elmo and Anna when they were drunk and, of course, Harriet herself. Now she thought her sister deserved some free time.

"The only responsibility you should have," she told Patty Jane, "is to keep that man of yours happy."

Resistance from the two people she loved most in the world made Patty Jane double her enthusiasm. She would make Thor and Harriet love the idea of the baby, paternity and aunthood by sheer force of will. Her feelings were growing like her body, from her ambivalent acknowledgement in the Leamington Hotel, moments after what she knew was conception, to acceptance a few days later, and now, building daily, a quiet joy of what was going on inside her and what was to be. She stood naked in front of the bathroom mirror, studying herself from different angles, running her hands across the curve of her belly, thinking, "Underneath my hands at this very moment, I might be giving my baby a backrub."

In the first and second months, Patty Jane woke up in the middle of the night to find her hand cupped protectively over her stomach and each time she almost wept, lying in the still dark night, awed by the wisdom of her body. A dark line appeared, beginning at her navel and disappearing into her soft brown pubic hair and Patty Jane thought it was the most marvelous thing, as if nature had bisected her with an obstetrical diagram: "Now, to the left of this line lies the baby's head, to the right its torso . . ."

The spot above her left eyebrow and the darkening of the skin between her nose and lip didn't bother her, either.

"It's the mask of pregnancy," she told Harriet proudly.

"Happy Halloween," said Harriet.

Because she had only spent a few hours of her marriage *not* pregnant, Patty Jane didn't know if her increased desire for Thor was a side effect of her condition or not; either way, the desire was great. Thor was a target for her passion at any hour, in any place, but the more her silhouette changed, the less willing a target Thor became.

"Honey, what's the matter?" Patty Jane asked him one night, tears filming her hazel eyes.

Thor was in bed, his back to her. The streetlight cast a thin rectangle of light between the window sill and the drawn shade.

"Nothing," said Thor. "I just want to get some sleep."

Patty Jane snuggled up behind him, pressing her cheek against the cotton ribbing of his sleeveless T-shirt.

"I know something that'll put you to sleep real good," she said. One of her hands climbed up his smooth hard thigh.

Thor batted her hand away as if it were something hot.

"Will you leave me alone for one minute? Can I have at least one night's sleep without you climbing all over me?" He twitched his shoulder. "Geez."

Patty Jane slid to her side of the bed as Thor fluffed his pillow by pumping a fist into it.

"Sometimes a man likes to make the first move, you know."

"Sorry," said Patty Jane, her voice plaintive.

"Just let me do the asking for once."

"Okay," whispered Patty Jane. Except that you don't ask anymore, she thought. It was as if her round stomach held something contagious that Thor did not want to catch.

Support came from another corner of her small family. Ione had booked a trip to Norway, her first visit back since she had left Stavanger as a young woman, but she canceled it when she saw Patty Jane's pregnancy was real and not, as Thor had told her, "something in her head." Ione wanted to be around to cook meals and scrub floors and pamper the woman who was carrying her grandchild. It seemed to her that Thor was not going to be big on pampering; she saw a change in her son that she neither liked nor understood.

Ione thought back to an evening when the newlyweds had invited her over for dessert and coffee. Ione had complimented the lemon cake profusely, even as she unobtrusively spit lemon seeds into her napkin.

After clearing away the plates, Patty Jane returned to the living room bearing a tray on which sat a triangular object, covered with a dishtowel. Patty Jane set it on the coffee table and with a flourish, pulled off the cloth.

"Ta da!"

Ione smiled expectantly, not understanding the game. "A birdhouse?"

Patty Jane laughed. "That's what I thought too. When Thor brought it home, I said, 'Oh honey, you built a birdhouse, how cute.'"

Patty Jane turned the house slowly. "But just look at it, Ione. Look at the detail. It's a model of our first house — the house your son wants to build for me!"

Ione looked at Thor, who was playing with his watchband.

"He said, 'I guess it's sort of like a birdhouse,'" said Patty Jane, "'in that it'll be our love nest.'"

A smile broke over Thor's face, even as he blushed vigorously. "Geez, Patty Jane."

"Well, it was so sweet, honey," said Patty Jane. "I just wanted to share it with your mother because it was so damn sweet." She touched the roof of the small wooden house. "Our love nest."

Before Patty Jane began to show, Thor had seemed incapable of *not* touching her; pushing a curl behind her ear at the supper table, squeezing her hand while they played Rook with Ione, laying his arm across her shoulders as he had on Thanksgiving before they ran out of Ione's door into the light swirling snow.

One month later, Ione saw none of that. On Christmas Eve, the first time she could see for certain that Patty Jane was indeed carrying, they gathered at Ione's small house near Lake Hiawatha. Flickering light from candles in their wall holders reflected onto the floors Ione had waxed twice. Straw angels and crocheted snowflakes hung from the Christmas tree and the smell of evergreen competed with the aromas of cider mulling in a blue speckled pot on the burner and the turkey roasting inside the oven.

To Patty Jane, it seemed a Christmas she had only read about. Elmo and Anna had celebrated the holidays by buying expensive liquor, leaving Patty Jane and Harriet to fend for themselves. One Christmas morning, Anna set a couch cushion on fire with a cigarette and Elmo doused it with a bottle of Jack Daniels.

"Idiot!" Anna had screamed. "Do you realize how much that stuff costs?"

She glows, thought Ione as they ate their turkey dinner. She could hardly take her eyes off Patty Jane and when she did, it was with great effort, hoping to find a complementary happiness in Thor's face. But she saw nothing there.

Thor's blank face had first appeared after the death of his father; his perfect six-year-old features set, as if frozen. Ione had thought he was adjusting well to his loss until one evening on her way to the bathroom, she heard a high-pitched squealing coming from Thor's bedroom. She quietly opened the door and saw her son sobbing into the pillow. Listening closer, she real-

ized the squeal was a chant, "Papa, papa, papa." She went to
him, her heart hammering, and sat on the bed beside him. He
jumped when she touched his back and looked at her with a
fury that seemed too old an emotion for someone so young.
She sat for a silent hour, her hand rubbing his back, until sleep
loosened his small tense muscles. She tried to talk about Olaf's
death the next day, gently asking her son questions, urging him
to talk, but the boy only looked at her and said, "Papa's gone,
Mutti. He's not coming back."

Ione knew that the calm face he wore now was like a glass-
smooth surface of water which, underneath, was disturbed by
sharks and riptides.

She saw how her son kept his fingers on his silverware, his
eyes on his plate, never once brushing Patty Jane's cheek with
the back of his hand, or winking at her when he thought Ione
wasn't looking. He was able to carry on a conversation, but
with the animation of a slug. Ione wanted to shake him by his
wide shoulders, hard enough so the still mask on his beautiful
face would shatter.

After dinner, as the two women did dishes, Ione reached out
her sudsy hands and patted Patty Jane's stomach.

"Uff-da mayda, I'm sorry," she said quickly, plunging her
hands back into the dishwater.

"Please," said Patty Jane and she stood facing her mother-in-
law, arching her back and thrusting her new belly outwards.

Ione dried her hands on the embroidered dishtowel and laid
her hands on Patty Jane's stomach and held them there, as if she
were warming them over a fire.

"I can't think of anything more wonderful to touch," she said,
her eyes shut.

Patty Jane held Ione's hands under hers, feeling Ione's hard
sharp knuckles against her palms.

"Thor doesn't like touching my stomach," whispered Patty
Jane. "I guess he thinks he'll hurt the baby."

In the silence that followed, Patty Jane wondered if Ione believed her. She herself desperately wanted to find some excuse for Thor's coldness. Ione gave a final pat to Patty Jane's roundness and then began attacking the turkey roaster with a shiny pad of steel wool.

Dishes done, the two women discovered Thor asleep on the davenport in front of the fire, his stockinged feet crossed and one big toe, pink and hale, poking out of a hole.

"Seems I never get to my darning basket," said Patty Jane. She didn't admit that she didn't have one to get to.

Ione was about to offer Patty Jane a glass of gooseberry wine, but reading the time on the small filigreed clock on the mantel, she said impulsively, "Patty Jane, Christmas Eve services are so lovely at my church — will you go with me?"

Patty Jane pulled the afghan up under Thor's chin. Normally nothing could tear her away from the privilege of watching her husband sleep. She could study each of his fine features, could watch the firelight play against his butter-colored hair. But these weren't normal times.

"I'd love to," said Patty Jane.

"You see, I usually go to the midnight service — there's such a sense of adventure getting out and about at that hour — but the eight o'clock has good singing — mostly the Chancel Choir — and if Thor's asleep . . ."

"Sure," said Patty Jane when Ione paused for breath.

A small shiver of pleasure zipped up Ione's spine. She was too shy to meddle, but the nonchurchgoing habits of Thor and Patty Jane nagged at her. She knew they weren't destined to hell because they didn't have a regular pew in the church, but still, she was certain God enjoyed the attention and shone His grace upon those who regularly added to the collection plate and knew the Nicene Creed by heart.

They drove the half-mile to Kind Savior's Lutheran Church in Ione's well-tended green Plymouth. Ione was an overly careful driver, leaning into the steering wheel as if she were trying to chin it; so close that occasionally her chest bumped the horn, startling her every time.

The church vestibule smelled of hot radiators and wet wool, and puddles of slush formed an irregular path to the double doors leading into the sanctuary. An usher greeted Ione and seated them. Ahead of them bobbed rows of haberdashery: special-occasion hats with velvet flowers and iridescent feathers, Russian hats of curly wool, long stocking caps, striped and tasseled.

"My Naomi Circle made the banner," whispered Ione. It read, "He is Born" in red and green letters and was draped behind the altar.

A long chord signaled the beginning of the service and the entire congregation rose to sing "Joy to the World." Ione and Patty Jane stood close, sharing a hymnal and Ione remembered how as a young woman she had loved sharing the book with her husband, his thumb solid and square-nailed on the left page, her small painted one on the right. The hymn could be a solemn dirge, such as "There Is a Green Hill Far Away," and yet Ione would be willing her heart to quit pounding, hoping to still her thoughts of Olaf's lips on hers.

She cocked her head slightly to better hear Patty Jane's voice. It didn't soar like her sister Harriet's, but it was serviceable and Ione summoned her thin alto to join her: "Let earth receive her king . . ."

Pastor Nelson's sermon was lively with humor and Ione was happy to see Patty Jane chuckling with the rest of the congregation. The deep-voiced minister imagined the holy birth happening in the city of Minneapolis — would the Dyckman or the Francis Drake Hotels turn Mary and Joseph away?

"Would you," he asked, and everyone felt certain he was speaking directly to them, "would you give up your sofa in the den to a poor couple, to a woman about to deliver? Or would you make feeble excuses about a lack of space? Would you eat your Christmas ham and linger over coffee and cookies, making jokes about the brazen, unkempt couple who wanted to spread fleas in your guest room?"

Patty Jane hugged her belly, imagining Mary's terror at laboring on a donkey, not knowing if she was going to give birth under a roof or a cold winter's moon. Considering the unusual circumstances of conception, surely Mary must have known everything was going to be fine? She probably wasn't even bothered by the contractions ("pains like a hatchet working its way out of your insides" was how her mother Anna put it); if God had chosen her to bear Jesus, she was probably the serene type who smiled while others screamed.

Pastor Nelson eased his grip on the pulpit and smiled.

"Friends," he said, and there was a collective relaxation of shoulders as everyone heard the shift in tone; they were off the hook and could stop feeling guilty. "Friends," the minister continued, "let us see in the faces of our loved ones, in the faces of strangers, the face of Jesus, for he truly does live in us all. Amen."

Patty Jane was startled when the congregation murmured "Amen." It was too abrupt an end to a sermon she wanted to go on and on; she wanted to think of Jesus in Thor's face (an easy task), to hear the resonant assurance in Pastor Nelson's voice.

Near the end of the service, after the gospel reading and the collection, the lights were dimmed and ushers standing at the end of the pews began to pass out small candles. Parishioners lit their candles from their neighbors' until all the rows were lit.

"This is my favorite part," said Ione, her head bent to her daughter-in-law's, watching the flame from Patty Jane's candle ignite the wick of hers.

F_{our}

NEW YEAR'S EVE turned out to be a stag affair for Thor and Avel. The original plan had been that the two couples would spend the evening dining and dancing at Avel's country club. But when Harriet and Avel arrived at the Rolvaag's, they found Patty Jane still in her robe, rheumy-eyed, standing over the kitchen sink gargling with saltwater. Harriet immediately offered to stay with her.

Patty Jane offered up a feeble protest between sneezes; she wasn't all that sick, and besides, she'd been dying to hear the Lance Jordan Orchestra, but Harriet said no, a woman in her condition shouldn't be out in 20-below-zero weather, with or without a cold, and she was feeling kind of achy herself. Why not give the boys a night out?

Harriet changed from a heavy black satin evening gown into a pair of Patty Jane's flannel pajamas. With her French-rolled hair and full coat of makeup, she looked like Hollywood's idea of a woman on her way to bed.

"Okay, you guys. Out," said Harriet.

"We're going to make popcorn and drink hot lemonade at midnight," said Patty Jane, sheepishly.

"Honey," said Avel, taking Harriet aside, "I don't want to abandon you on New Year's Eve."

"Avel, if I can't have fun with my own sister, who can I have fun with?"

"What about me?" he pouted.

Harriet picked up the top hat Avel set on the table and put it on his head. "We can go dancing at the club anytime, Avel. How many times can I help my sister, who's seven months pregnant and needs me? Hmmm, Sweetpie?"

The corners of Avel's mouth lifted. He loved being called Sweetpie. He called to Thor, who was getting Patty Jane settled under a quilt on the living room couch. "Looks as if our fate has been sealed, Thor."

When the two men walked into the wintry night, cold jumped them like a mugger. Avel had enlisted the services of his seldom-used white Cadillac limousine and his seldom-used driver. "My apologies, Clayton," said Avel as the man jumped out of the front seat to open the door for them. "I didn't think we'd be up there for so long. I trust you kept the heater running?"

"I'd be froze stiff if I didn't, sir."

Thor looked around the back seat, nodding. "My old Dodge looks pretty shabby next to this."

Avel chuckled. "It's not a bad way to get between two points."

Clayton adjusted the rearview mirror. "Are we all here, sir?"

"We're all here," said Avel. "This is the party."

Both men were quiet as the driver eased the limo through dark streets canopied by trees, their branches heavy and iced, chandeliers offering no light. Activity brimmed behind un-shaded windows where partygoers danced under streamers cascading from ceilings. At a stop sign, the car fishtailed. The roads were slick with a sheen of ice.

Clayton cleared his throat discreetly; he was proud of his driving (in the Big One he had driven colonels and generals — once Patton in Algiers — because his reflexes were quicker than anyone else's in his regiment) and wanted his passengers to know that just because the rear wheels had caught a little ice didn't mean he wasn't in control.

Avel leaned forward. "Have you any idea where we're going?"

"The club, sir?" asked Clayton, turning his head slightly.

"No, we don't want to go to the club without our dates. We'd be coerced into dancing with heavy-footed heiresses and their mothers." He leaned back in the seat. "We could always go see a picture, but that seems a defeatist thing to do on New Year's Eve." His sigh was short and businesslike. "Have you any ideas at all, Thor?"

Thor pulled at his gloves. "We could always just drive. Until we think of something, I mean."

Avel settled back into the seat and folded his arms across his chest. He hated indecision, especially indecision over something as inconsequential as where to spend a few stag hours, but it was apparent that neither he nor Thor was used to planning a night out. Avel had enough business and social obligations to occupy more time than he had to spare, and the only outside entertainment Thor ever sought was at a hockey rink.

At Lake and Minnehaha they waited as a freight train passed.

"Begging your pardon, sir," said Clayton, who enjoyed phrases he imagined English valets used, "but I read in this morning's paper that there's quite a party planned at the Calhoun Beach Club."

The caboose clattered by, its rear light beaming.

"Thanks for the tip, Clayton," said Avel, "but we're looking for something untried, aren't we, Thor?"

"I guess," said Thor. He was content riding around in the back of a limo; that was untried enough for him.

"Wait a second, slow down," said Avel, leaning toward the front seat. "That looks like a *boîte* of interest." He pointed to a bar whose name was outlined in flickering and burnt-out bulbs: *The Den Of.*

"Oh, no sir," said Clayton. "That's a pretty rough place."

"Good," said Avel. "Pull over." He rose slightly in his seat and adjusted his top hat in the rearview mirror. "And Clayton, take the car and have a night off. Happy New Year."

Before Clayton had a chance to put the car into park and open the door for his passengers, both men had already gotten out, each slamming his door shut, pausing for a millisecond to admire the forceful sound of steel clapping against steel. In synchronization, they straightened their backs and increased the length of their steps; it was the Dodge City Walk, the walk of men entering a new saloon.

The smell of beer and peanuts and pickles filled the room like a bad aftershave. Avel was energized. His cocktails had been drunk in the rarefied atmosphere of athletic clubs, drawing rooms or symphony hall lobbies. Since meeting Harriet, he had begun to discover the smells, the sounds and the sights of people who couldn't afford to pay for elegant surroundings. He was embarrassed that for so long he had hidden in the shelter of money.

"Sit at the bar?" asked Thor.

"Sure," said Avel, his eyes adjusting to the gloomy light.

They passed a line of hunched shoulders and sat at the end of the nicked wooden bar. A few balloons nudged the ceiling and a banner reading "Welcome 1954" was taped above the mirror behind the bar. The bartender, whose low-slung belt provided support to a huge and rolling belly, jabbed his chin at them in acknowledgment.

"Hamms," said Thor. "I'll have a Hamms."

"Ditto," said Avel, and the bartender cocked an eyebrow.

Foam drooled down the side of their mugs.

"Well," said Avel, hefting his mug, "here's to my future brother-in-law."

"Likewise."

They drank their beer in congenial meditation.

"Harriet's a good kid," said Thor finally. "Patty Jane thinks the world of her."

"It's a fine thing when sisters love each other."

"Sure is," said Thor, casting a furtive look at Avel, whose voice suddenly seemed tinged with melancholia. "You have sisters?"

Avel downed the last third of his beer and banged the bottom of his mug for a refill. "Two," he said, "and you'd have a hard time deciding which one was meaner and uglier."

Avel's statement shocked Thor. Although his own family had been fractured by death and Patty Jane's by drunkenness, he still believed in the ideal family (when a person was ready to start one), a family that served as an anchor against bad times.

"I didn't know you had kin," he managed to say after signalling for his own refill.

"Just two mean and ugly sisters," said Avel. "My parents met their ends years ago. My father was fifty-five years old when I was born, my mother just shy of forty-three."

Thor nodded as if that explained a lot.

"My sisters and I are in business together, but they don't have much import in my personal life."

The crack of a pool ball diverted their attention. There was an abrupt, high snicker, a laugh which seemed fueled by helium.

"You said the nine ball," said someone with a low voice, and if ever there was an invitation to a fight, this was it.

Avel and Thor, like the other men at the bar, swiveled their stools a half-circle to face the action.

"So you're a lousy shot and deaf too?" said a skinny guy with the unnaturally high voice.

"Take it outside before it starts," said the bartender. In his voice was the resignation of someone who says the same words every night.

"Okay, Hank. Let's go," said the man with the low voice.

The skinny one laughed. "Come on, Dean, finish the game, will ya? We can fight next year."

Dean scratched his earlobe, as if pondering Hank's suggestion. He was in the middle of chalking his cue when he smiled and nodded. "Next year," he said. "I get it."

Avel and Thor turned back to the bar.

"Shoot," said Avel, "I was hoping to see some fists fly."

"Night's still young," said a man feeding nickels into the jukebox behind them.

Les Paul and Mary Ford began singing "Mockin' Bird Hill" and the atmosphere of the bar changed perceptively, as if a page had been turned and a new, better chapter was about to begin. Avel lifted his beer mug.

"Thor, you're a prince of a fellow."

"Ditto," said Thor, clanging his mug against Avel's. He was enjoying his night out more than he thought he would.

Thor began to sing along to "Mockin' Bird Hill" in a three-note monotone:

"It gives me a thrill,
to wake up in the mornin',
to the mockin' bird's trill."

Avel squinted and appraised him like a jeweler. "You're no Harriet Dobbin."

"I know," said Thor, returning Avel's stare. "And you're no Clark Gable."

Avel laughed and coughed, swallowing his beer. "Just because you are."

"Amen to that," said a small woman with lips redder than blood, scrambling onto the stool next to Thor's. A dozen bracelets on her arm clacked together. "Course Mr. Gable's gettin' old," she said, putting her face inches from Thor's, "and you're not."

"No, I'm not," said Thor, "at least not right at the moment."

"My name's Faylene," said the woman, her breath condensing all the smells in the bar, "and this is my friend, Suzanne."

Suzanne rose up from behind her like a big shadow. "Hi," she said, her teeth bucked and flecked with stains.

"Ladies," said Avel, thinking that beauty had been on a holiday when these two were born, "join us."

"I'd say we already have," said Faylene as she hugged Thor's arm. "Suzanne, say hello to the little guy over there."

Obedient as she was homely, Suzanne sidled next to Avel, who thought she wouldn't be adverse to a friendly pat on the head.

"We've got a booth over there," Suzanne said, winking. Avel was fascinated that this woman had the courage to flirt. "Best seat in the house for anyone who wants to buy the beer."

Thor and Avel shrugged at each other, their eyes asking, "Why not?" The women skipped off to the table.

"Give me four more schooners, Skipper," said Avel.

With meaty hands, the bartender drew four mugs of beer and pushed them toward Avel. "Where'd you get this 'skipper' shit?" he said. "The name's Lionel."

Faylene and Suzanne kept Thor and Avel's trips to the bar frequent. During one run, the two men huddled near the jukebox.

"We're not being unfaithful in any way to the women in our lives, are we?" asked Avel. His bald spot was pink and dotted with sweat.

"Since when's conversation adultery?" said Thor, immediately proud of his answer. He narrowed his ice blue eyes at

Avel, whose image was not one hundred percent focused. "Or do you plan on doing more than talking?"

Avel shuddered.

"I'm nervous as a cat," Faylene said to the men, when they returned to the table. She took a long draw from the beer mug. "I sure hope they'll be nice to me." Beer dribbled down her chin and she swatted it with her fingers.

"Who do you hope will be nice to you?" asked Thor, fidgeting with the cummerbund of his rented tuxedo.

"The fellas. The audience." She and Suzanne giggled.

"Are you a chanteuse of some sort?" asked Avel.

Faylene pushed back a sausage of tightly curled hair. "If that's a fancy word for stripper, yeah, I am."

"Me too," said Suzanne eagerly. "Lionel's paying each of us twenty bucks to take off our clothes at midnight."

"Let me get this straight," said Avel, finally. "You are prepared to strip for twenty dollars?"

"Sure," said Faylene, "we've done it before."

"*You've* done it before, Faylene, not me." Suzanne shrugged her big round shoulders and smiled wanly at Avel and then, inexplicably, the corners of her mouth turned down and she burst out crying. Avel lamely patted her back. She said, sniffing, "Faylene's got boyfriends what pay her rent. She's got a good job at the dry cleaners. She's got kids what love her." She turned to Faylene and said in a whisper, "Why'd you make me say I'd take off my clothes with you?"

Faylene sat up in the booth, tucking her legs underneath her. "Lionel, can you get some coffee for Miss Crybaby over here? The beer's got to her again." She turned to Suzanne, who was drying her eyes on little square napkins imprinted with a cartoon of a naked woman inside a barrel. The caption read, "Tap this keg." "As I recall, Suzie, you said it would be kind of fun."

"Only 'cause I need the money."

Avel looked at Suzanne. "You're willing to strip for twenty bucks? In a dump like this?"

Suzanne's buck teeth scraped at her lower lip as she nodded.

Faylene laughed sharply. "Hey, it's no big deal. It's not as if we're going all the way down to the buff. We've got G-strings and pasties bigger than saucers." She looked at Thor. "I need 'em that big. My nipples got huge after my kids."

Thor opened his eyes in alarm.

Avel drummed his fingers on the table edge. "Listen, Suzanne, I'll pay you fifty dollars for *not* taking off your clothes."

"What?" said Suzanne.

"What was that?" interrupted Faylene. "Did I just hear moola being discussed?"

Avel sighed. "Okay, it goes for you, too. Fifty dollars for keeping your blouse buttoned."

"You a preacher or something?" asked Faylene.

"Hardly. Now is it a deal or not?"

Suzanne nodded, her head bobbing like a dashboard toy. Faylene lifted her chin and ran a hand full of rings down her neck. "Well, I sure do hate to deprive all the other boys."

Thor was at last forced to join the conversation. "Believe me," he said earnestly, "you won't be depriving anyone."

"Shut up, Sven," said Faylene, slapping Thor's thigh.

Jo Stafford was singing, "Shrimp Boats" and Hank, who had just beaten another sucker at the pool table, saw the little punk giving money to Fay and her ugly friend. A thought came over him: not only is the bitch a bitch, she's a whore.

"Wanna have some fun?" he asked Dean.

"What?" said Dean.

"Grab your stick and follow me."

With each step, the bar noises — the thud of glasses on wood, conversation — diminished. Behind the bar, Lionel folded his arms across his wide chest.

"Shrimp boats is a comin', a comin', a comin',
Shrimp boats is a comin' . . ."

Thor and Avel sat slumped in the booth, their chins just inches above the table top. Thor was debating the bathroom versus sleep, and when he was finally about to act, he found two men in front of him. Leaning on the table for support, he stood up.

"Excuse me, gennelmen," he said, "but if I don't get to the latrine in a hurry, we'll all be hosed down."

Hank clamped a hand on Thor's shoulder and pushed him down. "So you're selling your scrawny body now, Faylene?" Hank's fingers drummed the pool cue.

"What?" Faylene squinted as if she were looking at the sun.

Hank snapped his head toward Avel. "I saw the midget here giving you money."

Faylene giggled nervously. "Hank, this guy gave me and Suzanne money *not* to do our strip act. For some reason the guy doesn't want us to do our little routine and for fifty bucks I'm gonna say no?"

Hank regarded Thor and Avel. "You penguins fairies or something?"

"Beg your pardon?" said Avel.

"I have to go to the can," said Thor.

"I asked if you fairies in your penguin tuxedos were fairies."

"These guys ain't queer," said Suzanne. She looked at Avel. "Are you?"

Thor stood up. Anger and the immediate need to pee burned off some of his stupor. "Get out of my way," he said to Hank.

Hank moved like a snake but Thor saw his balled-up fist coming. As he deflected it, he punched Hank soundly in the stomach. Hank let out a sound like a deflating balloon.

Dean, in slow motion, raised his stick above his head. He stepped over Hank, who had fallen to the floor.

"Say your prayers," said Dean. He raised his stick high and Thor doubled his fist, but like a flying squirrel Avel sprang out of the booth. He grabbed the cue stick and for a moment was held aloft by it until both he and Dean crashed to the floor. On top, Avel began to pummel Dean's chest with his small fists.

Hank rose, staggering and swinging, and Thor landed a solid hit to his jaw.

"My jaw! My jaw!" Hank's voice was high as a soprano's.

"Avel, behind you!" screamed Suzanne. She and Faylene were perched on top of the banquette, out of harm's way. Avel felt a thump between his shoulder blades and he gasped, falling forward.

Thor felt Dean's fleshy fist connect with his left ear. As Thor wrenched away, his elbow smashed against the man's nose. Blood spattered to the floor.

Suddenly, a whistle blew and Thor looked up. The bartender stood before him holding a bat in one hand and yanking the whistle from his mouth with the other.

"Party's over," he said to Avel and Thor, "and I want you two jackasses out of here."

"Come on Dean, get that nose cleaned up," the bartender said to the big man, who wore a goatee of blood. He led Dean to the bathroom, asking him why he hadn't ducked. Hank had crawled away to the jukebox. Faylene sat on the floor next to him, holding a bottle of beer against his cheek. Suzanne still sat on the top of the banquette.

"Where's Avel?" asked Thor, hearing his own voice amplified in his throbbing ear.

Suzanne pointed. "Underneath the table."

Thor bent down and tugged Avel's pant leg. "Are you all right in there?"

With a groan, Avel crawled crablike from under the table. "I believe I slipped into another realm of consciousness for a while." He rubbed the fringe of dark hair around his head. "Did we win?"

Thor helped him up. "It'll be a tie if we get out of here."

Avel smiled at Suzanne as he dusted off his trouser knees. "So long, doll."

"I was rootin' for you," said Suzanne shyly.

Avel peeled off a bill and tucked it into Suzanne's hand. "I always appreciate a good cheerleader."

Suzanne's eyes widened as she looked at the folded square of money. "Whoa, Nelly!"

"Spend it on yourself," said Avel. He picked up his top hat, flattened in the mêlée, and bowed to Suzanne before he and Thor walked past men and women who alternately hissed and cheered.

"Don't take nothin' personal," said a man in the uniform of Peter's Pest Control. "Them guys fight anyone walks in here."

In less than a minute a cab appeared. "We're in luck," said Avel.

They rode a few blocks before Thor realized he still hadn't peed and asked the driver to pull over. He stood behind a tree, his sigh of relief a visible plume in the cold night air, his urine drilling a yellow hole into the snowbank.

Five

To Avel, the fight was a key that opened the doors of an exclusive club. He liked looking in the mirror at the purplish bump on his head (he had clipped his forehead on the bar's table edge) and found himself taking boxing jabs at his reflection.

"I've never been in a brawl before," he said to Harriet. They were sharing a bag of Vogstad's coconut donuts in the front seat of the Cadillac.

"Congratulations," said Harriet.

"No, you don't understand. I've wanted to, but the situation never presented itself. You can't exactly throw punches in a board room or an art museum."

"Why not?" asked Harriet.

Avel shifted on his new leather booster chair. "I suppose you could. Sometimes I feel it's much more than my physical growth that's stunted." Snowflakes splattered on the windshield and Avel sighed. "Is it every man and woman's curse to want it all and only get ten percent of it? Or do we ask too much?

Are we too selfish to see the beauty of our every days, to revel in our every hours, blinded as we are by what everybody else has?"

"Gee," said Harriet, lighting a cigarette, "I wish I knew."

Avel was partial to thoughtful debate, he said, having minored in philosophy at Brown. But with Harriet debates were usually monologues. Harriet had explained to him once that too much thought scared her, that she was happier doing than thinking.

"There are some things that no one's been able to figure out," she said, "so why should I?"

Everyone Avel knew had stock portfolios and trust funds and opinions, and he loved dealing with people who had no bargaining power other than their emotions. When he bought presents, there was true delight in receiving them. There were no refined thank-yous when he gave Harriet a new dress or Patty Jane a Motorola television set; there were yelps and shouts and hugs that squeezed the breath out of him.

He had been thinking of a gift — actually, a job — he could bestow upon Thor but he wanted to get Harriet's opinion first.

"Are you getting cold?" he asked. They had been parked in the Cadillac for over an hour. Harriet tossed the empty bag of donuts into the back seat and snuggled next to Avel.

"I've got my love to keep me warm," she sang.

Avel capped the thermos. "Harriet, what do you think Thor would think of a job that took a couple hours, paid him two hundred dollars, and brought him into millions of households?"

"I know I'd sign on the dotted line," she said, tapping an ash into the dashboard ashtray. "But what exactly are you talking about?"

Avel tucked his hand into the crook of Harriet's arm.

"As you know," he began, "there's not much that my sisters let me in on regarding the family business. Not that I mind, of course, I'd much rather smell the roses than send a memo. However, my talent for design is occasionally tapped. Last year, for example, I was a crucial participant in the 'Ames Yeast — It Rises to the Occasion' campaign." He paused and cocked an eyebrow at Harriet, waiting for a response.

"Pretty snappy," nodded Harriet.

"The public thought so too. It was one of our best years for yeast sales." He sighed happily, his breath steaming in the cold air.

"So where does Thor fit in with yeast?"

"Not yeast, my dear, Mighty Bites."

"Mighty Bites," said Harriet. "Are they like Toasty Bites?"

"Toasty Bites are an oat product. Mighty Bites are made from corn, plus they're sugar coated."

"Oh," said Harriet.

"The Gruesome Twosome decided I would be an asset in working with the art department. Thursday we looked at the first crop of models — a group of giants from the Gopher basketball team — but we were fairly nonplussed by what we saw. Did you ever notice how many basketball players have prominent Adam's apples?"

"No, I never did," said Harriet.

"Their thyroid glands don't know when to quit. In any event, we're looking for someone handsome, athletic, appealing — i.e., Thor — to hold a spoonful of Mighty Bites and grace our cereal box."

Harriet snubbed out her cigarette in the ashtray, nodding.

"Do you think he'd be interested?" asked Avel. "I know he's rather touchy about people calling attention to his looks."

"Avel, for two hundred bucks, I bet he'll let 'em look."

"Are you kidding?" asked Thor. "I pretend I'm eating a bowl of cereal and smile into the camera and I collect two bills?"

Avel nodded.

"Well, what the hay. It sure beats what Bill Blaine's paying me."

It was almost ten at night but Avel and Harriet had decided they couldn't wait to propose the idea to Thor and had driven to the Rolvaag apartment.

"Just think," said Patty Jane, wearing a bathrobe, "I'll be eating breakfast with my husband *at* the table and *on* the table."

"And you can put him away in the cupboard when he's a bad boy." Harriet smiled but Patty Jane heard the grit in her voice. Although Patty Jane hadn't said anything to Harriet about Thor's ambivalence toward her, a radar existed between the sisters and Harriet was receiving signals.

The photo session was held in a fourth-floor studio of the Ames Building. A square table draped with red gingham stood under a small forest of lights. A window had been painted on a backdrop; it displayed cheery curtains and through its panes several robins flew against a blue sky.

Avel and a small group of department chiefs clustered off to one side while a young woman touched up Thor's make-up.

"He is the perfect Mighty Bites man," said the head of the art department. "If only he'd relax a little."

"The guy's stiff as a stiff," said the head of product development.

"Yeah," said the head of marketing, "he looks tortured."

The photographer reloaded his camera and said, "Let's try some more," and the make-up girl, giving one more swab to Thor's nose, stepped out of camera range.

Thor dug his spoon into a bowl of dry Mighty Bites (the milk would be painted on later, he learned) and smiled broadly.

"Try not to look so strained," said the photographer.

"Strained?" whispered the head of the art department. "He looks constipated."

"Like he hasn't taken a dump in years," said the head of product development.

"Excuse me," said Avel. He walked across the room to the photographer and patted him on the shoulder. "May I have a word with him, please?"

"Be my guest," said the photographer. He turned to the make-up girl. "Betty, let's take five."

Avel, hands in pockets, strolled over to the table, stepping over lighting cables.

"I stink, don't I?" said Thor.

Avel shrugged.

Thor wiped away the sweat above his lip. "Geez, Avel, it's so hot in here and I feel so stupid being asked to smile a Mighty Bites smile. Just what the hell is a Mighty Bites smile anyway?"

Avel smiled; his wasn't a Mighty Bites smile, but it was sincere. He didn't quite understand Thor's discomfort; Avel loved to smile, upon request or not. He tugged up a few inches of his pinstriped pants and knelt.

"Thor, I think it would be better if you removed yourself from the situation."

"I knew it wouldn't work out," said Thor, rising. "I'm sorry, Avel."

Avel fluttered his hands. "Sit down, Thor, sit down. I don't mean remove yourself physically, I mean remove yourself mentally."

"Come again?"

"Think of Tahiti, the Caribbean — some paradise. Pretend you're there and when you look into the camera, you're seeing the most beautiful woman alive. Use your imagination, Thor."

The photographer and make-up girl returned with cups of coffee. Avel clapped Thor on the shoulder. "Let it fly."

Avel returned to the knot of concerned department heads. He pushed out his lower lip and nodded.

As Thor's forehead and nose were slapped with more powder

and the shooting resumed, he tried to imagine some idyllic island, but half the film was shot before he even left the continent. It was the photographer's sigh that cued him; he heard an
ocean breeze instead of the man's impatience and the hot lights
became the sun and he was on the Lido outside Venice — he
had a vivid memory of his father's stories of Italy's beautiful
women — and he looked into the camera pretending he was
looking into the face of an olive-skinned woman with a mouth
the color of red wine. He smiled.

"Good!" said the photographer. The camera clicked.

Several more pictures were taken, the photographer shouting "good" and "nice" and the knot of department heads moved
closer, their heads nodding in unison, their eyes shiny.

Thor held up a spoon of cereal. His smile was deep and held
all the promise of a young and vital American man. He looked
into the camera, only now he wasn't looking at the olive-
skinned Italian; he was seeing Patty Jane as she was a few days
after they were married. He was seeing her stepping out of the
bathtub, her body tight and taut, drops of water clinging to the
curves of her breasts, to her thighs. He was seeing her brush
back her wet short hair with one hand. He was seeing a smile
cross her face and a gesture, an uncurling finger, an invitation
that said, "Come here." Thor was seeing himself go to her.

"That's it!" shouted the photographer. "That's the Mighty
Bites smile!"

Six

THE PLATE RATTLED on the table as the waitress flung it in front of Patty Jane. Her movements slowed as she presented to Thor his tenderloin steak. "Medium rare, easy to chew, easier to digest," she said, leaning over him, her breast flattening against his shoulder.

Thor blushed and Patty Jane laughed. Other women's interest in Thor only confirmed her own good taste and the more brazen the flirtation, the more she got a kick out of it.

"Happy Birthday, honey," she said, once the waitress reluctantly turned her attention to the other tables in her section. She clinked her wine glass against Thor's, who added his own toast.

"To my wife, the most beautiful woman on this earth."

It was more surprise than modesty that made Patty Jane match Thor's blush; there had been a long drought in the season of his compliments.

In her eighth month, Patty Jane *was* lovely. She wore a rust plaid maternity dress which brought out the gold in her hazel eyes and the high peach tones of her skin.

Crossing the line between attentive service and peskiness, the waitress visited their table as many times as possible, until she asked if they cared for any dessert, to which Thor answered, "No, we'll have that when we get home."

And they did. For the first time in weeks, they made love. Thor rubbed Patty Jane's big belly with his hands and made it wet with his kisses, and when he looked up at her in the thin moonlight to ask, "Patty Jane, what have we made?" she cried out, a howl of joy and relief. Translated into words, the cry would have said, "Yippee! He loves us!"

Patty Jane later attributed Thor's demonstrativeness to one Manhattan and several glasses of wine and/or a celebratory birthday mood. Either way, it made no further appearances. The nearer she got to her due date, the further Thor drew away.

Patty Jane pleaded with him to tell her what the matter was, but how could he tell her that his impending fatherhood filled him with terror? On the rare occasion when he let his guard down, he daydreamed about his son or daughter (he even drew up a list of possible names), but pictures of himself rocking or feeding the baby were quickly blacked out by shadows of panic. His father's death had taught him early that within love lay the possibility of great pain. But he couldn't show his fear to his wife — what would she think of him then? — and so, like his other unwanted feelings, he buried it.

Patty Jane only knew that she was losing her husband. What she didn't know was the more he retreated from her, the more he began to brush the hands of women who came into Bill Blaine's, to engage them in conversation where words were superfluous to eye contact. He slowed down when women called to him between classes, agreeing to walk over to Dinkeytown, the commercial area near the campus, for a cup of coffee. He immersed himself in flirting as if it were a clear blue lake and he was learning to swim. It diverted him from the burdens of real love and, for the moment, it was enough.

As a consolation prize for his emotional and sexual withdrawal, Thor rewarded Patty Jane with conversation, but his words were of no great consequence: anecdotes about his teachers, his sales at Bill Blaine's, his plans to give Avel a lesson in auto mechanics. "Think of it, Patty Jane," he said, "the man's never even put a can of oil into his car."

"Why should he?" asked Patty Jane. "He can hire people to do things like that."

She was leaning on the handle of the shopping cart while the baby inside her danced a rhumba. They were shopping at Food Fair, following slushy tracks through the aisles.

"I'll tell you why," said Thor, putting a clump of bananas into the cart, "because a man should know certain things."

"Hmmmm," said Patty Jane, replacing the bananas.

"And did you know he's got a boat — a yacht, I guess you'd call it — that he keeps docked in some bay back east? He says we'll all have to go for a cruise this summer."

"Is that right," said Patty Jane. "A pound of liver, please."

The butcher behind the counter smiled the paternal smile most men gave her lately and, with tongs, he groped at the slick pile of brown-red meat. Thor turned away.

"I don't see how you can eat that stuff."

Patty Jane accepted the white paper package from the butcher. "It's good for the baby," she said and when she saw Thor roll his eyes, added, "*our* baby, remember?" She gripped the cart handle until her knuckles were white. "And for God's sake, try to acknowledge the damn thing, will you?" Immediately she sent a silent communiqué to her baby: I didn't mean to call you a damn thing, I'm just mad, that's all.

Thor felt the heat of a blush and turned toward the canned-foods aisle.

"Don't turn away from me, you bastard," said Patty Jane, spinning the cart on its wheels. "I'm sick and tired of you turning away."

Thor clenched his jaw and stared at a row of creamed corn. "Don't make a scene, Patty Jane," he said, his voice low.

"'Don't make a scene, Patty Jane,'" she said, mocking him. "What the hell am I supposed to do? How the hell do I get your attention, huh?" She jabbed the cart into his legs as she spoke.

"Cut it out, Patty Jane."

She rammed the cart into him again. The bottom metal bar banged at his ankles and he jumped forward.

"Cut it out, I said. That hurts."

"Oh, it hurts. Well, *excuse* me for horning in on your territory." She pushed the cart again, hoping to fling him over a pyramid of canned pork and beans at the end of the aisle, but Thor grabbed the cart and yanked it, so that it traveled a short distance on two wheels before knocking against a cart of cans marked "Half Off."

They stared at each other for a moment.

Thor reached into his coat pocket. He took all the money from his wallet and handed it to Patty Jane, along with the keys to the Dodge.

"Here's the money. Have one of the boxboys carry the groceries out." He stepped back and pointed a finger inches from Patty Jane's nose. "And now . . . just leave me alone." Patty Jane watched him walk away down the aisle, thinking that all the cruel things her parents had ever said to her were nothing, nothing at all, compared to the sentence her husband had just spoken.

Thor left the market, feeling as if he'd been expelled from school — frightened and thrilled at the same time. A wind caught the snow and sent it swirling around his feet. He paused at the corner to turn up his collar. The manners that Ione had instilled in him urged him to go back inside the store and apologize to Patty Jane, but the impulse was weakened by his giddiness. When the light turned green, he ran across the street as if someone had fired a starting gun.

That night, he called on his English professor (who had begged him to consult her at any time), and Mary Parker, a cheerleader for the Gopher football team.

The professor whispered, "Promise me you'll read Blake tonight," as he left her trembling under the chenille bedspread. Mary Parker, playing a game of peek-a-boo with her pompoms, had sung the Gopher fight song as he put on his clothes. "You made the play-offs," she shouted to him as he skipped down her front steps, "you lettered in love!"

Later as he walked along the quiet streets, shame crept up to him, at first like a skittish animal, one that he could ditch with the memories of the two dimples that lay on each side of Mary Parker's tail bone. But the more he walked, the more shame became a companion, a loyal hound. A pink band of dawn stretched across the eastern horizon above the Mississippi, and as he walked along River Road, the black tree branches rising from the bluffs like arthritic fingers, he could not shake the picture of Patty Jane sitting at the kitchen table, a quilt around her shoulders, waiting for him.

He burped dryly and his head pounded. He had drunk half a bottle of sweet wine at the English professor's and beer at the cheerleader's.

Maybe Patty Jane had fallen asleep by now, maybe she had read his textbook assignments ("I like knowing what you're learning"), maybe she finally thought, "This is it, I can't stay awake any longer." She usually slept with her mouth open and sometimes she jerked and squealed, like a sleeping puppy.

Such a deep tenderness touched Thor's heart that he thought he might cry. He hoped tears, plenty of tears, would fall and somehow absolve him.

"I *am* a lout," he said. But as much as he meant to disparage himself, he couldn't help but admire his colorful accusation.

Shame and guilt then darted behind a tree and his mind focused on another image of Mary Parker, who with the same passion she used on the sidelines at Gopher Stadium, had stood on the bed, nude, leading a cheer. Her thin, trim body was nothing like Patty Jane's, full and ripe with a baby. "*My* baby!" he thought urgently. "I'll try harder," he promised himself. "I'll hold her, I'll take her out for breakfast once she's done being mad at me and maybe then we'll go shopping for a — what do you call it? — a bassinette. For our baby!"

Thor began to run, enjoying the cold air in his lungs and against his bare head. The sky was lighting up and Thor, his arms pumping, thought he could run for hours. He saw some-one sliding down the hill of a large house on the block that faced the river. They waved to each other, conspirators at dawn. Between the trees lining the boulevard, the snowbank was high. He leaped over it to the street and then jumped back over it again because it felt so good. He thought of a newsreel he had seen once of Jesse Owens running the hurdles at the Berlin Olympics, how his legs had looked at the moment he cleared the hurdle, the sharp beautiful angle of bone and skin and muscle.

Increasing his speed, Thor jumped the snowbank again, his black coat following the lines of his legs, his arms bent at the elbow, lifting him higher, propelling him faster toward home.

A thought filled him: "I am a deer." It was his second-to-last thought as his feet slid on the icy crest of the snowbank and he hurtled forward. He was helpless before the speed and force of his fall and just before his bare, blond head crashed into the broad trunk of an oak tree, there was time for one last thought: "*Patty Jane.*"

When the telephone rang, Harriet was playing Mendel-ssohn's "Consolation" on her new Lyon-Healy harp. It was a beautiful instrument, its fore-pillar gilt, its soundboard painted with a scroll of flowers. Avel had delivered it to her apartment a week after her music lessons had begun. Harriet's full-time job now was practicing her harp and her trumpet, and she loved putting in overtime.

Avel, scheduled to leave in two days for a trade conference in Antwerp, Belgium, was lying on the antique couch he had also given Harriet, missing her already. He dozed intermittently and dreamed he was in heaven, being serenaded by the head angel.

Harriet was wearing a navy dressing gown of Chinese silk. Avel had seen the bolt of fabric in the backroom of his tailor's and had commissioned a gown for Harriet, who said shyly as she modelled it, "Well, it sure beats flannel."

Avel jerked reflexively when the phone rang. "Consolation" ended abruptly, as if the harp strings had been snipped. Harriet stood and her eyes locked with Avel's. Sometimes she got carried away, playing music until dawn, but who else was up and calling at four-thirty A.M.?

Avel watched Harriet's gown float around her as she moved toward the telephone.

"Hello?" she whispered, clutching the receiver with two hands.

"Harriet," came Patty Jane's voice over the line, "you've got to come over."

"Oh, Patty Jane, is the baby on the way?"

"No," said Patty Jane. "Just come."

Harriet hung up the phone, lit a cigarette with one hand and loosened the sash of her gown with the other.

"Start up the car, Avel," she said, her eyes squinting from the thin column of smoke that rose from her cigarette, "that was my sister."

The smells of Vogstad's bakery in full production accompanied them up to Patty Jane's apartment.

"He's run away from me, I know it," said Patty Jane. She ground the heels of her hands into her eyes, her fingers splayed in the curls on top of her head.

71

"Patty Jane," said Avel, "why would Thor run away? He loves you."

Patty Jane's bottom lip caught a rivulet running from her nose.

"No, he doesn't," she said. "He stopped loving me months ago."

Should they call the police? The hospitals?

"Go ahead," said Patty Jane, "no one will have heard of him."

She was right, no blond, extremely good-looking twenty-four-year-old male had been admitted to a local hospital or booked and fingerprinted at any nearby police station. By 7:00 A.M., Patty Jane allowed herself to lie down — "for the baby's sake" — and Harriet taught Avel how to play pinochle, their ears tuned like antennae to the footsteps they hoped to hear coming up the stairs.

When Thor did not return twenty-four hours later, Ione accompanied the threesome to the police station downtown to file a missing-person's report. Ione sat in the back of Avel's new red Kaiser Dragon. The flashy design of the car and its red-and-white upholstery clashed with the gloom of the occupants.

"You don't have to come," Harriet told Ione, to which Ione replied, "I must."

There was no conversation in the car. Ione cast a surreptitious look at Patty Jane, but her daughter-in-law's face was hidden by the furry rim of her jacket hood. "Lord help her," prayed Ione, "and help my son wherever he may be. And please dear God," went her silent coda, "don't let him be with my Olaf."

Sergeant Daniel Finn, hair standing up in a brush cut, typed out the m.p. report with two quick fingers and told Patty Jane not to worry.

"You'd be surprised, the number of expectant papas who skip town for a couple days." He pulled the report out with a thick red hand and the typewriter roller groaned. "I'll bet dollars to donuts he'll be back by tomorrow." His bushy red eyebrows lifted as he eyed Patty Jane. "Guy'd be a fool to stay away from a gal like you."

Later that afternoon, when Patty Jane had finally fallen asleep, Avel and Harriet left the apartment and drove to the Foshay Tower office of Milt Zims, Private Detective.

"Hard to get lost in a crowd with a mug like this," said Mr. Zims, studying a snapshot of Thor through thick-lensed glasses. "And you say he's how tall?"

"Six-two," said Avel, sitting straighter in the rickety chair next to a withering palm.

"Some guys have all the luck," said Milt Zims, pressing a plug of chewing tobacco into the channel between his gum and lower lip.

With tobacco-stained fingers, he wrote down the information Harriet and Avel gave him: Thor's class schedule, Bill Blaine's address. "No close personal friends, huh?" he asked, his ballpoint pen moving in scratchy angles.

Avel and Harriet shrugged.

"The goodlooking never do, do they?" said Mr. Zims.

Avel paid him a week's expenses in advance and told him to keep the editorials to himself.

From the detective's office, Harriet drove Avel to the airport.

"Forget it," said Avel when Harriet parked the car and pulled the keys out of the ignition. "I'm not going."

"Avel," said Harriet as she leaned over and kissed him with her thin, curvy lips, "we have been over this and over this."

Avel's eyes misted. "But I want to be near you. I want to help you."

Harriet tucked his scarf into the lapels of his coat.

"Avel, Patty Jane and I used to play this game. Whenever things were really bad at home, when both Dad and Ma were drunk and screaming and throwing things, we used to sit in the closet repeating over and over, 'Everything'll be all right.' And it might have taken a while, but it usually was."

"I don't want to go to Antwerp. I'm a coward for leaving."

Harriet smiled. "You're a businessman. Besides, it's just like that cop said, Thor'll probably be back by tomorrow."

Avel held her hands over his chest. "Do you still love me?"

Harriet kissed him. "Always and forever."

Avel kissed her back. "Ditto. Double ditto."

Two days later, on a raw March morning, Patty Jane gave birth to an eight-pound girl. She had refused any twilight sleep, any local anesthesia; she refused to obey the bullying nurse who told her to keep it down, for cripes' sake, did she want to upset everyone in the ward?

"Don't lecture me, you asshole," hollered Patty Jane, "I'll upset everyone in the whole hospital if I want to!"

An expectant father, reading a *Reader's Digest* in the waiting room, looked up from his "Points to Ponder," a smile lifting his mustache. Harriet, who sat next to Ione on the mud-colored couch, saw her ears redden. She squeezed Ione's hand.

"She's going to owe you a fortune in quarters, Mrs. Rolvaag."

Patty Jane's labor had brought on a cursing spree that surprised even Harriet. So she wasn't prepared for the giggles that suddenly escaped Ione's pursed lips. Harriet couldn't help but laugh, too; she hadn't laughed in days. The man shut his *Reader's Digest* and laughed with them. He was an old hand in waiting rooms, but he had never heard such caterwauling.

"They should put that one under," he said amicably, tamping Cherry Blend into his pipe.

The women's laughter was cut short. Ione drew up her shoulders, looked at him with a cold glare and said, "Mind your own business." This surprised Harriet more than anything said or screamed by Patty Jane and she encased the woman's shoulders with her arm. "Come on, Mrs. Rolvaag, let me buy you a cup of coffee."

Dr. Danielson, a young intern from Wilmar, hated his obstetrics round, finding labor and birth a thoroughly unpleasant experience. His intended field of medicine was podiatry; feet were neat and undemanding and patients were ever so grateful when a planter's wart or bunion was removed.

If this mad woman in the maternity ward didn't want any medication, why didn't she just stay home and have her baby? Or better yet, go squat in the forest? He had gently tried telling her that a little ether, a couple ccs of Demerol, would do her good, but when she had screamed, "Touch me with that needle and I'll sue you," he almost slapped her. Instead he spun on his heels and told one of the floor nurses to get him only when the patient was dilated ten centimeters and not a centimeter before.

Patty Jane had expected pain, but not the tornado of pain that threatened to turn her insides out.

When the contraction subsided, Patty Jane sat up from the damp pillow, her hair wet and matted against her skull. She had only made the decision to be conscious when labor first began. Thor was missing; she didn't want her child coming into the world with an absent mother, too. She tucked her chin into her chest and spoke to the huge mound that roiled under her thin hospital gown.

"Stop torturing me, baby," she said, her voice a hiss. "That's your daddy's department."

The baby's head was crowning when they wheeled Patty Jane into the delivery room.

"Push," said Dr. Danielson, putting on a rubber glove.

"What the hell do you think I'm doing?" said Patty Jane between clenched teeth.

"Now, now," said the young doctor, "let's not say things we'll regret later."

Patty Jane arched her back and ground her buttocks into the hard, papered gurney, letting out a scream that rattled the overhead lamp and the attending nurse. Like a letter into a mail chute, the baby slid easily into Dr. Danielson's hands. The nurse clamped the cord and the doctor held up the wailing newborn.

"It's a girl," he said, "and she sounds just like you."

After a three-day stay, Patty Jane left the hospital.

"Honestly," said the nurse who Patty Jane had called a slander to the name of Florence Nightingale, "what are you trying to prove? A week's recovery period is the minimum for our recuperating mothers."

"I'm not sick," said Patty Jane, packing the small green suitcase Ione had lent her.

"Honestly!" said the nurse again.

Patty Jane thought the policy of leaving the hospital in a wheelchair silly, but the nurse wasn't going to lose that battle. Ione and Harriet each held one handle of the chair while Patty Jane held the baby, and an orderly passing them in the corridor couldn't help but notice the grim determination of the three women.

As much as she dreaded it, Patty Jane knew she must get back to the apartment as soon as possible. Her real life included a husband who was dead or missing and she had to return to that life before she lost the courage to deal with it.

A wind made of equal parts motion and ice lifted the women's skirt hems and threw their scarf ends behind them as they scrambled from the car Avel had left for their use and up the stairs. Patty Jane held the baby, wrapped like a package in receiving blankets, whispering, "It'll be all right," as she climbed steps which seemed as high as Mt. Everest.

It was midafternoon five days later when Patty Jane and Harriet heard the knock on the door and they froze for a moment, locked in hope and fear: Was it Thor? Was it someone with news of Thor?

Harriet rose as Avel pushed open the door. Patty Jane's gloom lifted slightly, enough to allow for a chuckle when Harriet lifted Avel off his feet in a bear hug. But gloom was stingy with reprieves; sadness filled her again as she thought, "I could never have picked up Thor like that."

When Harriet finally put him down, Avel smoothed the front of his overcoat with dignity. "I had an inkling you might do that. That's why I left all the presents on the landing."

Although Harriet smiled, the silence that greeted this announcement told Avel everything.

"Oh, well, you can look at them later." He turned to the rack to take off his hat and coat, searching for something to say that might help.

"Patty Jane," he said and she rose to meet him. He gasped when he saw that despite being bundled in Thor's old terry cloth robe, Patty Jane had lost her round belly.

"A girl," said Patty Jane, nodding. She and Avel hugged and soon one lapel of the robe was damp with Avel's tears.

Patty Jane led him down the short hallway to the bedroom. He turned and mouthed to Harriet, "Thor?" and she answered him by shaking her head.

"Her name is Nora," said Patty Jane. "After 'The Doll House.' When Elmo and Anna were sober enough to read, they held a special loyalty to the Norwegians.

"She's exquisite," said Avel as Patty Jane lifted a satin-edged triangle of blanket. "She's even smaller than I am."

"Barely," said Patty Jane, and she wanted to kiss Avel for making her smile again. Instead, she took his hand and patted it. "I'm okay, Avel," she said, "I don't know what the hell is going on, but I'm okay."

With her finger, she grazed Nora's cheek. The baby's mouth worked as if she were suckling.

Harriet came into the bedroom. "Coffee's on."

"I've got something better," said Avel as they walked back to the kitchen. "Now let's get some glasses and then we'll figure out what to do."

Avel produced a bottle a French colleague had given him and Patty Jane said, "The last time I drank champagne was on my honeymoon." Immediately, she sank to her knees, her hands grasping the horizontal slats of the wooden kitchen chair. Her voice climbed to a high keen and both Avel and Harriet were on the floor with her, holding her, rubbing her heaving back. Underneath their hands, Patty Jane's spine was like a live wire.

"Come home, Thor," cried Patty Jane, holding onto the bars of the chair as if she were being held captive.

It was only when Nora awoke and punctured her mother's noises with her own that Patty Jane stopped crying.

Circles of wetness were spreading on the fabric of her robe. Avel asked, with great reverence, "Is that your milk?"

Patty Jane drew in a hiccup. "Sure is," she said. "I'm a regular dairy." She hurried to the bedroom.

A moment later, Nora's cries stopped abruptly. Almost roughly, Harriet pushed Avel into a chair and plunked down on his lap.

"Oof," he said.

"Oh, Avel, I am so glad you're home," said Harriet, her arms as tight around his neck as a starched collar. "It's been awful around here."

"Wait a second, Harriet," said Avel, squirming under her weight, "you've got to let me breathe."

"Sorry. I keep forgetting how tiny you are." She sprang up and sat on another chair and pushed herself toward him. She opened a fresh pack of cigarettes and lit one, waving the match out with a snap of her wrist.

"I have been so worried about her," she said, inhaling deeply.

"Today with you is the first time I've seen her smile. Nearly a whole week, I swear; no smiles, no laughs."

"Not even with the baby?"

"Well, that's different. Of course a mother's going to smile with her newborn. I'm talking about a regular, daily kind of smile."

Harriet was wearing her hair in a long braid down her back and as she talked, Avel took the band out and ran his fingers through the thick ribbons of hair, unraveling them.

"That feels better than anything I've felt in a long time," Harriet said. She sat still, her eyes closed, enjoying the feel of Avel's small, strong fingers against her scalp. Avel leaned to her and, holding her hair aside, kissed her on the neck. She snubbed out her cigarette. Their embrace was long and full and when it was over, Harriet tipped her chair back and pulled the glass knob of a kitchen drawer.

"Milt Zims brought this over yesterday," she said, and gave him a manila envelope.

Avel read a letter which was typed on University of Minnesota stationery:

> To whom it may concern, i.e. Thor's wife:
> I understand Thor Rolvaag's disappearance is under investigation. For what it's worth, he spent the night of said disappearance at my apartment. I don't think this means anything in and of itself, but I feel I have to tell you as it may be an integral piece of a larger puzzle. For professional reasons I am unable to reveal my name but please know that I thought Thor remarkable both in and out of the classroom.

Avel whispered softly. "So Thor was seeing another woman."

"Bastard," said Harriet. She lit another cigarette.

"He never said a word to me, Harriet." Avel lifted his narrow chin and probed it with his thumb and forefinger. "In our way, we were friends. I'd have thought he would have given me an inkling."

"He never gave anyone an inkling," said Harriet bitterly, "of anything."

Seven

MARCH WAS A MONTH of thaws and freezes. While the weather jumped erratically, the mood inside Patty Jane's apartment remained at a constant low. Harriet took up residence in Patty Jane's living room; she slept on the nubby-cushioned couch, folding up her sheet and blankets every morning and tucking them into the linen closet. Avel's chauffeur, Clayton, brought over Harriet's harp, cursing as he navigated the back steps. Harriet set up a concert schedule; she played at two in the afternoon and again at seven thirty with Patty Jane and the baby in attendance, seated on the wide velvet chair Avel had bought. To Handel or Debussy, Patty Jane nursed Nora and then both mother and child would fall asleep. Harriet's heart unfolded with tenderness seeing her sister and niece sleeping, both pink cheeked, their mouths slightly opened, and her heart clenched when she thought of Thor walking away from so much beauty.

Her sister's world seemed to spin on a skewed axis; just when it seemed fate was on Patty Jane's side, she was suddenly knocked over with little warning and no mercy. "Thank heaven and stars," thought Harriet, "that Avel and Ione are around to help." Although Avel reported that his sisters pestered him to make appearances at board meetings and scheduled conferences in which his attendance was "absolutely mandatory," he still was able to spend time each day cruising the streets of Minneapolis and St. Paul, looking for a sign, a trace, a single blond hair of Thor Rolvaag.

Ione kept her own strong and steady vigils. Each day, she awoke before dawn and went to church in the morning darkness, sitting quietly in the empty sanctuary, praying for her son. Occasionally, she wished the Lutherans hadn't cut themselves off from the Catholic Church; now, she could use the comfort of ornate ritual, of lighting candles for her son and hearing a kindly voice in a small confessional absolving her of Thor's absence. She didn't feel wholly responsible, but perhaps she had contributed to Thor's leaving his family without a trace. She wore guilt like a heavy scarf.

But guilt also stoked her energy, adding to her endurance, illuminating her simple promise: to help Patty Jane and her granddaughter.

After her daily communion in church Ione, like Avel, looked for Thor. Once, certain she had spotted him, she cried out and pressed down on her car horn, but the tall blond who turned around was a teenager whose sparse and wispy beard only partially covered his acne-mottled face. Donny Dahl, her employer at Dahl's Candies, was very understanding and let her change her hours or cancel them altogether. Ione had been making candy for Dahl longer than any of his employees and, as he had never compensated her for her peanut brittle and divinity recipes, he felt duty-bound to oblige her with an abbreviated schedule.

After her Thor patrol, Ione did the day's shopping, filling her basket with fresh fruits and vegetables that had been shipped in from warmer climes, selecting meat and poultry from a butcher whose floor was covered in sawdust. She brought her cast-iron pots to Patty Jane's and made rich and fragrant soups. She pummeled dough into loaves, making breads that Vogstad's Bakery didn't offer: whole-wheat raisin and dill rye and a black chewy pumpernickel. Ione served Patty Jane lunch on a tray and came back in the late afternoon to prepare dinner. She left only after every dish had been washed and dried.

"Ione, please, you're doing too much," said Harriet one evening as Ione wiped down the table covering.

"I love oil cloth," said Ione. "It's a miracle fiber, don't you think?"

"I'm going out for cigarettes," said Harriet, holding out Ione's coat. "Walk with me?"

Ione motioned toward the living room.

"They're asleep," said Harriet. "Three measures of Bach and they're out like lights."

"Uff-da mayda, it's that late already?"

"Time flies when you cook and clean all day," said Harriet. "Now come on, Del's closes in twenty minutes."

The night, comparatively speaking, was balmy. The temperature had climbed to the high twenties. Stars poked their light through the black cloth of sky and the streetlights shone yellow. Harriet took Ione's hand and tucked it under her arm. Ione admired people who could make companionable physical gestures that she was too shy to proffer.

"Your jacket's skjonn."

"Skjonn?"

"Beautiful."

Harriet laughed. "I know. Everytime I put it on, I think, how did Harriet Dobbin ever get inside a mink?"

"You look like a snow princess."

"Oh, thanks," said Harriet, squeezing Ione's hand. "Avel had a coat in mind but I said, 'Honey, I have to work my way up to that luxury.'"

Two boys holding hockey sticks, their ice skates suspended from their laces and hanging around their necks like sports jewelry, stepped on a snowbank to give the women room to pass on the sidewalk.

"Did you win?" asked Ione.

"Five-one," the boys answered in proud unison.

The women walked on.

"How old are you, Ione?"

"Fifty-one."

"You don't seem that old," said Harriet.

"I don't think I'm that old," said Ione. "Mostly I feel I am nineteen."

"Ione, I want to thank you for all you're doing for my sister."

"She's my daughter-in-law," said Ione quietly. "I only wish I could give her back my son."

Harriet's profile was lit against a street light. "Let's make a pact, okay? Let's promise not to talk about Thor for the rest of the night, okay? For this entire walk, not a word. Deal?"

"Deal," said Ione.

Harriet picked up their walking pace, and Ione, sensing a game, speeded up and passed her. They began a race, walking as fast as they could, holding themselves back from breaking into a sprint, and when they reached Del's Dairy Store, they were breathing hard, between laughs.

Del Jr., son of the store owner, was patiently explaining to a woman at the register that they did not open accounts to strangers.

"I'm not a stranger," said the woman in a voice edging hysteria, "I am a doctor!"

"Lady, I don't care if you're a hula dancer, we have rules for our credit policy."

"Fine," said the woman. She turned to Harriet and Ione and a smile crawled across her face.

"Looking for something?"

Harriet looked at Del Jr. but he only shrugged his shoulders. "Are you talking to us?" she asked.

"Could be," said the woman and she wiggled her eyebrows. "You look like you lost something." She turned toward the store keeper. "You, though. You and I were discussing credit."

"The discussion's ended. Cash only."

"Cash only?" Suddenly the woman's voice erupted into a baying laugh and with one arm, she swept to the floor the groceries she had placed on the register counter. A milk bottle crashed, eggs broke and a can of tomatoes dented. "That's what I think of your cash only!" She raced to the door and then turning quickly, she said to Harriet and Ione, "Hope you find what you're looking for." She ran out the door, her laughter trailing behind in the cold night air.

"Should I chase after her?" asked Ione.

"Nah," said Del Jr. "That one's crazy. I'd leave her alone."

Harriet and Ione helped him mop up the mess. He thanked them by not charging Harriet for a pack of Chesterfields and giving Ione a thick rope of red licorice.

"Dad tells me the customer is always right," he said in reply to her thanks. "I tell him, try working the night shift."

"Do you have the nerves about tomorrow night?" asked Ione as they walked back home.

Harriet lit a cigarette and the tip burned red as she inhaled.

"That's an understatement." Avel was bringing Harriet to meet his sisters for the first time. "I'm afraid it'll be like meeting Cinderella's stepsisters." There was a soft "puh" as Harriet inhaled her cigarette. "Of course Esme's eleven years older than Avel and Bernice is fifteen years older so you can see where there'd be a rift. Avel says they've always treated him like an intruder; he says the last thing he wants is to intrude on their empty lives."

Ione tucked the licorice, which was stiffening in the cold, into her pocket. "They will like you very much."

"I doubt it," said Harriet. "They think it's horrible Avel's seeing someone like me. They said if he wants to throw his life away on trash, he's going to wind up smelling pretty bad himself."

"Uff-da, Avel told you that?"

Harriet petted the lapel of her mink jacket thoughtfully. "Avel tells me everything."

"My husband didn't tell me much," said Ione softly.

Harriet looked at her in surprise. She had never heard Ione talk about her husband.

"Oh, it wasn't his fault. It's how we Norwegians are. It's hard for us to . . . to say certain things. We got so we even joked about it. Olaf used to have what he called the 'Vowel Theory.' To get our blood moving, he said, Scandinavians should breed with Iranians and Italians, Africans and Arabs; any person whose country began with a vowel."

Harriet thought for a moment. "What about Iceland?"

Harriet slipped on an icy patch of sidewalk and Ione reached out to steady her.

"Thor is even worse than me or Olaf. Getting information out of him is like pulling teats."

"Teeth," said Harriet, smiling. "But we promised not to talk about Thor, remember?"

Ione nodded.

"Good, then let's sing." Harriet threw her cigarette into a snowbank. "Do you know any Nat King Cole?"

"No." Ione smiled and her teeth clattered with cold and excitement. "But I could learn."

Avel, sitting in a hard and unyielding chair Esme claimed was from the Hapsburgs, smiled at Harriet as he took a sip of ersatz coffee the maid had served them. He shuddered. His sisters took their ties to the grain industry seriously, brewing pots of a formula modeled after Postum, rich with grain, devoid of coffee bean. "And for that matter, flavor," thought Avel.

"I advise you to skip the beverage, Harriet," he said.

Harriet nodded. Her hands had trembled so when lighting her cigarette, she wasn't about to attempt holding fine china. She did, as Ione put it, have the nerves. The decor of the sitting room wasn't helping her to relax either.

"It's early Transylvanian," Avel had whispered as they entered.

Heavy velvet curtains which somehow merged brown and purple hung from narrow, lead-glass windows. The walls were divided by a dark walnut wainscotting and forest green wallpaper from which hung portraits of stern and homely people.

"Please extinguish that cigarette at once!"

Harriet gave a small yelp and stared at the two small, stout women standing underneath the arched entryway. They looked like hairier versions of Avel, minus the charm.

"Harriet," sighed Avel, standing, "I'd like you to meet my sisters."

Bernice, the oldest of the siblings, fingered the brooch pinned to her collar.

"Esme's and my sinuses cannot tolerate tobacco smoke," she said.

"They're also allergic to joy and laughter," Avel stage-whispered, and then, in an act of solidarity, took Harriet's cigarette and inhaled deeply. His look of defiance was broken by a coughing fit.

"Stop this nonsense at once," said Bernice and, in a rustle of pleated organza, she marched to Avel and plucked the cigarette out of his hand. She flicked it, with keen accuracy, into the fireplace.

"Come on," said Avel, taking her hand and pulling Harriet up out of the scratchy horsehair chair. "This is abuse we don't have to take."

"Sit down," said Esme, her voice more gruff, if that was possible, than her billy-goat sister. It had the power to push Avel and Harriet back into their chairs.

"Let's get this over with," said Bernice. The two sisters sat on the Victorian divan, their short fat legs not quite reaching the floor.

"Our sentiments exactly," said Avel and he laughed but Harriet saw his nervousness. His hands fluttered about his face, smoothing his fringe of black hair, pulling at the knot of his necktie.

"Avel has no doubt expressed to you our trepidation in regard to your union," began Bernice as if reading from prepared notes.

"It's not you personally," said Esme, to which Avel, squeezing Harriet's hand, said, "Ha!"

"There are certain kinds of people who do better staying among their own kind," said Bernice.

"I.e., you're not smart enough to have rich ancestors," translated Avel.

Bernice squinted until her eyebrows met and formed one disapproving line. "Be that as it may," she said, "we are not meeting here today to ask you to cancel your wedding."

"But to merely postpone it," nodded Esme.

"What?" said Avel.

"You'll be in Colombia, Avel," said Esme, sweetness oiling her voice.

"As in University?" said Avel. "But I'm a Brown man."

"Colombia as in South America," said the sisters.

"We have an opportunity to be involved in a large grain exchange and some preliminary investigation needs to be handled," said Bernice.

"The board voted it be handled by you," said Esme.

"But I'm on the board," said Avel, "and I never voted that."

"We voted in your absence," said Bernice.

"Of which there are plenty," added Esme. "You'll depart May fifteenth and all business should be concluded by mid-July."

"You know that's impossible," said Avel standing, "I'm getting married in June."

"Not unless you know how to say 'I do' in Spanish," said Bernice.

"Avel," said Harriet, taking his hand, knowing he'd have no chance in a brawl with these women, "Avel, we can change our wedding date."

A bulge of vein throbbed on the side of Avel's head. "No, we cannot change our wedding date! We will be married on the twenty-third!"

Harriet saw the tears in Avel's eyes and heard the sisters' laughter as he pulled her toward the door. She had been spineless throughout the entire meeting but no one could bring her fiancé to tears and get away with it. Her abrupt stop yanked Avel a half-step backwards.

"Say girls," she said, her voice as light as the Avon Lady's, "I don't know why you're wasting your time in the grain industry when you're so obviously cut out for tag-team wrestling." She smiled her sweet, slightly crooked smile. "I'm sure you'd be a real crowd favorite — they love dirty fighters."

Avel laughed all the way out to the car.

"So what is so special about the twenty-third?" Harriet asked him later, when they had parked by Lake Hiawatha.

"I've just always had that date in mind when I thought of my own wedding," said Avel, petting her long brown hair. "I was so relieved when you agreed to it — I thought you might have a special day of your own picked out."

"Avel, the date doesn't matter to me; what matters to me is getting married."

Avel kissed the back of her hand. "My love," he said, "my Poet of Pragmatism."

"You old sweet talker," said Harriet, kissing his hand back.

A week later, Avel had another meeting. Milt Zims, Private Detective, called him into his office to tell Avel the search was finito, kaput, done and over. Zims curled a corner of a thin manila folder. "For all intents and purposes, Mr. Thor Rolvaag has vanished from the face of the earth."

"What about the two women he was seeing?"

Zims dug into a tin of tobacco. "From what I've gathered, they were one-shot deals." He chuckled at his pun. "You didn't get any calls from the posters?"

Avel shook his head. He and Harriet had taped up "Missing Person" posters of Thor in shop windows and on grocery store announcement boards, but no one — except a woman who said if they ever found him, could they give him her phone number — had called.

After that, Patty Jane asked them to go back and take down each poster. Every day she was becoming more and more convinced that Thor had not gotten lost like a straying dog, but had gone away on his own volition. What, then, was the point of bannering her pain next to "Lawnmower for Sale" and "I Babysit in Ur Home" signs?

Milt Zims opened the file. "I've checked every contact: classmates, teachers, the folks at Bill Blaines, guys he played hockey with, shop and cafe owners in Dinkytown, airport, train and bus ticket agents and . . . zip. The guy's done a better disappearing act than Houdini."

Resigned, Avel looked at the bill Milt Zims had discreetly been inching toward him. He took his checkbook from his vest pocket.

Zims's smile was filmy with tobacco juice. "My fee's low and my expenses are minimal," he said, watching Avel fill out the check. "But I do accept honorariums."

"I'll be in touch if I need your services again," said Avel. He blew the ink dry and turned the check over.

When Avel had left the shabby office, Milt Zims lifted the check and saw that it was made out for an extra two-hundred dollars.

He whistled softly. "Imagine the gratuity if I'd found the guy."

Eight

THOR'S ABSENCE PASSED the one-month mark and Patty Jane's depression began to grow mean.

Harriet strutted around the apartment playing Sousa marches on her trumpet, but Patty Jane only asked, "Does this look like a football field?"

Ione outdid herself in the kitchen, serving nearly-weightless homemade waffles, rhubarb jam and buttermilk biscuits, creamed soups with clam bits and scallions, and desserts that made one forget the presence of Vogstad's downstairs: powdered donuts, toffee bars glazed with chocolate and crushed walnuts, divinity fudge. But Patty Jane ate her food with a disinterest that frightened Ione, who remembered how lusty her daughter-in-law's appetite used to be.

"Now Patty Jane," she said, keeping her voice light, "I spent all afternoon on that angelfood cake and you're ignoring it."

Patty Jane looked up from her tray. "I don't know why you bother. You could serve me sticks and dirt for all I care. The only reason I eat at all is to keep my milk up."

Avel increased his gift load, filling the house with presents: a white enameled crib with a canopy, a rocking horse with a real hair mane and tail, a new refrigerator that defrosted itself, a velvet couch to match the chair and ottoman, and twenty bath towels of deep pile and varied colors.

Patty Jane took to watching *Queen for a Day* on the Motorola Avel had given them, staring impassively as women poured out their hard-luck stories to an audience empowered to anoint them with prizes.

"I could go on that show," she said to Avel, "Hell's Inferno, my story's as gruesome as theirs. Course my sister's marrying a Sugar Daddy, so why bother?"

"Patty Jane!" said Harriet, "You apologize to Avel."

Patty Jane rolled her eyes. "Fact's a fact." Almost belligerently, she opened up Thor's robe and her breasts spilled out. Nora awoke and scrambled for a nipple and there was a hard glint in Patty Jane's eyes as she looked up and said, "What do you think this is, a peepshow?"

Avel and Harriet conferred in the kitchen. The room smelled of baking ginger snaps.

"She needs help," said Avel.

Harriet's hands shook as she lit a cigarette. "She needs her husband."

Ione shut the oven door and turned to them, her arms folded. "It would be easier to find the help."

The three huddled at the table and decided that the time had come for Bryce Kolm, Avel's old college roommate and practicing psychiatrist, to pay a visit.

Two days later, a fragile spring sun warmed the crocus bulbs peeking through remnants of snow. Ione took her five-week-old granddaughter to a Naomi Circle meeting at church, as Avel and Harriet led Dr. Kolm into the living room and introduced him to Patty Jane.

"Oh," said Patty Jane, "so that's what all your whispered meetings were about. I'm going to have my head shrunk. And in the nick of time!" She threw back her head, stuck out her tongue and convulsed. The patchwork quilt on her lap flapped.

"You said nothing about epilepsy!" said Dr. Kolm, running toward her.

"Patty Jane, stop that!" said Harriet.

Still seated, Patty Jane froze her arms and legs, holding them rigidly in front of her. A moment later she collapsed, just as Dr. Kolm knelt by her.

"Very funny," said Harriet.

"Très amusant," said Avel.

"Get off your knees," Patty Jane told the doctor, "I'm not accepting any marriage proposals until I'm officially a widow."

"Patty Jane!" scolded Harriet.

Dr. Kolm rose slowly, his thin mouth holding a vague smile.

"Avel," he said, "Miss Dobbin . . . may I spend some time alone with Mrs. Rolvaag?"

"Be our guest," said Harriet, narrowing her eyes at Patty Jane.

Dr. Kolm sat on the new davenport, crossed one lanky leg over the other and smiled at Patty Jane.

"I understand you're going through some rocky times."

"Why, you must be a medical genius," said Patty Jane.

"Sarcasm," chuckled the doctor. "Some consider it a high form of humor." His thin fingers formed a steeple. "I don't."

"It's not my job to entertain you," she responded.

"What do you think your job is?" he asked and Patty Jane noticed several of his teeth were gold.

"Don't you think that's pretty flashy?" she asked, pushing up on her elbows and sitting straighter in her chair.

"I beg your pardon?"

"Those gold teeth of yours." Patty Jane tapped her corresponding teeth.

Dr. Kolm shifted as if his tail bone itched. "Gold is a very strong alloy, far outlasting porcelain." He cleared his throat. "But that's really not the issue here, is it?"

Patty Jane shrugged. "You tell me, you're the doctor."

The man uncrossed his legs. "See here, miss — "

"Ma'am."

"Ma'am. I understand abandonment by one's husband can leave one's psyche bruised, and I also understand that some verbal hostility is cathartic, but let's not overdo it to the point of denying help, hmmmmm?"

"Is one married?" asked Patty Jane.

"Yes . . . but I can't see that my marital status has any bearing on your case."

"Feature this, doc," said Patty Jane, leaning forward. "Your wife gets up one day and never comes back. She leaves you with a brand new baby — a baby she's never seen — and she never comes back. You sit by the window, night after night, watching for her to turn the corner of your street, to stand under the street light and wave. Are you following me, doctor?"

"Yes."

"Good, because it's important. Now. You hold on because you've got this little baby, okay? You hold on when you're taking a bath, even though it would be easy to slip underwater and not come up. Sometimes, if you can get into the kitchen your mother-in-law has practically closed off to you, you might take a butcher knife and wonder how it would feel if you jammed it up under your heart. Like this." Patty Jane lunged forward, her balled-up fists under her ribs.

The doctor flinched. "Are you saying there's some friction between your mother-in-law and yourself?"

Patty Jane laughed. "Try to hear what I'm saying, doctor. The man I love has left me. No one can tell me where he is or if he's still breathing. I think of killing him for what he's done — and sometimes I think of killing myself."

"I could prescribe some medication," said the doctor.

"No thanks," said Patty Jane adamantly. "Besides, I'm breast-feeding."

The doctor sat forward. "Now that's interesting."

Patty Jane lifted the quilt up to her shoulders and said nothing.

"Good luck," he said finally. "If you're so opposed to psychotherapy, it's luck you'll need."

"Close the door on your way out," said Patty Jane.

"She's very hostile," said Dr. Kolm as Avel and Harriet met him in the hallway. "Full of anger, that one."

"She *has* been under a lot of pressure," said Harriet defensively.

The doctor sniffed. "Something has to explain her terrible manners."

"Does she need treatment, Bryce?" asked Avel.

"Oh yes," said Dr. Kolm. "Plenty of it. But not from me." He put his hat on, tilting it at a rakish angle. "Avel, I'll see you at the reunion next fall." He flicked the brim of his hat. "And I'll direct the bill to your office."

He bumped his briefcase against the door as he left.

Avel's voice wavered, "I hope Patty Jane told him off good."

"I did," said Patty Jane. She stood leaning against the new refrigerator, her hands in the pockets of Thor's robe. "And please don't ever do that to me again. I don't need a shrink." She sighed and pressed her cheek against the side of the gleaming white freezer door. "It's my heart that's broken, not my head."

To the chagrin of his sisters, Avel edited his itinerary so that he would be home in time for his planned wedding day.

"Now for the honeymoon," he said to Harriet. "Las Vegas?" They were having lunch at Charlie's Cafe on 7th Street, along with crowds of businessmen and tourists.

"No, that's where you go to end a marriage," said Harriet.

"Imagine the lights and the glamour."

"Divorce Town USA. Just read *Photoplay*."

"New York City!" said Avel. "A suite at the Waldorf and a honeymoon ride in a hansom cab.

"What's a handsome cab?" asked Harriet. "And what's so hot about riding around in a taxi?"

"New Orleans," said Avel. "Spiced-up French food, great jazz and wrought-iron balconies where we can sip dark coffee."

"I had a girlfriend who went there once," said Harriet. "She ate fish stew and raw oysters and puked up the whole lot."

Avel expanded his suggestions to include cities outside the continental U.S. — Honolulu, London, Paris, Baghdad, but Harriet seemed to have valid reasons for saying no to each.

"Okay," said Avel, his patience leaking like air out of a bad tire. "Where do you suggest?"

Harriet looked at her plate. Avel thought how he wanted to push aside her long dark hair and kiss her lovely neck.

"The Wisconsin Dells," she said quietly, not looking up.

"What?" said Avel, straining to hear.

Harriet leaned toward him, a cheap brass pendant as well as a string of pearls he had given her dangling above the relish tray.

"The Wisconsin Dells. Dad always promised us we'd go there but we never did. Ever since I was seven years old, I've wanted to go to the Wisconsin Dells . . . and camp."

"Good God," said Avel.

"In a tent," said Harriet. "No cabin."

"Barbarian!" said Avel, laughing.

"We'll fish in the morning, swim in the afternoon, and . . ."

Avel reached across the table for her hand. His white cuff grazed a pile of creamed herring.

"And love, love, love each other at night."

Harriet's smile was beatific. "In one sleeping bag."

After lunch, they joined the surging traffic on 7th Street ("For a Cow Town," said Avel, trying to change lanes, "Minneapolis is getting pretty sophisticated") and drove to Wanda's Bridal on La Salle Avenue.

Wanda Durnam had celebrated her seventieth birthday that winter and she liked letting everyone know it, for it never failed to elicit disbelief and the same refrain: "Why, you don't look a day over fifty!"

"Attitude," she would say, her ruby red lips parting in a smile, "that and black hair dye."

As Wanda stood in front of an arrangement of three mirrors, holding a bridesmaid dress, swaying with it as if it were a dance partner, the chimes above the door jangled and she turned, adjusting her harlequin glasses.

"May I help you?" she said, putting down the dress. There was slight disapproval in her voice — she was opposed, on aesthetic principle, to short men with taller women.

"We're looking for a wedding dress," said Harriet, squeezing Avel's shoulder.

"The loveliest dress for the loveliest bride," said Avel.

"Well, well, well," said Wanda, smiling, "let's just see what we've got." Physically mismatched or not, she found their giddiness appealing. Usually couples or, most often, brides-to-be and their mothers, looked at dresses with the seriousness of attorneys selecting a jury. "Have a seat, please," she said, gesturing toward two soft-cushioned floral chairs. "Show starts in two minutes."

She returned cradling yards of tulle and organza, net and lace, voile and taffeta. She dumped the white cloud on a small couch, then lifted a padded satin hanger. A crêpe de chine gown unfurled like a celebratory banner.

"That's beautiful," said Harriet. "I'll take it."

The dress had a sweetheart neckline, a fitted waist and a panel train.

"I've got some real honeys here," said Wanda, tossing aside

the crepe de chine. "Now this one with the Venice lace appliqués is a stunner and this one here is my personal favorite . . . the one I'd wear if I were twenty instead of seventy. Look here, Juliette sleeves, for your Romeo."

"Thanks all the same," said Harriet, picking up the original dress and touching the seed pearl buttons, "I've got the one I want."

Wanda took out a pencil from its mooring beneath her turban. "She makes up her mind fast, doesn't she?" she said to Avel.

Avel nodded, his hands folded in his lap. "She did with me."

"You'd be a perfect size six," said Wanda in the dressing room, "if your hips weren't so tiny." She recorded the last measurement in her notebook and snapped its cover shut. "Now, you're sure your sister doesn't need to be fitted?"

"She's a perfect size eight," said Harriet, stepping back into her dress. "She's got more hips and a bigger bust than me."

"I wear a size seven," said Wanda, rolling up the measuring tape, "and I'm seventy years old."

Wanda promised the dresses would be ready for the first of June and when Avel paid the deposit, she held the check at a distance, narrowed her eyes and said, "Avel Ames. My goodness, are you with the Ames Grain people?"

"That's my lot," said Avel, screwing on the top of his pen.

"Well, I'll be," said Wanda, "I start every morning with Ames Oatmeal. On my face," she amended, "That's my beauty secret. Oatmeal facials . . . and attitude, of course."

"One more stop," said Avel, sliding up onto his car's booster seat. "We'll save the camping gear and the marriage license for tomorrow, okay?"

Harriet nodded and lit a cigarette. Her smile would have been as enigmatic and alluring as Mona Lisa's, except for the plume of smoke she expelled from her nose.

She was filled with a glorious congress of feelings: love and joy, accomplishment and excitement. She breathed deeply, smelling smoke and car leather and Avel's cologne.

"Say 'This is my wife, Mrs. Avel Ames,'" she said.

Avel was about to turn the key in the ignition but he stopped and touched her face with the back of his fingers. "This is my wife," he said, "Mrs. Avel Ames." He sniffed.

"Avel, you've got to learn to say that name without crying."

A block before their destination, Avel asked Harriet to close her eyes. He turned into a car lot, telling Harriet, "Keep them shut," as he got out of the car. Approaching the man in the lot he asked, "Is it here?"

The pudgy young salesman who wore a big smile and a bad suit nodded.

Avel opened the door for Harriet. "Grab my arm, love," he said, "and don't peek."

Giggling nasally, the salesman led them behind the small office trailer and mouthed to Avel, "There it is."

"Open your eyes, darling," said Avel and when Harriet did, she found herself standing in front of a pale pink 1954 DeSoto Powerflyte.

"Keys're in there," said the salesman, smiling and rubbing his hands together.

"What is this?" asked Harriet.

Avel took her hand. "One of the prettiest cars made, precious." He squatted in front of the car and pulled Harriet with him. "See the grille? I'm especially partial to this grille."

"Oh, Avel. Where'd you ever find a pink car?"

"We had it customized in the factory," said the salesman, increasing the velocity of his hand-rubbing.

"Now get in, sweetheart," said Avel, "and let's cruise."

Laughing, Harriet jumped into the car and started the engine.

"Let's take a drive along the river," Avel said. He exchanged a smile with the salesman as Harriet put the car in gear.

"Wait for me, dear," he began but Harriet had found the gear she wanted and plunged into the street, tires squealing.

"The minx," said Avel, laughing. He ran back to his car.

"The minx," agreed the salesman. He stood rocking on his feet, chuckling, until his boss rapped on the window of the office trailer, summoning him inside.

"Lutefisk" almost ended the combination bridal shower/going-away party Ione threw for Avel and Harriet the night before Avel's departure to South America.

"I need medical attention," gasped Avel after taking a huge bite of the Norwegian delicacy. His eyes watered and the top of his head pulsed red. "What is this stuff?"

"Codfish," said Ione sweetly.

"Aged in lye," added Harriet.

Presents followed coffee and cake.

"Ione, these are exquisite," said Avel, fingering the edges of a set of hand-embroidered pillowcases, their monograms planted inside a garden of blooming flowers. "I forgive you completely for trying to poison me."

"You're wonderful," said Harriet.

"Uff-da mayda," said Ione, her face reddening. She reached under her chair and pulled out another present. "This one is just for you, Avel."

Avel opened up a box of stationery and saw that all of the envelopes were pre-addressed to Ione.

"When you get tired of writing love letters to Harriet," said Ione, "drop me some lines. I am dying for hearing about South America."

Harriet unwrapped a final present, a sheer nightgown, its bodice covered in leaves of lace. It came with a matching robe and its card said the gift was from Patty Jane.

"Patty Jane, I can't wait to wear this," said Harriet, planting a loud kiss on her forehead. "Thank you."

Patty Jane shrugged. "Thank Ione," she said, turning back to the window which she had stared from through most of the party. "She bought it." Rivulets of rain streaked the window panes.

"Let's have some music!" said Ione, turning on the radio she had brought in from the kitchen.

Doris Day was singing "Secret Love" and Avel took Harriet in his arms. They danced on the small rectangle of floor that was bordered by furniture.

Ione noticed how smooth Avel was. Patty Jane stared out the window, completely still, except for her foot tapping unconsciously to the beat.

When the song was over, Patty Jane got up.

"Goodnight, everyone," she said, cinching the belt of Thor's robe. She bent to pick up Nora but changed her mind and went to Avel, pulling him up out of his chair in a tight hug.

"Have a wonderful trip," she said, kissing the top of his head. Then, cupping her hand to his ear, she whispered, "Sleep with her tonight, Avel. I mean it."

Blushing, Avel smiled and whispered back, "Why, thank you, Patty Jane, perhaps I will."

His knees trembled as he and Harriet said their good-byes. He was remembering that past winter when he proposed to Harriet, and she had asked him if they could begin sleeping together. They had already been dating for three months, and their kisses were passionate, their grapplings frequent, but every time consummation appeared likely, he would push Harriet away as if she were pulling him down into water over his head.

"I'm sorry, honey," he had said while Harriet furiously buttoned her dress in the front seat of the Cadillac. Steam had turned every window opaque even though the temperature was in the mid-thirties.

"Oh, for pete's sake," Harriet had said, her teeth biting hard on an unlit cigarette. "*You're* sorry."

Holding onto the steering wheel, Avel bowed his head. "I respect you too much, honey."

"Avel, I don't want your vote for president, I just want to sleep with you!"

The knuckles of Avel's small hands had turned white as he flexed them around the steering wheel. When he spoke, his voice wavered and cracked. "Harriet, I love you. I want to marry you . . . and I'm afraid that if we sleep together . . ." he pressed his forehead on the top of the steering wheel, "well, then you won't want to marry me."

"What?" said Harriet, inhaling a throatful of smoke.

Avel's shoulders hunched. "Harriet, I'm no Casanova. There was even a time in my life when so much was made about my being oversensitive, I was certain I was queer. It wasn't until I went away to college and met women who weren't preselected by my family that I realized most women *weren't* like my sisters." Avel had spoken to the center of the steering wheel, afraid to look at Harriet. "Still, I've only been with women — in the biblical sense, that is — well, I can't even count the times, not that there have been many. But what makes my memory fail is that each time was . . . not memorable."

"Why?" asked Harriet.

Avel had turned to her, resting his cheek against the wheel. "Probably because I didn't love any of them the way I love you."

"Makes sense, I guess," said Harriet, rolling the window down a crack to throw out her cigarette. She shivered as the cold night air rushed in. "Patty Jane's pretty much told me the same thing."

Avel sat up, thinking: "Patty Jane, my ally."

Harriet looked at Avel in the darkened car interior. "But she slept with Thor after their second date and said it's an entirely different thing when you truly love someone." She touched her hand to his chest. "Now I've found someone I truly love and I want to share myself."

"Harriet!" said Avel. "You are a prize I never imagined winning!" Agony worked itself around his features. "But please, let's wait, all right?"

Harriet had subsequently confided to Patty Jane that Avel wouldn't "do it" with her until they were married.

"Well, he's a lot older than you are," said Patty Jane. "I guess he's more old-fashioned."

Harriet shrugged. "Afraid's more like it. He's afraid I won't marry him if we sleep together first."

"Is he impotent?"

"What?"

"You know, does it work?"

Harriet blushed. "Well, yes. I mean I think so from the . . . limited exposure I've had with it."

"Well, he's a little guy, maybe he's bothered about his size."

The conversation had taken place just as Patty Jane had begun to notice something was wrong in her own bed; Thor seemed to be losing interest in what had given them pleasure, so she wasn't sure how to counsel her sister.

"If he wants to wait," she said finally, "let him. Hell, there might as well be one Dobbin who's a virgin bride."

Now, celebrating their first spring together, Avel and Harriet loaded up his car with their presents and drove to the river in a night fragrant with new rain. They parked the car and stood on top of a rocky, tree-filled bluff with a steep grade that led to a narrow white sand beach lining the Mississippi. On summer nights, high school boys carried kegs of beer down the incline for "river parties." It was a precipitous undertaking, occasionally resulting in a dropped keg bounding down the jagged trail, bursting as it crashed into a rock or pine tree.

"I'll lead the way," said Avel, taking Harriet's hand. "If you trip, I'll break your fall."

"If I trip, I'll break your neck," said Harriet, letting go of his hand.

Curtains of clouds shrouded the moon and they took several baby steps, their eyes adjusting to the darkness.

Stopping a too rapid descent by lunging at tree branches, walking on all fours, crab style, down grades they couldn't navigate in an upright position, they traversed the hill in a zigzag course of fits and starts.

"Call in the rescue squad," said Avel, hugging the trunk of a tree and gasping for breath.

"We're almost there," said Harriet. "I can see the river."

Avel let go of the tree trunk and ventured a few feet to where Harriet stood, her hands on her hips. He craned his head and saw the wide band of the river, dark and full of motion.

They joined hands and climbed down the last quarter together, their feet breaking twigs and dislodging stones. When the land leveled off, they ran toward the river's shore, their laughter filling the night-silent basin.

A barge moved through the dark water. Avel and Harriet sat on the bank watching it.

Avel asked, "Are you cold? Let me warm you up."

Harriet kissed him and the kiss he returned was warm and urgent. He guided her gently to her back and lay on top of her.

"I mean *really* warm you up." His lips were in her hair and his hands climbed under her dress and began roaming Harriet's body.

"Avel," whispered Harriet, "I'm warming up."

When he began pulling down her panties and garter belt, Harriet said, "Avel, do you know what you're doing?"

"Absolutely," he said. "Now unbutton my fly, would you please? Let's liberate the Ally."

As they rolled and undulated, leaving imprints of their bodies in the wet sand, Harriet thought "This is like a musical score, and I'll lose consciousness at the crescendo." When Avel arched his back and cried out, Harriet joined him, her voice like an animal's she had never heard.

They lay together, holding tight until they stopped trembling.

"Thank you, my darling," said Avel, smoothing a tendril of hair from Harriet's face. "Thank you for the most exquisite moment of my life."

"You're welcome," said Harriet and gently bit his lower lip. "Now let's go to the car for another round."

They dressed each other as breaking clouds raced across a pale moon and an owl watched them from a tall dark pine.

At the airport, Harriet and Avel clung to each other.

"I'm not going to bathe for the entire trip," said Avel. "I'm going to wear your smell the whole time. And as soon as I get on that plane, I'm going to fall asleep so I can dream of last night."

Avel drew Harriet away from the commotion of a family counting their luggage. "Do you realize," he said, "the next time we stand together we'll be taking our vows?"

Harriet swallowed. "I took mine last night."

Tears sprang to Avel's eyes. "Harriet, you say things that tear my heart out." He grabbed her around the waist and kissed her. "You find words I thought were too profound to speak."

Harriet kissed the top of Avel's head. "Sure I do, honey."

Avel boarded the plane at the last possible moment.

"Oh, I almost forgot this!" he said, running back to Harriet.

He withdrew an envelope from his vest pocket and gave it to her. "Mad money. Fritter it away on anything and everything — when we're married I'll be tightening the reins."

"Avel, now we both know you ride bareback."

Avel's eyes widened. As he ran to the plane, he turned, and shouted, "June twenty-third, my love. God, I love you! Oh, happy day!"

After the steps had been removed and the plane began to back out, Harriet waved frantically to Avel, whose face was framed in the small window. She watched the plane until it was a speck in the blue spring sky. Then she drove slowly to her sister's apartment, that sad place where love had fled like a delinquent motel guest.

Nine

Pᴀᴛᴛʏ Jᴀɴᴇ ᴡᴀs conducting an experiment: if one expended as few feelings as possible, was there a correspondent decrease in pain? What she felt for Nora was expressed openly, but these feelings rose from a maternal core and were not negotiable for anyone else. She was convinced that by putting a lid on her emotions, the flame of pain might be snuffed out.

On May twenty-seventh, Patty Jane's twenty-second birthday, she received a letter from Avel written on thin blue airmail paper. Its timing was perfect. Her inertia had begun to bore her and yet she couldn't find the impetus to move.

> As you probably know already, I took your advice (by far the best I've ever received) and made wonderful love with your amazing sister. That act of love filled me with a joy that is still with me. Business is going splendidly. Everyone I come in contact with likes me because, I feel, they sense this joy. Either I will soon be running the entire South American grain industry or I'll be elected El Presidente.

My hotel proprietess, Senora Rosa, leaves fresh gardenias on my bedside table, the scent of which fills my room and my dreams of Harriet. I sweat profusely eating the spicy pepper-laden food. Life is spectacular.

And now, Patty Jane, since I was the recipient of your wonderful advice, perhaps you'll allow me to offer mine. Know that you are loved and deserving of all the love that is swirling around this universe. Whatever caused Thor's departure, I'm certain, was the work of his own demons and not yours. Even though it would seem all evidence points to the contrary, I know he loves you.

Oh, Patty Jane, heal your precious heart. Happy Birthday, my almost-official sister-in-law.

Love, Avel

P.S. The enclosed check is for wild spending only.

The enclosed check was made out for five hundred dollars.

"Nora, I think I just got my wake-up call," said Patty Jane to her sleeping daughter. She took off Thor's robe, her uniform of the past two months, and pressed it to her face, searching for his lingering smell. As she stood naked in front of the bathroom mirror, she was not kind in her assessment. "My God," she thought, "if Thor could see me now he'd leave me all over again." Her hair was matted and lustreless and her hazel eyes were sunk into their sockets. "I look as thin as Harriet," she thought, her hands exploring the sharpness of her cheek and chin bones. Her ribs were visible through the skin of her chest, an odd contrast to the swelling of her milk-full, blue-veined breasts.

Too hurried to wash her dirty hair, she tied a scarf around it and pulled on clothes without attention to pattern or color.

Fashioning a sling out of a thin flannel baby blanket, she tied it around her shoulder and tucked Nora into it, next to her heart.

She breezed through the living room, waving cheerfully to Ione, who was embroidering a baby dress, and to Harriet, cleaning the spit valve of her trumpet, and went out into the spring air that up until that moment she had only known through a window.

Inhaling the sweet May breeze, Patty Jane walked with wide strides, taking in the action of her modest commercial street as if this were the first time she had observed it.

Every fiber of her hair, every pore of her skin, seemed now to awaken; she watched new green leaves fluttering, sudsy lilacs spilling lavender by the Henrickson's Hardware parking lot, robins flitting around a nest in the eaves of the Spiffy Wash laundromat.

Patty Jane walked to Lake Street and into the Flour City Bank. Nora slept and did not wake up until Patty Jane had split Avel's check into two accounts, one of which had her name on it.

"Pretty baby," said the accounts assistant, who smelled of violet sachet.

"Hungry baby," said Patty Jane as Nora began to cry, "is there a restroom I can use?"

"Sorry," said the accounts assistant, "it's for employees only."

"Okay," said Patty Jane, "this chair'll be fine." Before she had her middle button undone, the bank manager rushed over and escorted her to his office.

"You'll probably be more comfortable here," he said, gesturing toward a large leather chair.

"Thank you," said Patty Jane as the manager walked, in great haste, from the office.

With the visit to the bank, Patty Jane ended her hermetic existence. After that, she left the house at least once a day. She always took Nora with her and she always walked, despite offers from both Harriet and Ione to use their cars.

Her legs, shapely as a showgirl's, grew stronger. Her thighs became smooth and solid, hard to the touch. She walked miles: to Page Airport to watch the planes take off, down Washington Avenue to the train station. She took Nora to the observation deck of the Foshay Tower and held the cooing baby up to the window. Together they looked at the unfolding city below them.

"We've got the world at our feet," Patty Jane whispered, "at least for right now."

Each walk invigorated her, but once back at the apartment, she would undergo reverse metamorphosis, fold up her butterfly wings and crawl into her cocoon.

To support her sister, while Avel was away, Harriet had moved in with Patty Jane. Ione still slept at her own house, but spent most days at her daughter-in-law's, acting as chief cook and housekeeper. One day, while she was out, Ione stripped Patty Jane's bed linens and took the load of sheets and blankets down to the washer in the basement. When she was finished washing, she hung the clothes up to dry on the backyard line. She was not prepared for a hysterical Patty Jane to tear the laundry basket out of her hands as she returned to the kitchen.

"Where is it?" screamed Patty Jane, and for one alarming moment, Ione thought Patty Jane had misplaced the baby.

"Aha!" she yelled, pulling at the belt of Thor's robe, "you did take it!"

"What?" said Ione, her hands clutched to her chest.

"Thor's robe! You washed Thor's robe!" Patty Jane pressed the fabric to her face. "You washed him all away!"

Harriet found the two women in Patty Jane's bedroom, her sister sobbing into her pillows as Ione stood by the bureau, her hands hanging limp and helpless at her sides.

"Uff-da, I am so sorry," said Ione, her face blanched. "I washed her bed clothes. Thor's robe was with them . . ."

"It smells like Duz!" wailed Patty Jane. "I can't smell Thor anymore!"

Harriet sat on the bed, petting her sister's hair. "Honey, that robe might have smelled like Thor once, but you've been wearing it for over two months. It had gotten pretty rank."

Patty Jane beat at a pillow with her fists. "I don't care! I could still smell him in it!"

"Patty Jane," said Ione, "I am so sorry." A squeak escaped from her throat. "Min sonne," she said quietly. "I miss him, too."

Shame intruded on Patty Jane's grief but she didn't console her mother-in-law. Ione might have lost a son, but it was his wife he had run from.

"Could I be alone for a while?" she asked, her voice thin, and then she cried herself to sleep.

Harriet had put her music lessons on hold during the first month of Thor's disappearance but as his absence lengthened, she started them up again. Her teachers were planning to feature her in their individual department recitals. Stella Amundsen was giddy with the idea of pairing Harriet and her best baritone, in a medley of show tunes. She thought her protegés equal to, if not surpassing, Nelson Eddy and Jeanette McDonald.

Harriet held an enormous measure of gratitude for the McKern School of Music, for inside its walls she was surrounded by the thing more elemental than her own heartbeat: music. She loved entering the building and greeting the receptionist. She loved walking down the corridor and hearing different music behind each door: the string quartet warming up, a forlorn oboe solo, a jazzy piano duet. She loved carrying her trumpet case; she was as proud of this badge of identity as a doctor is of his black bag. She loved sitting down at the school harp in Evelyn Bright's room, smoothing her skirt with studied decorum. She loved opening the door to her voice class and hearing Stella Amundsen's happy trills welcoming her.

Avel had requested that she provide all the music for their wedding: "Trumpet Voluntary" for the processional ("I'm supposed to play the trumpet as I walk down the aisle?" she asked); "Claire de Lune" on the harp before the vows, and after the minister's pronouncements, she was to sing "Ave Maria." "Avel," she had said, "I don't want to be a one-woman combo on my wedding day; I just want to be the bride."

She was, however, working on a song with Evelyn Bright. It was a surprise for Avel, his wedding gift.

One morning, Evelyn Bright showed her the melody she had been working on. Harriet had enlisted Evelyn's aid not only because she was her favorite teacher, but because she was a successful song writer, having penned not only the "Minnie Delany Radio Hour" theme song, but also the White Bluffs beer jingle.

Evelyn was delighted to be involved in Harriet's conspiracy, confessing to Harriet that she and her husband Cornelius were "quite the lovebirds" after twenty-one years of marriage and that "surprises" were largely responsible for keeping zip in their marriage.

"A note tucked in his lunch box, a love poem whispered to him before he goes to sleep, a drop of your perfume on the inside cuff of his shirt — it's the surprises, Harriet, the surprises of romance that keep a love alive." Evelyn Bright nodded sagely, her fleshy chin dipping in and out of her ruffled collar. She sprayed water into her mouth with an atomizer and hummed what she had composed for Harriet.

"Pretty," said Harriet. "I think I'd like the A flatted though." She pointed to a measure on the sheet music Evelyn had propped on the music stand.

Evelyn hummed the changes. "Right on the money, Harriet," she said, making a notation. "Have you come up with any lyrics, dear?"

"Just a line," she said, flicking her hair over her shoulders: "The mortgage will never be paid to Avel, landlord of my heart."

Evelyn giggled. "Oh, for cute. So contemporary." She sang the line to the beginning bars of her music. "It fits perfectly. Oh Harriet, I'll bet we could sell this song. Couldn't you just hear Perry Como singing it?"

Harriet smiled. "He's going to croon to 'Avel, landlord of my heart'?"

"Oh, for funny," said Evelyn Bright. "Okay, then Peggy Lee."

May washed into June. Patty Jane tucked Nora under her yellow rain slicker and wore buckle-up rubber boots on her five-mile walks. Essential practicality had begun to prick her consciousness. She knew she must begin rebuilding her life, that her future days couldn't be composed only of long walks and the care and feeding of her baby daughter. She had to take the shutters down, throw away the "No Trespassing" sign, and start letting people in.

The weeks of quiet Patty Jane had prescribed for herself had another surprise benefit. They had afforded her the opportunity to watch and listen to her sister and mother-in-law, to study them together and alone. She was touched to see how well Harriet and Ione got along. Their mutual reserve had evaporated like a smoke signal on the wind. They played Rook and ate popcorn at the kitchen table, read aloud their letters from Avel. Patty Jane faked naps on the wide velvet chair, eavesdropping on Harriet and Ione when they sat in the living room, working companionably on separate projects: Ione practicing the precise Norwegian art of rosemaling painting; Harriet reading through a musical score or pinning up rows of her hair, searching for the perfect style for her wedding.

One afternoon, after one of Harriet's harp concerts, Nora slept in her mother's arms while Patty Jane enjoyed a drowsy state of consciousness in which reality was a dream and every dream was good. The windows had been pushed up and a fresh breeze picked up the hems of the sheer curtains like the hands of naughty boys. Duke Ellington played on the radio.

"Ione," said Harriet and Patty Jane heard the strike of a match, "how old are you again?"

"Fifty-one."

"Is that scary?"

"Uff-da, nei. Why do you ask?"

Patty Jane opened her eyes to look at Harriet, who had drawn her feet up under her on the couch, staring at the smoke that untangled from her cigarette.

"I just can't see myself as anything but young," said Harriet.

Ione was bent over the coffee table. She drew a flower pattern on a wooden plaque with dustless chalk. Then, as her mother and grandmother had done, she would "rosemal" the pattern with oil paint.

"When you're young, that's how you think." She held the plaque away and admired her own work. "But once you get not-so-young, you find out getting old is not so bad . . . even better."

"Really!"

"You milk my words."

"That's *mark* my words," said Harriet.

Ione squirted a curl of russet oil paint onto her palette. "Well, this is my way of thinking. There is inside all of us, I think, the soul of an eight-year-old. Time and experience and motherhood — especially motherhood, because my stars, then you're in charge of someone else! — make you wiser, but underneath it all is still that little eight-year-old center." Ione selected a fine brush and pressed it into the paint. "I'm fifty-one, but it's a number without meaning."

Harriet held her cigarette a half-inch from her mouth, her eyes fixed thoughtfully at a point on the ceiling.

"Avel's thirty-five," she said, "and he isn't at all what I'd expect a thirty-five-year-old to be. In fact, I think I act older than he does."

"That's what I am saying," said Ione. "One single number can't measure all that is age."

"Damn right there," thought Patty Jane. "I just turned twenty-two, I could pass for sixteen and I feel about one hundred and four."

The alterations of Harriet's wedding dress had been completed and Ione accompanied Harriet to Wanda's Bridal to pick it up.

"Why, hello, Mrs. Ames-to-be!" said Wanda, resplendent in a gold-flecked caftan and matching turban. "Oh, and this is your mother?"

"No," said Harriet, smiling. She introduced the two women and gasped as she saw her dress hanging behind the register desk. Her walk toward it was shy, as if she were approaching a godchild she'd never met. She lifted it gently off the hook and carried it to the dressing room and when she came out, Ione's hands flew to her mouth.

"Oh, my stars," she said under her fingers. "Oh, my heavenly stars."

"Yes, dears, we cinched the waist perfectly," said Wanda. She stood behind Harriet and they looked into the floor-length mirror. "See how it flares out? Makes you look like you've got some hips."

After Harriet changed, Wanda pulled a dress bag over the gown. "Have a marvelous wedding," she said to Harriet. She smiled broadly, displaying ruby red flecks of lipstick clinging to her incisors, and then asked Ione, "Guess how old I am?"

Later in the car, convulsed in giggles, Ione told Harriet she didn't know what came over her that had made her say, "Oh, I don't know . . . eighty-five?"

There was a big calendar on Patty Jane's kitchen wall, compliments of Bill Blaine's Sporting Goods ("We Help You Play the Game Right") on which Harriet celebrated a small nightly ritual: the crossing out of each number enclosed in its small box. She liked standing in the silk robe from Avel, her face just washed, teeth brushed, the small light above the sink shining from its bell-shaped glass shade, drawing an X through another day. She liked seeing the progress of time's march and felt an affinity with each day as she stood before the calendar with a black crayon: Yes I spent you, you existed for me, thank you. She liked the pattern the black Xs made and one night Harriet smiled, noticing the closer they got to her wedding day, the more beautiful patterns the Xs made.

T en

IN SOUTH AMERICA, Avel acquired a golden tan and half a dozen suits made by Bogota's premier tailor. He took to wearing Panama hats and diamond stick pins under the knot of his tie, and seeing himself in hotel lobby mirrors, he laughed, thinking, "Who is this little guy who looks like the owner of a Latin dance hall?"

At parties hosted by diplomats and wealthy businessmen, parties in which sad-looking musicians plucked the strings of their guitars and guests spilled out of tiled dining rooms and onto patios lush with blooming bougainvillea and birds-of-paradise, beautiful women, their thick black hair piled on top of their heads in loops and knots, would form tight circles around Avel, begging him to dance, to help himself to another glass of wine, another deep-fried dessert from the local pasteleria.

Avel was courtly and debonair in the midst of so much attention but the clusters of black-eyed, brown-skinned beauties were not sources of temptation. They were flowers in the extraordinary bouquet of womanhood, the bouquet in which his Harriet was the perfect center rose.

He flew to Buenos Aires and toured the great wheat fields of the Pampas, courtesy of a Harvard-educated ranch owner whose front tooth was studded with a ruby. Avel met with ministers of agriculture in Brasilia and Caracas, interviewed gauchos on crop yields and rainfall, rode a pack mule with the mayor of Cordoba and got drunk on the finest beer he'd ever tasted with a group of economics students at the railway depot in La Paz.

He chuckled over his sisters' foiled plan — their conviction that they'd exiled him. In reality, his punishment had turned into the journey of his life. In Bogota, where he based his operations, he kept a notebook on his bedside table and he was often seized by an idea that had to be written down — thoughts on sorghum derivatives and rotation planting, cooperative ventures. The last thing he did at night was write his bride-to-be. In a letter dated June 10, 1954, he wrote:

Dear Harriet,

Immediately after our camping sojourn to the Wisconsin Dells, we must extend our honeymoon and come here. I have shown Senora Rosa, my housekeeper, your photograph — the one we took by the statue of Hiawatha carrying Nokomis — and she sighed greatly, saying, "Muy bonita." She has given me a rosary, which she says will bring luck to our marriage.

I am missing you, Harriet, but in a happy way. Your love is alive inside me and it has fueled me. I find a confidence in myself and my abilities, and an interest in the family trade that never would I have expected to bloom and, my lovely wife-to-be, it is all your doing.

My darling, I was on my hands and knees digging in a furrow of rich alluvial soil with a Pasto Indian who was as old as the Andes and without language. We talked for a half hour about a precious sprig of wheat.

Harriet, of course I cried and the old Indian nodded as if he understood!

It's as if my life has been an exceptional orchestra poised and ready to play and at last the conductor has arrived to lead it into its first movement. I can feel it's some mighty Mozart, too!

Adios until the next second I think of you,

Avel.

Harriet kept his letters in an empty Mighty Bites box under the couch, dreaming of gardenia bushes, crowded bazaars and woven wool ponchos bright as crayons.

All necessary business was taken care of, to a degree that far exceeded Avel's expectations. His briefcase was heavy with proposals and letters of intent, facts and figures that his sisters would pore over with a dry lust. As he boarded a plane for home he imagined his presentation to the group of business people who thought of him as more a court jester than a colleague.

Avel watched Bogota disappear beneath him. He hummed a song about a gold mine he had heard street musicians play and as the plane rose to its cruising height, the sadness of saying good-bye to the place where so much had happened was pushed aside by the anticipation of his wedding day. Nodding to the businessman across the aisle from him, Avel officiously sprang open the locks on his briefcase, took out a legal pad and began to do something he had never before done: write a memo. In bold capital letters across the top of the page he wrote:

THINGS TO DO

Marry Harriet!!!
Honeymoon!!!
Better acquaint self with family lawyers, particularly
M. Sumner re: real estate and stock holdings, existing

will and changes naming Harriet benef., house on Lake Minnetonka — available for summer occupancy?

Patty Jane — offer of schooling? Work? — Possibly firm-related?

Avel filled the page and when he was finished he accepted a pillow from the stewardess and, idly fingering the rosary Senora Rosa had given him, he fell asleep.

The mailman passed the paperboy as the twelve-year-old was folding the afternoon edition of the *Minneapolis Star* outside the paper shack.

"Beautiful day," said the mailman, nodding.

"At least the rain's stopped," said the paperboy, a dreamy kid who was saving his collection tips to buy a ham radio.

For both of them, it was a routine day and a routine day's work.

Harriet, dressed in a navy houndstooth suit, stood in front of the bathroom mirror, fussing with her hair.

She was going to the airport to meet Avel's plane and iron-winged butterflies flapped in her stomach. She hadn't been able to eat the breakfast or lunch Ione had prepared. Caffeine and nicotine were the only nourishment she'd had. By seven that evening, she and Avel would be married at Lake Calhoun, where nearly a year ago they had shared a first-date Chinese dinner.

She pulled her hair out of its bun and a wave of electricity fanned a section of it upward. She was brushing it over one eye when a scream from the living room knocked the hairbrush out of her hand and sent her reeling from the bathroom. Patty Jane, her face white-washed, was slumped against the front door. In her hand she held a lined piece of notebook paper.

"Patty Jane?" said Harriet, her voice a gust of fear.

Patty Jane lifted her hand and, trembling, Harriet pulled the paper from her sister's grip.

She read its typewritten message once as she and the paper shook, and then she read it again for comprehension. It said:

> Dear Patty Jane.
>
> I'm alive. Forgive me and then forget me.
> Sorry.
>
> Love,
> Thor.

The sisters stared at each other, their faces mirroring shock. The silence that filled the room swallowed up a thousand words.

"He's alive," said Harriet finally.

"I'll kill him," whispered Patty Jane.

Ione, returning from a shopping trip with Nora, picked up the folded rectangle of the *Minneapolis Star* from the middle step. She parked the stroller in the small entryway, next to Thor's bicycle and, her arms full of Nora, the paper and a bag of oranges she had picked up at Del's Dairy, she climbed the stairs. She nudged the front door open with her foot, then gasped as she saw Patty Jane's and Harriet's faces. The newspaper fell from under her arm.

The bag of oranges slipped from her grasp and thudded down the steps. The women stood listening until the oranges reached the bottom of the stairs.

"What?" Ione asked. Patty Jane took Nora out of her arms and pressed the letter into her trembling hands.

"Min gutt er i livet! Min gutt er i livet!" Ione kissed the piece of notebook paper and held it to her chest. "My boy is alive!"

"Not if he comes around here," said Patty Jane.

Harriet laughed because laughter seemed the best way to diffuse the shock. Her laughter ended in abrupt silence, as she bent to pick up the paper Ione had dropped. Half of Avel's picture appeared on the front page. His whole face emerged as Harriet, in slow motion, unfolded the paper.

The headline read, "AMES GRAIN HEIR PERISHES IN PLANE CRASH."

"What kind of sick joke . . ." began Harriet, her voice pleading for mercy.

Avel's smile began to disintegrate into tiny dots, and the newsprint swirled in front of her: "Crash landing in Port-au-Prince . . . witnesses report engine fire . . . no survivors." The dots jumbled together into a black page and Harriet fell backward into Ione's and Patty Jane's arms.

Part Two

Eleven

NEEDLEPOINT SAMPLERS and magazine cut-outs of hairstyles hung on the fake wood paneling above the row of hairdryers and the shampoo sink. Tucked into wide-framed mirrors facing four barber chairs were home-made Mother's Day cards and operators' licenses. The linoleum floor of the room was sun-faded and all the equipment was used or "reconditioned." Slashes of electrical tape patched the vinyl chairs and the metal domes of the hair dryers were dented, but Patty Jane thought there was not a snazzier beauty salon in the entire free world. On a wooden sign cut to look like a wavy head of hair, Ione had handpainted the words *"Patty Jane's House of Curl"*, and the sign's namesake wanted to turn a cartwheel every time she looked at it. The shop was attached to a stucco house on Nawadaha Boulevard, a tree-lined street of one-family houses. The down payment had been made by Ione, who was now living with Harriet and Patty Jane and Nora. They all worked, in their separate fashions, at the House of Curl.

"More coffee, Crabby?" Patty Jane asked an iron-haired woman who sat roasting under a hair dryer. Nicknamed for the brusqueness she had acquired as a W.A.C. during World War II, the woman held out her cup.

"Don't skimp on the cream this time and get me a couple more of those spice cookies while you're at it," Crabby said.

She, like the other customers at the House of Curl, wore a freshly-laundered, monogrammed smock and ate heavily of Ione's baked goods. They all knew they could ask to pay for their haircuts or body waves on a tab if money were tight, and if they had an important appointment but no babysitter, they could drop off their children. For the women of the Longfellow neighborhood, Patty Jane's salon was their poker room, their pool hall, their general store — a place where they could share their stories and receive a flip or pageboy in return.

The beauty parlor had held its seventh annual Holiday Cookie Exchange a week earlier and there were still cookies left — spritz and pfeffernuss and chocolate pinwheels that Ione arranged on trays and set on the appointments desk, a former card table to which she had attached a flounced skirt.

Patty Jane got Crabby Bultram her order and sat down next to Harriet, who was playing the final bars of "Für Elise" on her harp.

"Pretty," she said.

"You can't go wrong with Beethoven," said Harriet.

"If he's a man," said Bev Beal, sweeping up snips of hair, "you can."

Clyde Chuka, at his manicurist's table, shook his head. "One day you'll be lucky in love, Bev, and change your tune."

The hair stylist patted the black lacquered dome of her hair and shook her head. "I can't change the way the music's written."

Nora charged into the room, her cheeks red from building a snow fort. "Mail call!" she said, riffling through a handful of letters. "Mail call for Mrs. Thor Rolvaag!"

Patty Jane steeled herself. The only one who addressed her that way now was her husband, in his semi-annual missives.

The letter, postmarked this time from La Crosse, Wisconsin, *was* from Thor and it contained, as usual, $50 and the typewritten message, "I'm fine. How are you?"

Angry tears welled up in Patty Jane's eyes.

"I'll be right back," she said, even though everyone knew it would be hours before she composed herself and reappeared. In ten years, Patty Jane had come far but every terse letter from her long-lost husband was a reminder of what a long, hard journey it had been.

At Avel's memorial service, Harriet had astonished the churchful of mourners by sitting at her harp and playing the song she had cowritten as a wedding present, "You Are the Landlord of My Heart." The Ames sisters had arranged the service and up until then, it had been dry as kindling. It was clear from the minister's eulogy that he hadn't known Avel well and the soloist had sung "You'll Never Walk Alone" off-key. It was only when Harriet's beautiful and plaintive voice ("Others have tried to own it, tried to stamp it with their mark, but I only pay my love to you, 'cause you're the landlord of my heart") met with the music of her harp that everyone rummaged in their bags and pockets for handkerchiefs.

On the church steps, Harriet had maintained her composure as a stream of people offered their sympathies. She nodded somberly as Detective Milt Zims told her no one would ever get him on a plane, no siree, he was a train man through and through, and she hugged a large woman who claimed to have met Avel in a bar called *The Den of* on New Year's Eve.

"Thanks to him and the money he gave me, I decided to get my life on track," said Suzanne Wojinski. "I'm going to be an LPN."

Harriet even had the courage to approach Avel's sisters, telling them it had been an honor to love their brother.

"Thank you," said Bernice dryly, and then she and Esme skittered away to greet the mayor and his wife.

It wasn't until Harriet, Patty Jane and Ione were inside Patty Jane's apartment that the facade of control broke and Harriet crumbled like a condemned building broadsided by the wrecking ball.

"I don't know what to do for her," said Ione one muggy August afternoon two months after Avel's death. Harriet was submerged in a slough of grief that narrowed her activities to crying, smoking and sleeping. On that day she had combined the three, setting her hair on fire.

"I'd say dousing the flames was pretty good." Patty Jane let herself laugh at the memory of Ione standing at the kitchen sink, aiming the rinse hose at Harriet.

"I was scared of my wits," said Ione, shaking her head.

"I was scared *out* of mine," said Patty Jane. She looked at the grocery list. "Are you sure you'll be all right with her? I should really get the shopping done."

"She's asleep, Nora's asleep, I'll be fine."

"Anything else you can think of?"

"Some brown sugar — and how are we doing on coffee?"

Patty Jane smiled; theirs was a household that could run out of toilet paper or soap but never dessert fixings or coffee.

Having just chosen the laundry detergent that offered a free dish towel over the one that included a glass tumbler, Patty Jane wheeled her grocery cart into the cereal aisle. Her scream brought store personnel and a half-dozen shoppers to her side.

"What's happened?" asked the breathless assistant manager, scanning the aisle for broken glass and worse, blood.

"My husband!" wailed Patty Jane.

"What's that about a husband?" asked an old man to the butcher.

Patty Jane grabbed a box of Mighty Bites off the shelf. "This," she said, slapping the box, "is my husband."

"She wishes," muttered a housewife in pincurls.

The assistant manager mustered up his customer-is-always-right smile, rarely an effortless reflex.

"Why don't I get you a nice cool root beer?" he asked, thinking it a reasonable offer to someone suffering from delusions in his grocery store.

"I don't want your damn root beer!" Patty Jane shouted. She threw the cereal at the shelf and boxes of Mighty Bites tumbled to the floor. "I just want him!"

"Who could blame her?" asked the housewife, watching Patty Jane race out of the store.

The telephone message given to Esme Ames by her secretary was full of asterisks and exclamation points.

"Those signify profanities," said the secretary, her ears reddening.

Esme Ames did not take any of the dozen similarly profane calls Patty Jane made to her within the next two days, but finally dictated the following letter:

9/1/54

Dear Mrs. Rolvaag:

Your husband signed a model's release and we are well within our legal rights to continue marketing Mighty Bites as is. That he left you is unfortunate, but the circumstances that put your husband's picture on our cereal box were set into motion months ago and it would be quite impossible to warehouse an existing and successful product.

Sincerely,
Esme Ames

Ames Grain

P.S. If you persist with your telephone calls, I shall report you to the police.

Patty Jane's was the lone voice of dissent. There had never been a more successful cereal in Ames Grain history and from the letters that poured into customer service, it was due more to the delectability of the model than the "corn-crunchy goodness" of Mighty Bites.

"That handsome gentleman on the box," wrote "Extra-Satisfied" of Baltimore, Maryland, "sure keeps me coming back for seconds!"

"It's just one bad joke on top of another," said Patty Jane to Harriet. "Next they'll probably market Avel's face on boxes of shortbread."

Harriet stared at her cigarette smoke.

"Come on, Harriet, that was a joke. *Short*bread, get it? Oh, never mind." She slapped her sister's thigh, trying to get anything — even Harriet's circulation — going. "How about taking a walk with me?"

Harriet's long sigh was her only answer.

"Oh, fine, the silent treatment. I love the silent treatment, don't you Nora?"

The baby, strapped in a pack on Patty Jane's back, gurgled.

"Last offer, Harriet. Going once, going twice."

Harriet sighed again.

"And we're gone." Patty Jane brushed at the sleeves of her

jacket. She had sympathy for Harriet, but patience wasn't one of her strong suits. "We won't be gone long. Try to move at least one body part, okay?"

When the hikers returned home, Eddie Fisher, at full volume, was singing about his papa.

"Pipe down, Ed," said Patty Jane, turning off the kitchen radio. She hollered at Harriet about disturbing Vogstad's customers downstairs, but secretly she was pleased; she couldn't remember the last time Harriet had summoned up the energy to turn on the radio.

"Really, Harriet," she said, walking down the hallway to the living room, "if Mr. Vogstad didn't have such a crush on you, he'd have evicted us by now."

A shadow flickered in her peripheral vision, so slight that she barely acknowledged it and yet she was immediately filled with dread.

"Harriet?" she said weakly, stepping backward to the bathroom door.

"Ah-ah?" said Nora in her little pack.

The sunsplashed bathroom with its windowsill lined with blooming African violets looked cheerful and benign except that Harriet was sprawled over the bathtub.

For a moment Patty Jane wanted to believe that her sister was doing nothing more than scouring away lime deposits, but as she took a few shaky steps forward, she saw the bright red splashes of blood on the linoleum. Nearby, a razor glittered.

"Harriet!" Her scream triggered one in Nora and the bathroom was suddenly a horror chamber — full of screams and blood and Patty Jane's search for life in her sister.

Patty Jane pulled Harriet off the rim of the tub and then nearly dropped her back again when she saw Harriet's wrists were intact.

"Owww," moaned Harriet. "My head."

Patty Jane frantically riffled through her sister's scalp, feeling for dampness. She found none, but a purpling lump was forming above her left eyebrow.

"Oww," said Harriet, touching the bruise and shifting her position. She saw the blood on her leg.

"Hey, I'm bleeding," she said weakly.

"Harriet, honey," said Patty Jane, "what happened?"

Harriet stared at the bathroom tile, thinking. "I don't know," she said finally. "I was changing the razor blade — I was going to shave my legs — and I . . . well, I guess I passed out." She put her index finger in her mouth and pressed it to the cut below her knee.

"You weren't trying to kill yourself?" Patty Jane's voice was a whisper.

"Kill myself?" Tears formed in her eyes as quick as a blink. "Oh, Patty Jane, I already feel dead."

The sisters held each other until Nora, bored and hungry, started to cry.

"Do you believe her?" asked Ione, as she and Patty Jane sat at the kitchen table having a late-night conference.

Patty Jane nodded. "If I didn't, I'd go crazy with worry. She doesn't have the heart to hurt anyone including — knock on wood — herself."

"I'll never forget when our dad threw her trumpet out the window," said Patty Jane, shaking her head. "She went to get it, and cradled it like it was a baby, petting its dented horn while these big tears rolled down her face. Elmo and Anna were meaner to her, I think, because they knew they could hurt her more.

"No matter how drunk and mean they had been the night before, Harriet would still make them breakfast in the morning — oatmeal and boiled eggs and coffee that watered-down way Anna liked so much. And she was always smiling, running to get them aspirin and light their cigarettes, and me, I'd be in the living room taking my time reading the sports section because I knew that was the part of the paper Elmo wanted most.

"From an early age, Ione, I knew that just because my parents tried to make me feel like crap, it didn't mean I really was. I mean, I even feel that way about Thor: he ran out on me, but he's the dumb jerk, not me."

"Thor was —"

"But Harriet doesn't think the same way," interrupted Patty Jane, not wanting to talk about Thor. "Go figure, Ione. She's got the voice of an angel — she's this musical genius who taught herself to read notes the way some kids teach themselves to read words — and yet she's always needed someone to take care of her."

"To be good to yourself," said Ione, shaking her head, staring into her coffee cup. "Sometimes it seems that takes a special talent all its own."

Patty Jane's own self-esteem took a dip one day when, home early after a walk, she surprised Ione at the kitchen table, writing out checks to the electric and gas company.

"I feel like such a damn stupid idiot!" Patty Jane said. "How could I go charging groceries, turning up the heat, how could I do anything without realizing I was sponging off my own mother-in-law!"

"Uff-da," said Ione, "who said anything about this sponging? I want to help you."

"Oh man," Patty Jane said, "you've been paying the rent too, haven't you?"

Ione carefully pulled a stamp from its perforated border. "Avel had been taking care of it when Thor left." She licked the stamp and applied it to the envelope with a quick roll of her fist. "When Avel left us, I took over."

"Oh, Ione, I'll pay you back! I'll pay you back with interest!"

Ione's nostrils quivered. "Patty Jane, it's the littlest I could have done."

"Well, I'm going to get a job and pay you back."

Rudy Holtz of Holtz Automotive laughed in her face when she applied for work as a car salesman.

"Honey," he said, clamping his smile on a big cigar, "the day I hire a gal to sell my cars is the day I go out of business."

She had no better luck at the two department stores where she applied.

"Why do you want to work in appliances?" asked the personnel director.

"I'd like a job with commissions."

"We don't have one single woman in appliances."

"Don't you think it's about time?" asked Patty Jane.

"I most certainly do not," said the personnel director. "A man's got to support his family. How can he do that when women want to take his job away from him?"

"How am I supposed to support my family?"

"There's a job opening in women's toiletries," he said.

Patty Jane gathered up her purse and coat. "Don't make me tell you what you can do with your toiletries."

Patty Jane spent a day in the library researching careers after Ione told her she would pay for a trade school tuition.

"Dental hygiene and court reporting were in the running," she said when she came home, her face flushed with excitement, "but the winner is . . . ta-da . . . beauty school!"

"What does this 'beauty school' mean?" asked Ione, thinking beauty was something you were born with, not something you could study for.

"It means that you'll have free haircuts for life!"

When Clyde Chuka walked into Patty Jane's House of Curl to apply for a job, he liked what he saw. A thin woman with long hair was plucking "The Twist" on a harp while a group of smocked women, some in curlers, others with wet hair, danced around the room.

"Man on the premises, man on the premises," shouted the first one to notice him.

A pretty woman laughed. "Honestly, Bev, you sound like we should take cover." She walked over to the man, her hand extended. "Hi, I'm Patty Jane."

"Of the House of Curl," Clyde Chuka surmised.

She looked around the room. "Here to pick someone up?"

"No," he said. "I'd probably go to a bar to do that."

Patty Jane laughed. "I mean are you here to give someone a ride home? Myrna, is this the new man you've been telling us about?"

"No, Clint's tall," said the woman. "No offense to you, sir."

"No offense taken," he said, nodding in her direction. "Actually, I saw the sign outside."

Patty Jane studied the broad-shouldered, compact man and furrowed her brow before realizing what he was talking about. "Oh, the 'manicurist wanted' sign." She still remembered the humiliation she'd suffered when she had applied for unconventional jobs. "Okay, then. Would you do my nails — a sort of test run?"

"Be my pleasure," he said.

"And you are . . . ?" Patty Jane asked.

"Clyde Chuka."

"Chuck-a?" Bev Beal said from across the room, where she was cleaning her combs. "What kind of name is that?"

"Czech." He smiled. He pulled off his Millers baseball cap and a long black braid spilled down his back. Some of the women gasped. "Actually, I'm mostly Indian. Lakota. But my great grandfather was from Prague. He was a fur trader, partial to ladies of the native persuasion."

"Sounds like my husband," muttered Alva Bundt. "Except he's not picky."

Patty Jane quickly seated Clyde Chuka at the manicurist table.

"So, you have had experience," said Patty Jane, watching him work on her pinky.

"Yeah. I used to do my relatives. The women, that is. There's something about holding a woman's hand that gives me a lot of pleasure."

Patty Jane withdrew her hand from his. "You're not some kind of pervert, are you? This doesn't . . . excite you in the wrong way, does it?"

"Patty Jane," scolded Harriet.

Clyde Chuka laughed. "No, it doesn't excite me . . . in the wrong way." He took Patty Jane's hand back in his. "See, I'm an artist — I sculpt — but I do odd jobs on the side to pay the rent. Manicure is a pretty odd job, but I'm good at it."

He was, and Patty Jane hired him.

"None of you gals mind, do you?" she asked. No one did, although Bev Beal later took Patty Jane aside and said she wasn't so sure her boyfriend would like her working with an Indian. Patty Jane advised her to get another boyfriend.

They were figuring out his work schedule when the door burst open.

"I could show you all something!" cackled a woman with wild eyes and premature grey hair who entered.

"Excuse me," said Patty Jane to Clyde Chuka. "Can I help you?" she asked the woman.

"You'd like to think you could, don't you? But maybe then I'm the one who could help you." Her laugh was an eerie bray.

"She comes in every year or so," Harriet whispered to Clyde Chuka. "Where she should really be is in a psycho ward."

"What I'd like to know," said the woman, walking through the salon, swinging her pocketbook from its thin chain handle, "is why I'm not more welcomed here."

"Okay, that's it," said Patty Jane, trying to turn the woman around.

"Don't touch me! Nobody touches me!" The woman composed herself and coyly dusted her sleeve. "Well, almost nobody." She laughed again.

Paige Larkin's baby, sleeping in the corner playpen, woke up and began to cry.

"I want you out of here," said Patty Jane.

"It's a free country!"

Clyde Chuka stood up. "Need some help, Patty Jane?"

"Oh, Chief Sitting Bull, ready to go on the war path!"

It was a struggle, but Clyde Chuka and Patty Jane and Ione managed to get the woman out the door and to her parked car.

"So what did you really hire me as?" said Clyde Chuka as they watched her drive away. "Manicurist or bouncer?"

"Feel free to express yourself anyway you want," said Patty Jane. "It's that kind of place."

Nora pushed aside the pleated door that separated the House of Curl from the dining room and sat in one of the unoccupied chairs.

"Is Mom back yet?" she asked Clyde Chuka. She felt the guilt of the messenger — she had delivered the letter from Thor — wondering why her dad never stuck in a "Hi kid, how ya doing?"

Clyde Chuka shook his head. "I'm free until my two o'clock. Want your nails done?"

Nora nodded happily. She was only nine years old, but when she had her nails done, she felt like twelve. She had her father's pale blond hair and crayola blue eyes, but she was far scrappier than the average cherub. She was the one who locked Karen Anderson, daughter of Patty Jane's precision barber, Dixie Anderson, in the fruit cellar after suffering one too many of Karen's socks to the stomach. Karen and Nora were both engaged in a struggle for any show of attention from Bev's son Ricky, who was several years older than them and, in the vernacular of the day, "dreamy." And once, while doing laundry, Patty Jane found a crumpled note in Nora's overall pocket. It was from her second-grade teacher. The note explained that Nora must stay after school for the entire week — for fighting.

"Lois Lombardi started it!" Nora wailed when Patty Jane demanded an explanation. "She's the one who was making fun of me — because I don't have a dad."

Patty Jane gave up any thoughts of lecturing her daughter on restraint. "Your dad was very wrong to leave us, Nora," she said instead. "But it was his fault he left us — not yours, not mine. Some people have a lot of reasons for doing things that make other people feel bad."

"I only had *one* reason for hitting Lois Lombardi," sniffed Nora. "I hate her!"

"Your father didn't hate us, honey, he just . . . I don't know. I guess he thought he was too young to be a husband and a father. He made his own choice."

"Well, I hate his choice too," said Nora.

"I know you do, baby." Patty Jane pushed aside the towel she had been folding and refolding and took her daughter into her arms, wishing she could hold her like this always, keeping her from pain and hurt and from jerks like the Lombardi kid.

But one thing that always brought out Nora's best behavior was sitting in the House of Curl, listening to the women talk; she felt as if she were in a special club overhearing top-secret information. Plump and pretty Myrna Johnson brought tales of bargain shopping. Whatever you needed, from oven mitts to girdles, she knew where you could get it cheaper. Inky Kolstat, who wore her hair in a white cloud, worked as an usher at the

Orpheum Theatre. As a young woman she had had coffee with Mr. John Barrymore.

"He wanted more," she said, "but I wasn't about to be anyone's passing fancy, theatre legend or not."

Alva Bundt's husband was cheating on her, which didn't bother Alva much because "the more he gets in on the outside, the less he'll ask it of me."

Fair and regal Paige Larkin had hemorrhaged so badly after the birth of her son that she had needed a blood transfusion and if her husband thought they were going to have a third child, "he has another thought coming."

Sometimes, if the conversation leaned toward the juicy side, a client might purse her lips and nod toward Nora but Patty Jane, bobby pins clenched between her teeth would say, "Oh, don't mind Nora. I imagine she'll be hearing worse things in her day."

They were talking about the recent assassination of President Kennedy.

"It's a conspiracy," said Karen Spaeth who taught French courses for Berlitz, "Oswald kills Kennedy and Ruby kills Oswald . . . something big set off those dominoes."

"Oh, for crying out loud," said Alva, her hair wrapped in goop and plastic, "this is America."

Clyde Chuka knocked over the bottle of "Flamingo Pink" polish Nora had selected.

"He should have chosen show business over politics," said Inky Kolstat, who dispensed movie gossip ranging from the dating advice George Hamilton gave Elvis to the box office gross of *How the West Was Won*. She shook her head. "Name one star handsomer than he was."

"No, it was the work of one deranged man," insisted Alva. "One nutcase who got what he deserved."

"I myself would have preferred a trial," said Clyde Chuka in his low, even voice. "Would have been some interesting things coming out of that one."

"Not me," said Bev Beal, holding a customer's head under a spigot. "I'm only sorry I didn't get to see the guy fry."

"Honestly, Bev," said Dixie, who wondered if her styling specialty — the Jackie Kennedy bouffant — would continue to be her customers' favorite request.

T welve

After a successful three-year run, Thor's picture on the Mighty Bites box had been replaced by a cartoon character named "Mr. Mighty Biter." Patty Jane was so relieved that she wrote Esme and Bernice Ames a letter thanking them for "finally letting me shop for cereal in peace." While Bernice scoffed, "As if we did it for her," Esme was touched by a graciousness she didn't practice herself. She telephoned Patty Jane, opening lines of communication that had once seemed irrevocably disconnected.

Esme then made occasional appearances at the House of Curl, and it was at the last Holiday Cookie Exchange that she had approached Patty Jane and Harriet with the idea of a "communion" with Avel.

"I've been exploring different spiritual paths," she explained. "I've had the good fortune of linking up with an eminent parapsychologist who's out of this world!" Esme giggled, a tight little snort.

Ione was thoroughly opposed to the idea of a séance, thinking it un-Christian, if not downright devilish.

"It's just Esme's way of apologizing," said Patty Jane. "She feels bad about the way she treated Harriet and Avel and now she wants to make amends. If this'll help her, who am I to say no?"

"Well, I want not a part of it," huffed Ione. "You go ahead and tempt the devil; I will take Nora to a movie."

The eminent parapsychologist was the palest guy Patty Jane had ever seen, a man named Wesley who wore a red paisley bow tie and perfumed his hair. He had everyone sit at the dining room table and hold hands. It was quiet for a long time before Wesley started to twitch his head as if he were trying to get a bug out of his ear. Then he started yapping like a chihuahua.

"Avel, Avel Ames, there are some people on the earth plane who would like contact with you. Are you willing?"

A loaded silence was interrupted with a big thump. Harriet looked wildly at Patty Jane, and was somewhat comforted to see her sister's smirk.

"Avel, I'm sorry about the shameful way I treated you," said Esme, her voice tremulous. "Will you forgive me?"

There was another loud thump.

"He forgives you," translated Wesley.

To Harriet, it was obvious that Wesley was rapping the underside of the table with his knee. But still, it was unsettling. Avel had been dead for nearly ten years, but Harriet had kept his memory alive in a brave little flame of love, and now felt the séance cheapened Avel's real spirit. She excused herself early and slipped out into the backyard for a smoke, shivering from a loneliness far colder than subzero Minnesota temperature.

The others left the séance more satisfied: Wesley was fifty dollars richer, Esme felt she had been gifted by her brother's forgiveness, and Patty Jane was spurred to think of some special events of her own.

On a chilly March evening in 1964, when the window shutters rattled under a persistent wind, Patty Jane announced she had some new plans for the House of Curl. Something in her voice made Nora turn off *The Patty Duke Show* and Ione put down the travel section of the newspaper.

"Listen to this." Patty Jane tapped her pen on a steno pad and cleared her throat. "'Patty Jane's House of Curl presents its Famous People Lecture Series. For one dollar — refreshments included — you can listen and learn from people who've made a successful and creative life for themselves.'" Patty Jane looked up. "Well?"

The tapping of her pen punctuated the silence that followed.

Finally Ione coughed and said, "Patty Jane, do you know any famous people?"

"The title's subject to change," she said irritably. "If any of you can think of something better, by all means, let me know."

A look passed between Harriet and Ione and Nora. Harriet lit a cigarette and exhaled the smoke through her nose, a gesture Nora thought looked half glamorous, half demonic.

"You might want to elaborate a bit, Patty Jane," she said.

"Okay, that's all I'm asking for, a little interest," said Patty Jane, turning to her mother-in-law. "Ione, who do people tell their troubles to?"

Ione looked to Harriet for help but Harriet was watching her smoke rings disintegrate in the air.

"Their families?" Sometimes the way Patty Jane asked a question made Ione feel she'd better guess the right answer or a buzzer would go off and she'd be penalized.

"Sure," said Patty Jane. "But I mean outside the family. Who do they go to?"

"Their ministers?"

"True, true. But who else?"

After a silence, Patty Jane sighed as if she were the only one in the room with an IQ over one hundred.

"Hairdressers," she said, answering her riddle. "Everyone knows people tell their hairdressers everything, right?"

They murmured their assent, happy Patty Jane was through with the quiz.

"And you know what I hear while I'm working everyday as a hairdresser?"

"That Alva Bundt's husband is cheating on her?" asked Nora.

Patty Jane and Harriet laughed.

"Uff-da mayda," said Ione, trying to hide a smile, "this is the kind of education she gets by having a free train in that place?"

"That's a free *rein*," said Patty Jane.

Nora didn't understand the reaction her simple question elicited; to her, "cheating" meant that Alva Bundt's husband padded his score in Yahtzee or moved his checker forward when he thought no one was looking.

Patty Jane stood up and began pacing in front of the fireplace. "Now, what I was trying to say before I was interrupted by my daughter the comedian, is that most of the gals who come in here are looking for something more in their lives." She read the look on Ione's face. "Yes, even the church-going ones. Most of these women have husbands and children and a yearning they just can't put their fingers on."

Her hand waved aside one of Harriet's smoke rings and she said to her sister, "See, they're all looking for something but they don't know what it is."

"Love," said Harriet, dramatically.

"Happiness," piped in Ione.

"Fun?" said Nora.

Patty Jane winked at her. "All very good answers," she said, "but to get them, you need one basic thing: a sense of self. A sense that we're not just mothers or children or wives or girlfriends."

Looking coolly at her audience, Patty Jane stood in her red gingham blouse and tight red capri pants. Nora's ten-year-old heart pounded, thinking there was not a person on the entire planet she could love as much as her mother.

"I just want to open up the world a bit for people who think it ends on the border of Hennepin County," said Patty Jane. "I want to do it for them. For us." She pushed back her hair with one hand. "Come on," she said, invitation in her voice. "It'll be fun."

The plan that had come into Patty Jane's head, she felt, would serve her own curiosity as well as that of her clients and friends. She would offer lectures that could branch off into classes of interest, taught by people interested in their subject, attended by interested people. In the seminars Patty Jane imagined there would be no picking of nail polish, no perpetual yawning.

"Sort of a salon within a salon?" asked Clyde Chuka when Patty Jane outlined her plan to him. They were on afternoon break, sitting at the dining room table, helping themselves to Ione's apple crisp.

"Exactly," said Patty Jane, "it'll be a gathering place for artists and other notables." She nodded her head, excited. "That's what I'll call it: 'Patty Jane's House of Curl presents the Artists and Other Notables Lecture Series.'"

"It's a mouthful," said Clyde Chuka.

"But it says it all," said Patty Jane and they finished their break in silence, watching grey drizzle fog up the windows behind the ivory lace curtains.

"What is all this nonsense about famous and notable lectures?" asked Crabby Bultram, waving one of the flyers that Patty Jane regularly mailed to her clients.

"We're going to try a little something new," said Patty Jane.

"Well, who's going to attend to my coif?"

Ione, arranging toffee bars on the refreshment table, whispered to Harriet, "Shouldn't she take care of her own cough?"

"Coif," said Harriet. "Hairstyle."

Crabby had a standing Saturday morning appointment for a wash and set, but she used The House of Curl as a social club too, dropping in often to help herself to seconds of Ione's treat of the day, leaving plum lipstick stains on her coffee cup. Nora was afraid of her; the old woman never remembered her name and spat when she talked.

"Mrs. Bultram," said Patty Jane, "The House of Curl routine won't change. The seminars will be in the evening."

"Oh." Crabby adjusted her harlequin glasses and looked at the flyer. "So this is at night. Well, I guess I'll have to come on by then and see what the hub-bub is about."

Nora, holding a stack of freshly scented bandanas, passed Crabby, who grabbed the child's thin arm and pointed her in Ione's direction. "Norma, dear, do me a favor and fetch me a toffee bar."

For the first Artist and Other Notables Lecture Series, Patty Jane pressed Clyde Chuka to do a slide presentation of his sculptures, but he said he'd rather not subject himself to the criticism of his clients. Instead, he agreed to Patty Jane's second choice, to "find someone interesting in your artists' circle." He enlisted Geoff Bell, who introduced himself to the women assembled in Patty Jane's living room as "an avant garde filmmaker."

After Bell had projected two of his films on a section of wall above the fireplace and the lights were turned on, he saw his audience had shrunk from twelve to four.

"Well, then," he said, rubbing his hands together, "I see that my art spoke rather loudly to some of you."

"Yeah," said Bev, who had giggled throughout the presentation, "and it said, 'Get out before the cops raid the joint.'"

Both films — jumpy 16-mm black-and-whites — featured nudity. *Morning Glory* portrayed a naked woman romping through a barnyard while a farmer plucked feathers off a dead chicken, and *Ozzie William's Detour* was about a stockbroker who, naked, climbed a billboard and played reveille for a band of marching female soldiers. After they receded into the distance, the man sat down on the edge of the billboard and ate sauerkraut from a can while reading *The Wall Street Journal.*

Ione had been the first to slip out of the darkened room. She put on a pot of coffee in the kitchen and waited for the storm of women she was sure would follow. She felt a great relief that none of the Naomis, her church circle sisters, had attended the program, choosing instead to serve cake and punch at Oscar and Lucy Patterson's fiftieth wedding anniversary.

The modesty taught by the Lutheran Church had always been at odds with the basic ease with which native Scandinavians regarded their bodies. So it was not so much the nudity Ione minded, but Mr. Bell's obvious delight in shock value. Show-offs generally irked her, unless she agreed that what they were showing off was absolutely wonderful.

The party in the kitchen grew until only Patty Jane, Harriet, Bev and Clyde Chuka remained to applaud when the final images flickered and vanished from the living room wall.

"I'd love to stay and shoot the breeze," said Geoff Bell, rewinding the spool of film and replacing it into a canister, "but I'm scared as hell." He nodded toward Clyde Chuka. "Give me a hand with the projector, would you?"

The two men walked silently to Bell's car and it was only as he fumbled with the trunk lock that the silence was unbuttoned. Clyde Chuka had to put the projector on the curb because laughter sapped the strength from his arms.

"I owe you one," said Clyde Chuka finally.

"You're telling me," said the scorned artist, getting behind the wheel and turning the ignition key. "But I guess that's what I get for trying to bring art to the masses."

"Good gravy!" said Crabby Bultram, inside the kitchen, her hands fisted and her chin pulled toward the ceiling. "If I wanted to see smut, I would have gone down to the Avalon Theatre on Lake Street!"

"If that's art, I'm Queen Elizabeth," said Alva close behind.

"Why on earth did you allow that pornography in your living room?" Crabby barked, and Patty Jane wished she had a rolled-up section of the *Minneapolis Star* to swat her with.

"Art," said Patty Jane through clenched teeth, "that was one man's art."

"One man who should be arrested," sniffed Crabby.

There were a few echos of assent from the group congregated around the kitchen table. Patty Jane's eyes sent her sister a signal asking for help, but Harriet, a faint smile playing on her lips, shrugged her shoulders and lit a cigarette.

"Ladies," said Patty Jane, drawing up her shoulders. "I'm sorry if many of you were offended . . . It was an experiment, that's all."

The back door opened and a gust of night air swept in with Clyde Chuka, his eyes still tearing from laughter.

"Ummm," he said, "cup of that coffee if you're pouring, Ione."

The momentary silence that greeted his entry was broken by over a dozen irate female voices.

"Ladies, ladies," he said, holding up one hand while accepting a cup of coffee with the other. "If I had known you were interested, I would have asked the artist to stay and answer some of your questions."

"Questions!" said Crabby Bultram. "Here's one: why isn't that man serving a jail sentence?"

"Why doesn't he try to make a good movie?" asked Inky Kolstat, feeling that her cup of coffee with John Barrymore long ago made her opinion doubly relevant. "Something like *Singing in the Rain* or *Tammy and the Doctor*."

"Does the guy who played the stockbroker make personal appearances?" asked Alva Bundt.

"Ladies, ladies," said Clyde Chuka, smiling. "Geoff Bell's

work is very well known in art circles. He and I thought it might be fun to widen those circles a bit and he thanks you for the opportunity to show what he knows is controversial work."

Clyde Chuka's dark brown eyes and warm, Dakota-accented voice were so earnest that the women quieted.

"None of you had to leave the safety and comfort of your homes," he continued. "You could have stayed in your rec rooms watching Ed Sullivan, but you came out on a chilly Sunday night."

Patty Jane noticed a collective change of posture as the women listened to Clyde Chuka. Spines straightened, chins lifted, and a general feeling of pride seemed to wash across them. The women exchanged smiles as if to say, "Well, aren't we something!"

Clyde Chuka took a sip of coffee and his eyes scanned the room. He focused on Crabby Bultram. "Life, according to Helen Keller, is either a daring adventure or nothing," he said, "and thank you all for participating in it."

The women gave Clyde's speech a silent ovation, nodding and smiling.

Soon, they collected purses and coats and children (Dixie's oldest daughter had been watching them in the basement for thirty-five cents an hour) and said their goodnights. Patty Jane sidled up to Clyde Chuka, who was standing at the door, seeing them out.

"Quite a speech," she said.

"'Night Alva," said Clyde Chuka, holding the door open to the last of the guests. "Watch the walk — it's slippery."

"Thanks," he said and, locking the door, he turned to Patty Jane. "I was quite an orator at the Indian School. Until my infamous General Custer speech."

Patty Jane turned off the back porch light. "What was that?"

"I pretended I was Crazy Horse, reporting from battle." Clyde Chuka took his coffee cup to the sink and rinsed it.

"And?" said Patty Jane, following him.

Clyde Chuka sighed. "And there was a dispute between me and the teacher as to what was fact and what wasn't. See, there he was, a white man, trying to teach a bunch of Lakota and Oglala kids that the greatest warrior in the Sioux Nation was some kind of barbarian. I said it was like me coming into a classroom full of white kids and telling them that George Washington was a pervert."

Patty Jane laughed sadly. "So that ended your career as speechmaker, huh?"

"That ended my career as a student. Our words blew up into a fight and we broke each other's noses. I was thirteen when I got expelled — the teacher probably got a commendation." He dried the cup thoroughly, pushing a dishcloth into it and turning the base of the cup in quick revolutions. "Expelling me was a formality. By the time the school notified my grandmother on the reservation, I was already on the freeway, hitching a ride to anywhere."

Thirteen

W HEN BUSINESS WAS LIGHT, Clyde Chuka joined Patty Jane for her afternoon walks. That she, a natural speed walker, had to slow her pace for him was more than compensated for by his company. Solitude on a day's walk was not sacred to Patty Jane; she had been urging Harriet to join her for years and remembered fondly when Nora was strapped to her back. No, she had had enough solitude to last her life.

On the day after what was, in time, referred to as "The Artists and Other Notables Porn Festival," they walked along the stone wall ringing Minnehaha Falls. The falls were eerie and phosphorescent, their motion frozen into a white curtain of ice. Patty Jane and Clyde Chuka were alone except for a man setting up a camera on a tripod.

"I stayed up late last night, Clyde Chuka," said Patty Jane, "thinking, thinking, thinking what my customers would like as far as the lectures go. I finally came to the bright conclusion: let them tell me."

"For the people, by the people."

Patty Jane smiled, the dimple high on her cheek flashing.

She pushed her hands into her pockets. "I got out of bed, dug a shoe box out of the closet, covered it in shelf paper, cut a slot on it and presto — a suggestion box. The gals are going to tell me what they'd like. Crabby Bultram is going to tell *me* how she'd be willing to pay money to learn how to —"

"Drive a Sherman tank."

"I'm sure she already knows. She was in the War, you know."

"Well then, maybe she'd like to know how to skin a deer."

"A live one."

Their laughter rode puffs of vapor in the cold air. They walked along the stone wall that lined the bluff, stopping at the steps that zigzagged down the steep hill to the creek basin where the falls emptied. Packed snow and ice covered the steps and the Park Board had placed a wooden barrier at the head of the stonewalled staircase stencilled with the words "Do Not Enter." It was a sign of temptation more than deterrence.

"Let's," said Patty Jane. Ducking under the barrier, Patty Jane grabbed the handrail at the top of the stairs. "See you at the bottom," she said, "dead or alive."

She loosened her grip on the handrail and her feet, their hold tentative, slid out from under her. She hobbled back into a standing position. "That hurt like hell."

"You want to forget it?" asked Clyde Chuka, brushing snow off the back of Patty Jane's jacket.

"Are you kidding?" With her hands on the rail, Patty Jane sat down on the packed snow of the stars and began sliding down. She picked up speed, her mittens on the metal rail. All her senses were enveloped in exuberance and terror as she whooshed down the giant ice slide, and from the yelps behind her, she knew Clyde Chuka was feeling the same way. They were kids again. Nothing mattered but speed.

When Patty Jane reached the last steps she rolled a way down the bank and came to a stop, panting and laughing. In a

matter of seconds Clyde Chuka was next to her, and toge..
they lay on the ground, their laughter puncturing the winter
stillness. They rolled until their bodies were pressed together
and suddenly their laughter ended and their lips touched.

Clyde Chuka's lips were warm and rich on Patty Jane's. Covered with snow, she burned inside.

"Holy shit," she said when the urgency of their kiss faded and
their lips gently parted. "I could get used to that."

"Yeah, me too," said Clyde Chuka and he kissed her again, a
quick dry kiss, and they both sat up, slapping the snow from
their knees and jackets.

When she had first hired him, Patty Jane, finding Clyde
Chuka attractive — she also thought his wearing a long black
braid both brave and sexy — dropped heavy hints, but if Clyde
Chuka had caught any, he wasn't saying. Finally, during a break
a month after he started working at the House of Curl, Patty
Jane asked, "Clyde Chuka, why in hell-nation are you playing
so hard to get?"

Clyde Chuka stirred his coffee and set his spoon delicately
on the saucer.

"Patty Jane," he said and his clear brown eyes met hers. "I'm
not playing anything."

Patty Jane fiddled with the china cup, her fingers running
along the filigreed edges. "Well, for cripes' sake, most men find
me very attractive."

"You are very attractive."

"So?" she asked, batting her eyelashes, hating the cheap flirtation but unable to stop herself.

Clyde Chuka peeled the paper skin off a cranberry muffin.
"So what?"

Patty Jane slammed the flat of her hand against the table.
"Damn it, Clyde Chuka, do you need a written invitation?"

a rested his hand under his chin and a small sigh
lders. "Patty Jane, it doesn't matter what kind of
t, I'm not taking you up on it."

sputtered in frustration. "Well, why not?"

"......., he said, biting into his muffin, "this is good." He ate it slowly and deliberately, until Patty Jane wanted to sock him. "Not that it's any of your business," he said finally, wiping the crumbs from his lip, "but since you're so gung-ho about making it your business, I'll tell you this: I'm celibate."

A hinge loosened in Patty Jane's jaw and it dropped open. "Celibate?"

"My body's enjoying a little quiet time." He rose, pushing back his chair. "Too much sex is like too much talk. Sometimes it just gets noisy and nothing is said at all."

Able to relate to Clyde's words, Patty Jane clamped her mouth shut. It wasn't as if her sexual calendar were fully booked, but in the past few years she *had* slept with several men. Among them had been a divorced man she'd met at a PTA meeting and a repairman who'd fixed her washer. It was after a night spent thrashing with a carpet salesman that Patty Jane realized that rather than filling her up, sex without love had hollowed her out, and she was tired of being in the arms of men who left her with only the residue of loneliness.

But now, as she and Clyde Chuka walked down the snow-packed path that ran along the frozen creek, past the open field known as the Deer Pen and to the Mississippi, Patty Jane wondered if Clyde Chuka had decided to end his celibacy.

"So what did that mean?" she said, breaking the silence that followed their last quick kiss.

"It means we shouldn't go sliding together."

"Clyde —"

"Shhh." He pulled her gently to him and pointed a gloved hand at a clump of bare bushes. "Look."

A doe and her fawn stared at them through the tangle of

branches, their ears held upright like antennae, their noses twitching.

"Oh, I wish Nora could see this," whispered Patty Jane.

The fawn looked at its mother, who raised her head, ruffling a white streak of fur on her throat. She leaped sideways and ran into the glen, the fawn following. They vanished so quickly that it seemed they had been nothing more than grey shadows on the snow. Clyde Chuka dropped his arm from Patty Jane's shoulders and took her hand.

"Patty Jane," he said, tucking her hand, with his, into his jacket pocket. "I like you too much to sleep with you."

"I don't follow your logic," said Patty Jane. "And what about that kiss?"

They began to walk. Silence yoked their shoulders and rode between them.

"That kiss," said Clyde Chuka finally, "was our trophy for getting down those steps alive."

"So you reward dangerous behavior with sex?"

"Patty Jane," he said, and she heard the seriousness, "I have plenty of reasons for wanting to sleep with you and plenty for not. And the way I see it, the 'for-not' side stacks up higher."

"Well, tell me the reasons you have for sleeping with me."

"Quit fishing, Patty Jane. You can figure those out." He softened the stony expression the cold and the conversation had imprinted on his face. "But here's why I don't, and not necessarily in order of importance: One, I don't want to mess up a friendship that means more to me every day; two, as a matter of principle, I don't sleep with bosses, teachers or circus performers, and three, I don't want to get tangled up with Thor."

"Thor?" said Patty Jane, stopping in her tracks.

"Yeah, Thor." There was a hint of resignation in his voice. "Here's the way I see it, Patty Jane. We're alloted one great love — and some of us are lucky enough to find it. That love is sort of our pilot light and when it goes out . . . then it's out for

157

good." He blew out a big breath puffing his cheeks. "Now, I could be a burner and warm you up a bit, but I'd never be what I'd want to be, that pilot light. So I guess I'd rather stay away from the stove altogether."

"Chicken," said Patty Jane, and shut her eyes against the tears she didn't want Clyde Chuka to see.

Fourteen

In 1967, Nora became a teenager, and to Patty Jane it seemed as if her daughter had crossed a street, leaving her explicit instructions not to follow.

"It's just a phase," reassured Dixie, mother of four. "What do you expect?"

"Common courtesy, a little respect."

Dixie hooted. "Where you from, Patty Jane, Mars?"

If there was a reprieve in their daily skirmishes it was after supper, when Nora dumped the contents of the Suggestion Box on the kitchen table and read them aloud. The suggestions were not signed, so Nora mimicked the voice of the client she thought the author.

"'Subscribe to better magazines,'" read Nora in Inky Kolstat's high-pitched whine, "'*True Confessions* is cheaper than *National Geographic* and a lot less boring.'"

"It doesn't say that," said Harriet laughing, reaching for the scrap of paper.

Nora held the suggestion above her head. "Does too, and there's a P.S." Her voice climbed back to an upper register.

"'And how come Harriet never plays any Rolling Stones for dance breaks?'"

Nora cleared her throat and when she spoke there was a growl to her voice. "'How many times do I have to ask this: why can't the ceramics class be moved to Thursday morning? Everybody knows I clean Father Donahue's office on Fridays.'"

Patty Jane put her feet on the bottom rung of Nora's chair, and blew on her coffee. "Crabby Bultram, right?"

"Uff-da mayda, that woman already takes my Advanced Crochet class," said Ione, setting out a plate of peanut butter squares. "I wish I had the nerves to expel her."

"Oh, Grandma," said Nora, "just give her the old crochet hook," she made a stabbing motion, "right to the butt."

Harriet laughed and Ione tried to downplay her smile by tsking, but Patty Jane looked at her daughter without expression and said, "Watch your mouth, miss."

Nora rolled her eyes. "You're one to talk."

There was relatively little that could affect Patty Jane's opinion of herself, but criticism from her daughter scratched and stuck to her like burrs on wool socks.

"Just read the suggestions," said Patty Jane, trying to keep her voice even.

Nora wiped peanut butter crumbs from the side of her mouth with an extended pinky. At thirteen, it was obvious she was going to be beautiful, dangerously beautiful. Most people would ask nothing more of her than her looks. Patty Jane knew that she, herself, was one hell of a looker, but Nora's beauty was like Thor's; it passed all expectations and sallied into a rarified country.

"Next suggestion," said Nora clearing her throat and looking wide-eyed at her mother, "'Find a hair color you like and stick to it.'"

Now that she was abstaining from loveless sex, Patty Jane had turned to hair dye for kicks. She was sampling every color between platinum blond and jet black; at present her hair was red with a pinkish cast.

Something that was hinged in Patty Jane unfastened and her hand, darting out, smacked Nora on the side of the mouth.

"Mom!" cried Nora.

"Oh, God," said Patty Jane. She jumped up and wrapped her arms around Nora. "I'm sorry."

Harriet and Ione found excuses to leave the room. Patty Jane half-knelt, half-stood over her daughter and although bent at an odd angle, gave her a hang-onto hug.

"I always said I'd never hit you," she said finally, backing into her chair, her neck stiff and her shoulder wet with Nora's tears.

"Well," sniffed Nora, "you never did . . . much."

"Just the time you put Paige Larkin's son in the clothes dryer."

"He liked it!" said Nora. "And don't forget the time I pushed Karen Anderson off the trellis in the backyard."

"Oh yeah," said Patty Jane softly. "And now. That makes three. Three more times than I promised myself." Patty Jane shifted and studied her short, square fingernails. "My mother and father hit Harriet and me a lot."

"I know," said Nora.

"Only when they were drunk, but I still remember the rage I felt." She sighed deeply and touched her hair. "So you really don't like it, huh?"

Nora shook her head. "It's pretty weird. I mean with that pink in it."

"Maybe I'll darken it a little. There's a new color out — Cinnamon Blaze.

Nora shook her head, biting her lip.

"Well, come on Wonder Girl, you don't expect me to reform just like that, do you?"

Harriet and Ione finished their coffee in the living room and practiced their vocabulary list. They were both taking Gudrun

Mueller's Beginning German class and felt cosmopolitan asking each other for more *küchen* or *kaffee mit schlagge und zucker*. But Harriet was restless and as she looked out the window at the still sunlit evening, she suddenly had the very novel idea of going out.

"I need to stretch my legs," she told Ione. *"Auf Wiedersehen."*

Harriet walked several blocks west to Minnehaha Avenue, where she caught a city bus. Taking her seat, Harriet shivered as an astonishing thought occurred to her: she hadn't been out at night by herself since Avel died. Over thirteen years, she thought, shaking her head. She took a hasty inventory. There were occasional Minneapolis Symphony concerts with Evelyn Bright, shopping with Ione, movies at the Leola and suppers at Embers with Patty Jane and once, a Rook game at Bev Beal's, but that was the extent of her nightlife.

Of course there was plenty of entertainment within the walls of Patty Jane's House of Curl, especially now that classes and seminars crowded the basement and dining room; classes that Harriet both took and taught. She had assembled a small choral group and to her amazement found Crabby Bultram to have a sweet and sure soprano. With her music and the company of her family, she hadn't felt the need to go anywhere alone.

"Shoot," Harriet thought, "you've been scared and that's all there is to it." Her heart quickened as the bus rumbled past the apartment where Thor and Patty Jane had lived as newlyweds, the apartment Harriet and Patty Jane had shared as "semi widows." Vogstad's Bakery was now Bab's Baked Goods, Mr. and Mrs. Vogstad having retired to Arizona.

Harriet clenched her jaw muscles and folded her arms tightly, her hands on each shoulder as she came to the street corner where long ago Avel had pulled his oyster-colored Packard up to the curb and offered her, a twenty-year-old girl with a long brown pony tail, a ride. "Yes," she thought, "that's why I don't go out alone. There are ghosts out there."

For more than a year after Avel's death, Harriet had often crawled into Patty Jane's bed in the middle of the night, feeling such loneliness and grief that she was certain she would be crushed by it. Time helped, but she knew her heart had been permanently damaged. Unlike Patty Jane, she had neither the desire nor the courage to meet new men, even as her heart felt shriveled from lack of sustenance. She had learned how to mollify her pain; being out by herself around her old haunts was not in her lesson plan.

"I must get off this bus right now," thought Harriet. Panic seemed a living thing trying to scramble from her chest and into her throat. "Breathe," she willed herself. She gripped the signal cord so hard it cut a line across her palm. The bus door belched open and the driver and a half-dozen passengers watched the skinny woman stagger down the steps and careen to the curb.

Harriet walked blindly, holding her purse to her chest. Passing cars honked and an old man watering his lawn asked if she needed help, but Harriet ignored them all, continuing her simple chant: "breathe, breathe, breathe."

"I have been down Minnehaha Avenue lots of times," she thought. "I have seen these landmarks of my life over and over — there's the laundromat with the washers that eat quarters and the hardware store that gives a free lollipop with every purchase, and there's the house of that boy who got stung by a bee in the seventh grade and his arm swelled up bigger than a Christmas ham — there's nothing scary about these places."

But as she passed Del's Dairy, the grocery store she once used for cigarette runs, her panic continued to roil. She saw what used to be Dugan's Door and Fixtures was now the Come Right Inn.

"I'll do that," she thought, looking both ways before stepping into traffic.

By her second beer, she had abandoned all her panic and some of her balance. Her father had always said, "Ahhh, this hits the spot," after his first swig and now she knew what he meant. It hit a spot that made everything feel better, and she giggled at the discovery.

There were not many people who accepted the Come Right Inn's invitation. Two booths in the back were occupied and Harriet was the only one sitting at the long bar.

"Haven't seen you here before," said the bartender.

"The name's Harriet," she said, holding out her hand. "I've never been to a bar by myself before."

The bartender, whose sideburns were miniature replicas of the state of Florida, wiped a hand on his dirty white apron and shook Harriet's. "I'm Augie. I own this place."

"And a fine one it is," said Harriet.

Augie lit her cigarette. "Another one?" he asked and held up her empty glass.

"You're the boss," said Harriet, leaning forward like a kid at a soda fountain to watch him work the tap.

The heavy door of the bar opened and a man and woman, both small and dark, entered. The man took a seat and the woman went to the bar.

"Two, Augie," she said, holding up a hand as smooth and plump as a child's. "Well, say. Hello, Miss Dobbin."

Harriet turned her head, which seemed to be getting less support from her neck than usual.

"Well, hello!" she said, hoping her enthusiasm would hide her lack of recognition.

The older woman smiled and the mystery was solved; the brilliant white smile was the same as her son's, Clyde Chuka's.

"Mrs. Chuka, how are you?"

"As good as you after a couple a these." She took the green bottles Augie handed her. "Come on and meet my neighbor."

Holding onto the lip of the bar, Harriet slid off the stool and gathered up her purse and cigarettes. "Do I pay now?"

"Are you done?" asked the bartender.

Harriet looked at her half-empty glass. "I don't think so."

Augie leaned toward her and Harriet could see pale red hairs growing out of his nose. "Well, I'll just keep a tab going then, okay?"

Merry Chuka had been the featured guest at one of Clyde Chuka's Indian Studies classes. She had brought several pieces of clothing that had passed to her from her great grandmother. The women assembled in the dining room for the Tuesday evening class had "oohed" and "ahhed" at the craftsmanship of a pipe bag and a pair of moccasins, all sewn with sinew and covered with beadwork depicting buffalo, eagle feathers and arrows pointing in four directions. Merry had looked constantly to her son for reassurance. Clyde had badgered her for weeks to come to this "Beauty Salon of Higher Learning."

"Why would a bunch of white women want to see an old Indian's shoes?" she had asked him.

Harriet had been transfixed, feeling the butter-smooth leather of the pipe bag, holding it to her face to smell the old animal hide and the hands that had worked it.

"My friend Melvin," said Merry as Harriet sat in the booth next to her.

Melvin smiled, toothless. The deep wrinkles around his mouth lifted his round, pockmarked cheeks.

"Miss Dobbin here works with Clyde at that beauty place."

"Hmmmmm," said Melvin, still smiling.

"Call me Harriet," she said.

"And me, Merry," said Clyde Chuka's mother. "Like in Christmas."

Merry and Melvin weren't speedy drinkers, but they were steady, and it seemed to Harriet that no sooner had Melvin gotten another round than he was up at the bar, ordering again. He would return from these short, frequent trips with hardboiled eggs on a chipped plate, or with dark wrinkles of beef jerky and little bags of cheese popcorn.

"I am really sloshed," said Harriet, surprised.

"I'll drink to that," said Melvin.

Merry licked the foam lathering her top lip and winked at Harriet. "I didn't know you liked to get burned."

"How's that?" said Harriet.

Merry laughed and winked at Melvin. "It's a term me and Melvin here thought up. You get burned on firewater, get it?"

Harriet nodded solemnly. "Yeah, I get it." She put her face in her hand and wrinkled her nose. "Now where were we?"

Melvin shrugged. "Here, I guess."

Merry laughed and winked at Melvin. Harriet had never met a person who winked so much. "I was saying to Rita here that I didn't know she was a drinking gal."

"Oh yeah," said Harriet. She pondered the mouth of her beer bottle. "What'd you say my name was again?"

"Rita?"

Harriet made a buzzer sound. "I'm sorry m'am, you forfeit the Amana range but we have some lovely parting gifts."

"Come again?" said Melvin.

"She's joking," said Merry.

Harriet took a sip of beer and, after she swallowed, wiped her tongue with the back of her hand. "Yuck, this thing has changed flavors."

Merry laughed and winked. "I knew you weren't no drinker."

"My folks were," said Harriet. "Maybe it's in my blood."

"I don't know nothing about that. Look at Clyde. He'd rather eat a buffalo chip than take a shot."

Harriet felt a sudden urge to sleep. She made a rectangle of her folded arms and put her head inside it. She had closed her eyes when she felt a hand on her shoulder.

"Well, speak of the devil," said Merry, belching.

"Harriet, honey, you okay?" Clyde Chuka's voice was gentle.

Patty Jane had sent him to look for Harriet and passing the

Come Right Inn, his mother's favorite hangout, he decided to step in and say hello.

With effort, Harriet lifted her head.

"Hey, Clyde," she said. The smile on her face was drowsy.

Clyde Chuka sat next to Melvin, who leaned closer to the wall, as if he were afraid of his seatmate. Harriet lay the side of her head on her arm and smiled again.

"Ma," said Clyde Chuka, his voice as pleasant as a weather announcer's, "what the hell's going on?"

Sticking out her small, round chin, Merry pondered the question. "Same thing that always goes on here, I guess. We're having a party."

Clyde Chuka lifted up an empty beer bottle and smeared the wet rings underneath it. "How'd you all hook up?"

The couple from the back booth left, the woman holding the man's arm like a policeman escorting a lawbreaker into the station.

"Come on," the woman said as they passed, "we haven't got all day and even if we did we'd have to go anyway."

Something flickered in Harriet's memory, some recollection of that shrill and half-crazy voice, and she lifted her head just as the woman with the unruly grey hair opened the door, pushing the man ahead of her. Harriet was surprised to see it was dark outside.

"Harriet, you want me to take you home?" asked Clyde Chuka.

Harriet sighed, wishing she had more options. "Yeah. I guess."

She dug a five-dollar bill out of her billfold and put it under a beer bottle.

"Hey, you get change," said Merry.

Harriet waved her hand.

"Well, I owe you one," said Merry, winking.

The air in the kitchen was dense with pine cleaner as Clyde Chuka helped Harriet in. Patty Jane was on her knees, wearing a big blue shirt that read "Phil's Plumbing" over short-shorts. Her arm and shoulder flexed as she scrubbed the floor with enough force to strip a layer off the linoleum. Seeing Harriet and Clyde Chuka, she let go of the coarse bristle brush and rested her hands on her haunches.

"Where in the universe of hell have you been?" she said.

A rebellion kicked up in Harriet, hearing Patty Jane's voice. She was of age, after all.

"You give me a cramp," she said. She flicked her hair back behind her shoulders, remembering for a moment how Clyde Chuka had held it back for her when she threw up into a lilac bush a block from the bar. Now, holding the edge of the counter, she went to the coffee pot on the stove.

Patty Jane lifted the brush and threw it into the bucket, splattering water onto the floor.

"Jesus, Harriet, you've been drinking. I can smell it from here."

Harriet plucked a cup from a mug tree next to the toaster.

"Good. Maybe it'll kill some of this Pine Sol," said Harriet. "It smells like the North Woods in here."

Clyde Chuka stood back, like a wary referee. He couldn't remember seeing the sisters fight.

Patty Jane stood against the sink, arms folded, watching Harriet with narrowed eyes. "You're spilling, you know."

Harriet set the coffee pot back on the burner. "The maid was in the parlor hanging out her clothes," she sang, "along came a blackbird and snipped off her nose."

Patty Jane sighed. "Doesn't it matter that I was worried about you?"

Harriet sipped at her coffee and some dribbled down her chin. "Patsy Jane," she slurred, drawing the back of her hand across her mouth, "I can take care of myself."

"News to me."

Harriet turned to the sink and very carefully, as if she were handling Ione's precious china instead of thick ceramic, washed her cup. She wiped her hands on the back of her shorts and walked, in almost a straight line, toward the door to the dining room.

"Goodnight, Clyde Chuka," she said, and her voice rose in singsong as she added, "goodnight, warden."

Fifteen

IN LESS THAN A MONTH, tension between the two sisters rose as if fueled by yeast. Since Avel's death, Harriet had suffered sporadic bouts of eczema and now it flared up on her forehead and under her left eye and in bubbly lines along the sides of her fingers. After each song on her harp, she stopped to light a cigarette. There were no dance breaks in her concert repertoire now; she played somberly and sometimes discordantly, and customers exchanged uneasy looks under their hair rollers. She was not present at any of the evening classes and Ione couldn't find the words, in any language, to answer Gudrun Mueller's inquiry, "Was ist los mit Harriet?" Harriet asked Evelyn Bright to take over directorship of the choral group, with the explanation that she needed time off.

It soon became clear that she needed time off to drink. A small, rational part of her heard Patty Jane pleading, but that part was shoved aside by the need to put down the pain she had been lugging around for so long. She couldn't believe how good she felt when she was drinking, how entertained — and entertaining — she was, how light and easy life seemed.

After a late lunch by herself, leaving opened cans of tuna and frying pans sticky with scrambled eggs, Harriet would leave the House of Curl and visit local and not-so-local bars. Alcohol and its effects gave her a bravery that led her to explore hotel bars downtown, Irish hangouts in St. Paul, dance bars near the river.

She took Patty Jane's keys to the pink Desoto one afternoon, but Patty Jane, hearing the engine of the old car fire up, left Alva Bundt leaning her head into the shampoo sink and ran out to the curb, jumping in the car just as Harriet ground the gears, lurching backwards.

She reached over and snatched the keys from the ignition and put them into her smock pocket.

"This is my car!" screamed Harriet. "Avel gave it to me!"

"And you gave it to me!" said Patty Jane, matching Harriet in volume, "and I don't want you smashing it into any goddamn person, place or thing!"

The fury was interrupted as they realized the car was still in motion, traveling backwards at an increasing speed down the sloping street.

"Put it in park, for God's sake," said Patty Jane. She scrambled over Harriet and slammed her foot on the brake, two feet shy of their neighbor's new yellow Mustang. Patty Jane's chest rose and when her heart stabilized, she turned to Harriet, hopeful, willing to share the joke, but Harriet was letting herself out of the passenger's side.

"Go ahead!" yelled Patty Jane through the open window. "Go get drunk, you stupid bitch!"

"Clyde, what's going on?" asked Nora. She had cornered him taking his break at the dining room table.

"With what?" said Clyde Chuka, washing down a swallow of chocolate cake with coffee.

"With Mom and Aunt Harriet. Come on in the kitchen where Grandma is."

Ione was at the table, fiddling with a dried flower centerpiece and looking like a co-conspirator.

"We've got to do something," she said as Nora and Clyde Chuka sat down.

"Harriet's getting drunk a lot, isn't she?" asked Nora.

"Yeah," Clyde Chuka said and his shoulders rose and fell. "About every night from what I can tell."

Ione buried her small fist into her cheek and shook her head. "I thought at last Harriet had come around the bends."

Nora looked at Clyde Chuka. "Why is she drinking?"

"Nora," he said and his voice was a step above a whisper. "I'm going to tell you a story. Trouble is, it doesn't have an ending." He sat for a while, rubbing his forehead with both hands. "I come from a long line of drinkers," he began. "Nah, make that drunks. Because it's different — see, some people can have a few and wave good-bye and others have a few and wave their empty glasses at the bartender for more. I was raised by my grandmother because my mother was too drunk to do the job herself. My father, drunk, wandered onto a train track right in front of a moving locomotive. He was drunk and a second later he was dead drunk. The prettiest girl in the whole world with eyes as shiny as black agates, well, she had a few too many and drove my pickup into a ditch outside Jamestown, North Dakota. I was sitting in a little cabin thinking about her when someone knocks on my door like there was a fire and it's her brother telling me she's dead." Clyde Chuka folded his hands in his lap and stared at the table centerpiece for a long time. "You make this in Alva's class?"

Ione nodded. The silence grew until it was a pulse in Nora's ears.

"Alva's got a good eye," said Clyde Chuka, "I'd like to see what she could do with a blowtorch and some scrap metal." He blew on his coffee although it was long past being hot.

"Is that the end?" asked Nora softly.

"No," said Clyde Chuka. "I told you this story didn't have one. The only two people in my family who don't drink are me and my grandmother. She never did and I did for a while until I saw I was headed somewhere I didn't want to go." He put two fingers in the corner of his eyes. "Shit," he said softly. "What I've seen, Nora, is booze is like a mean old cur who goes after those who won't bite back. People with big hearts and sad souls." He touched his chin to his chest and two silvery tears slid down the planes of his face.

A cold fright gripped Nora. Something very serious was happening and if her mother, her grandmother *and* Clyde Chuka couldn't do anything about it, who could?

One rainy Saturday in October, Harriet sat down at her harp, played a few glissandos and stood up suddenly, as if she had just remembered having left the iron on. Nora, who was helping a walk-in into a "VIP" smock, looked to her mother, but Patty Jane didn't turn her attention away from Myrna Johnson's hair.

"Pressing engagement," said Harriet.

Nora saw her mother pat Myrna's shoulders, tug at the hem of her skirt, and follow Harriet into the front room.

"Excuse me," said Nora, fumbling with the smock snap. Whispers fused into a loud buzz as she, too, left the shop.

She caught up with her mother and aunt in the kitchen where Patty Jane was trying to block Harriet's exit by leaning against the door.

"You're not walking out on your job," Patty Jane said, her teeth clenched.

"Excuse me, *boss*," said Harriet, trying to push her aside.

Patty Jane pushed back and then their hands turned rigid and they began slapping each other.

"Stop it!" screamed Nora.

Footsteps, like accelerating knocks on a hollow door, rose from the basement steps and Ione and Clyde Chuka, who'd been setting up chairs for Paige Larkin's Decorating with Fabrics class, burst into the kitchen.

Patty Jane got in one more slap before they were separated. Harriet's cheek was red; her long hair, loosened from its barrette, was wild. The sisters breathed heavily, their mouths open.

"What's all this — " began Clyde Chuka, but Patty Jane spoke to Harriet over his words.

"I don't want you in this house if you're drinking."

Harriet rotated her jaw and laughed bitterly. "Well, I don't want to be in this house if I'm not."

She turned and opened the back door, and cold wet air and a flutter of amber leaves blew against the screen. The room was silent as everyone stood framed in the kitchen door, watching Harriet walk through the backyard and into the alley.

"Go after her, Mom," said Nora, her whisper amplified in the quiet.

Patty Jane watched the backyard elm shake itself of leaves. "I can't," she whispered back. "She's already gone too far."

On Halloween Nora got her first period. She made this discovery between classes, while she was in the girls' bathroom with her best friend, Lori Mellstrom.

Lori, who was carefully leeching the color from her lips with white frosted lipstick, offered the tube to Nora, who had just come out of a stall.

"No thanks," said Nora, "it would clash with my complexion."

"Everything clashes with your complexion."

The student body of Nokomis Junior High had voted to come to school in costume. Nora was dressed in witch's regalia: black dress, cape and hat and pea green face and hands. Her joke, however, was that she wasn't impersonating a witch but Mrs. Stevenson, the math teacher who liked to test the resiliency of her ruler on the knuckles of lazy students.

The warning bell rang and a crowd of princesses and sultans

and gangsters surged through the hallways. The girls at the bathroom mirrors dispersed and Lori, dressed like a Carnaby Street modster, dropped her makeup into her shoulder bag.

Nora grabbed her arm and held it until they were the only two left in the bathroom.

"What's the deal?" asked Lori. "If I'm late for English, Hagen gives me a demerit."

"Cousin Charlotte's here," said Nora.

Lori's eyes widened under the weight of her false eyelashes. "You're kidding me."

"Cousin Charlotte" was their code name for menstruation. They liked none of the other popular euphemisms — "friend" was too sappy and "the curse" was too harsh; "And besides," explained their hygiene teacher, "ovulation doesn't deserve such discredit."

Both girls had waited for Cousin Charlotte's arrival — Lori more anxiously than Nora for she was fourteen already, six months older than Nora, and by right deserved to enter Glorious Womanhood first.

Nora put her green hands on her hips. "Why would a woman like me tease a girl like you?" She went through the day with a thick sanitary pad pinned to her underpants, part of the necessary equipment she had carried in a calico envelope for six months.

She and Lori left school early, ducking up the side aisle during assembly. Walking home in thoughtful silence, they didn't make their usual stop at Del's Dairy for Milk Duds or penny candy. Their good-bye at the corner where their routes separated was short and tense.

At home, Nora took a bath, picked at her dinner, dried the dishes in a trance and then crawled into bed with *Betsy and Tacy*, one of her favorite childhood books.

"I didn't think you were asleep," said Patty Jane, coming in after one unacknowledged knock.

Nora thought of saying something sarcastic, but when she opened her mouth one word came out with a wail: "Mama!"

"I got my period today." This announcement set off a new round of tears.

"I know, Nora. I know."

Irritation cut into Nora's mourning. Couldn't she do anything in private?

"How did you know?" she asked, wiping her nose with the heel of her hand.

"I'm your mother, Wonder Girl," said Patty Jane. "I know everything about you."

Nora considered the ramifications of this statement.

"Besides," said Patty Jane, "I saw the pad in the waste basket. We're tampon women in this house."

Nora reached for a Kleenex in the decorative box Ione had made in Paige Larkin's class. She was disgusted with herself for leaving such an obvious clue.

"I don't want to be a woman yet," she said, blowing her nose.

Patty Jane smiled. "You're not, hon."

"I am, too. I could have a baby."

Patty Jane pulled the lapels of Nora's robe close together, as if she were dressing her for winter weather.

"Just because some of your insides are maturing doesn't mean the rest of you is keeping up with them."

"I hate the word 'mature.' Our hygiene teacher uses it all the time, and she pronounces it that funny way — 'ma-tour.'"

"I remember feeling exactly the same, Nora," said Patty Jane, lying back on Nora's bed. "Becky Subseth was what we called mature — she had breasts and hair under her arms in the fifth grade — and I never saw a more miserable sight in my life. I thought, If this is mature, count me out." Her fingers rubbed the furrows in the chenille bedspread. "Now, Harriet, she was a different case. When she got her period, there was never a more pleased person in the world. She made a little calendar out of pink stationery that read, 'A Record of My Menses.'"

"Menses?"

Patty Jane smiled. "Yeah. She liked the clinical sound of it and she kept up that calendar until she was at least seventeen, marking every entry with one of the little pencils our dad used for scoring golf games."

Nora leaned her head on her mother's shoulders. "Mom, is Aunt Harriet going to be okay?"

Patty Jane sighed and stared at the Beatles poster above Nora's desk without really seeing the Fab Four.

"I don't know, Nor."

They sat holding each other until they heard doorbell chimes.

"Hey," said Patty Jane, "we can't leave your grandma downstairs with all those trick-or-treaters."

Sixteen

At the Thanksgiving table that year, the turkey got rave reviews and everyone praised Ione's sage and onion dressing. Alva Bundt's gourds-and-straw centerpiece was striking and could anyone polish silver better than Nora? But compliments flew in an atmosphere of forced gaiety. No one had heard from Harriet in a week.

She had camped out at Evelyn Bright's house until Evelyn's husband Corny gave his ultimatum: "Either she goes or I do." Evelyn, dabbing at tears with a lace handkerchief, had driven Harriet downtown, at her request. It was the last anyone had seen of her.

Anxiety tightened Patty Jane's stomach, and she pushed her food around her plate until the cranberries colored the mashed potatoes pink and the corn was buried under yams and gravy. Harriet's empty place at the table chastised her. Yet something kept Patty Jane from hunting her sister down. She had known from childhood that drink couldn't be bullied out of a person, and now she felt herself paralyzed by that same helplessness her parents' jags had inspired.

She thought of the Thanksgiving Harriet had sung grace and three-year-old Nora had made her sing it over and over again. She thought of the time Harriet stuffed the turkey and instead of sewing it up, stapled it. She thought of the Thanksgivings she and Harriet had listened to the Macy's Day Parade over the radio while their parents drank in the living room.

After the dishes were put away and Ione whipped cream for the pumpkin pie, Patty Jane and Nora pulled the wishbone. Nora got the bigger piece but Patty Jane shut her eyes and made a wish anyway, for the safe and sober return of her sister.

Harriet's Thanksgiving was not spent in a dinner line at the Salvation Army. Nor was she hauled down to the police station and charged with vagrancy. She had a nice turkey dinner — a little dry, but it was good — at a hotel restaurant with a man she had met at the train station.

The man, a metal parts salesman from Kansas City, afterwards invited her back to his hotel room. She said "sure" as easily as if he'd asked for a light and there, under stiff sheets whose hospital corners were impossible to loosen, she felt a man inside her for the first time since she and Avel had rolled on the riverbank under a universe of stars.

He was gone by the time Harriet woke the next morning, but there was a five-dollar bill and a note thanking her "for the laughs." It occurred to Harriet that she wouldn't have to sleep in bus or train stations as long as there were men far from home.

In her lucid moments — soaking away her hangover in a hotel room bathtub — she faced herself and vowed that after she dried her hair and dressed, she would call Patty Jane. She usually managed to pick up the receiver, but fear and shame paralyzed her fingers and she would remember it was Patty Jane who had kicked her out, who, if you thought about it, was responsible for her predicament. It was then that she placed the receiver back in its cradle, wondering when the man she was sharing the room with would come back and take her out for a drink.

Harriet knew there were other names for these men who paid her to keep themselves happy and drunk, still, she called them "chums," and Bon Drake was the eighth.

Harriet had been with him almost a week. He was an attorney from Fargo, N.D., handsome and silver haired. Bon never mentioned his age, but Harriet thought he must be fifty; his waist sagged a little and the flesh under his arm was loose.

But she liked putting her arm through his as they walked the streets of downtown Minneapolis. Christmas decorations were up and snow fell and she imagined herself happily married. That they were usually drunk and laughing did not undermine Harriet's fantasy. If she were to see herself and Bon on the street she knew she would think, "what a happy couple."

Then the wife Harriet didn't know existed called. She and Bon, stretched out on the hotel bed, had been watching *The Beverly Hillbillies*. Harriet fled to the bathroom.

"What's that stuff on the side of your face?" Bon asked conversationally, sticking his head in the door.

Harriet pulled her hair down over her cheek where a red scaly patch had risen.

"Eczema," she said, "I'm prone to it."

"Are you prone to this?" asked Bon, hitting her, and the next thing Harriet knew she was on the floor next to the toilet, her pulse crashing in her head like a wild surf, and Bon was on top of her. "I'll pretend I'm dead," she thought, "if I'm not already." A minute or an hour passed — Harriet had no way of knowing — before Bon lifted himself off her, muttering black words that Harriet could barely hear. She heard a drawer close, or maybe it was a door. She only knew she wanted to lie on the floor and sleep for a long time.

Winter of 1968, settled in like an immigrant with no plans of going back to the homeland. Patty Jane found herself constantly checking the thermostat; despite long underwear and sweaters, she was never warm enough. In the middle of a comb-out or a dye job, terrible pictures crept into her head: images of Harriet blue and frozen under a bridge abutment, or bloody and broken, the victim of a driver who didn't see her stagger into his path. She would duck her head against the wave of dizziness that accompanied these pictures while her customers asked if she was all right and did she need some water?

An armistice had been signed between Patty Jane and her daughter. Nora sensed that with Harriet's departure, Patty Jane needed all the support she could get. Nora got up early and made the morning coffee, a gesture that touched her mother. After homework, they often built a fire and sat watching television, or listening to some of Harriet's albums.

But tonight Nora had gone upstairs early, to soak in the bathtub, which had become her retreat.

The electric clock hummed above the refrigerator and Patty Jane, looking at her reflection in the window, was sickened by how many times she had seen the same mirrored image, how many times she had sat at kitchen tables, waiting for someone to come home.

"What's the matter with me?" she asked her reflection. "Why does everybody I love leave me?" She laid her head on the table but tears and their solace had abandoned her, too. She pushed herself away from the table and shouted up the staircase that she was going for a walk.

Wet flakes of snow fell like feathers and Patty Jane tied the hood of her parka tight. She usually loved walking on snowy, windless nights, when the sound of footsteps was absorbed by the carpet of fresh snow. She walked down the Parkway toward

Lake Nokomis and was both surprised and disheartened when, after she had walked a mile, her bad mood hadn't lifted.

She slipped and skidded down the hill that led to the lake and when she got to its snowy banks she threw herself onto a drift and rolled until she lay exhausted. She lifted the hem of her parka and dug out hard chunks of snow from above her waistband; her skin was numb. She looked over the frozen surface of the lake and decided to do what she had always warned Nora not to do: walk across it.

Skating was allowed on the edge of the lake, on a small rink the Park Board made by clearing off a rectangle of snow. The moon, unseen above the flurries, gave off pale light as Patty Jane walked toward the big beach and the warming house.

She knew the lake was frozen solid, but still, she had heard many stories of fishermen on foot who had fallen through ice they had driven their car on the day before. With each step, her feet kicked little arcs of snow, and when she reached the middle of the lake, she stopped and made a full turn, arms outstretched like a figurine. Then, very deliberately, she jumped high, knees bent, and jumped again. She expected to hear ice cracking, to see a dangerous line cutting through the snow and ice like a thick black snake, and when she didn't, she jumped again and again. When the jumping exhausted her, she fell on her knees to the ice.

"Why?"

Her voice had the effect of a slap and she looked around, embarrassed and confused. She stood, gingerly, and walked a few steps on tiptoe and then broke into a sprint, running fast and hard until she reached the bank.

"Hold on, hold on," she thought, "I can't be going crazy." She climbed up the wooden ramp to the warming house and walked twice around the sanded sidewalk that rimmed the dark building. She was cold and wet and bereft until two words came into her head: Clyde Chuka. "He can help me," she thought, "he always has before."

Clyde Chuka had described his home to her often. It was on the second floor of a building with a butcher shop, a religious bookstore, and a small insurance agency on the first floor. It was on Park Avenue, near the Swedish Institute, and Patty Jane knew she could find it easily. With a destination in mind, her head cleared and her pace became vigorous. Twenty minutes later, she was standing under an awning by a doorwell, ringing the bell that read "Clyde's Place."

A look of surprised pleasure animated his features as he saw her through the small oblong window in the door.

"Why, Patty Jane, what a treat," he said, pulling her inside. "You're soaking wet."

"I had a run-in with some snow." She stamped her feet and took off her parka.

"Come on up, I'll make some coffee."

The narrow staircase smelled of mildew and wet carpeting. Mexican music played loudly and when Clyde Chuka pushed the door open, Patty Jane said "Yikes," sidestepping a six-foot creature made of wire hangers and pieces of fur.

"That's Bob," said Clyde Chuka, "he's my watch gerbil."

Patty Jane petted its back. "Where'd you get all the fur?"

"Salvation Army, Goodwill, secondhand store coats. His whole backside is foxtails."

Past the entryway was a large room, with a wall of windows on the south side, containing a dozen pieces of sculpture in what looked to Patty Jane like various stages of completion.

There were open paint cans and dropcloths everywhere. A sawhorse painted with peace signs on which tin and plastic soldiers perched stood near a real potted tree, its branches hung with broken glass. Bird forms of chicken wire and rags stiffened with corn starch froze in midflight on pedestals of wood. A rusty axe plunged into the center of a huge blue and green globe.

"So this is what you do when you're not pushing back cuticles?"

Clyde's smile was wide. "Yup. This is what I do. Make yourself at home in the parlor."

"The parlor?"

"The couch over there behind *Remorse*."

"What?"

"*Remorse* is the name of that piece over there." He pointed. "The baling wire and cement blocks."

"On second thought, help me make the coffee."

She followed him to the kitchen. Clyde Chuka measured coffee into the tin basket of a blue speckled pot. Colorful dishes sat in a drying rack and the tile counters and range top were wiped clean.

"You're quite a housekeeper," said Patty Jane.

Clyde Chuka tilted his head and looked at her. His hair was unbraided and it fell below his shoulders.

"Patty Jane, I'm glad you're here, I really am. But why did you come?" His eyes were as gentle as his voice.

Patty Jane pressed her back into the edge of the counter top and her chin trembled.

Clyde Chuka poured two cups, grabbing the handles of both with one hand. With the other, he took Patty Jane's hand and led her to the couch. He set the cups on a coffee table fashioned from corrugated tin and they sat down on the worn corduroy couch.

Patty Jane tried to take a sip of the fragrant coffee, but she set her cup down and fell back against the couch, sobbing.

"I miss Harriet so much!"

"Me too," said Clyde Chuka.

"I'm always losing the people I love."

"Me too."

It seemed to Patty Jane that her brain, like a broken television set, had turned to fuzz. She had no consciousness of anything but Clyde Chuka's lips on hers, his strong hands on her back. Somehow, they managed to stay on the narrow couch, their bodies fitting together, moving together like familiar dance partners. Patty Jane's clothes came off but she didn't have any memory of unbuttoning and unzipping; they somehow seemed to dissolve and regain their form on the floor beneath her.

She felt Clyde Chuka's smooth, hard body, his hands that couldn't stop moving. His chest was hairless and hard-domed muscles covered his arms and shoulders. He was inside her and they rocked together until their bodies mutually celebrated the Fourth of July.

They lay facing together, each petting the other's hair.

"Shit," said Patty Jane.

Clyde Chuka smiled. "Aw, you're such a romantic." He ran his fingers through her red hair. "I can't remember what color your real hair is. Oh yeah, it's a light, shiny brown."

"It was. It's probably got a bunch of grey in it now."

"I love you."

Patty Jane's instinct was to look behind her shoulder, at the curve where their conversation had swerved.

Clyde Chuka laughed. "You should see your face, Patty Jane. The word 'stricken' comes to mind. Haven't I told you the same thing plenty of times before?"

Patty Jane nodded.

"Haven't you told me the same thing?"

"Yes, but it's been a brother-sister thing. I hear it after we make love for the first time and it has a different meaning."

Clyde stretched his arms. "Maybe it does. Are you hungry?"

Without putting on their clothes, they finished the pot of

coffee and made some French toast. Patty Jane found herself giggling — she had never stood naked with a man in a kitchen, eating French toast and drinking coffee. She had never known a man as comfortable in his own skin as she was in hers.

Clyde Chuka pushed a piece of toast from his back teeth with his pinky.

"I tell you, Patty Jane, I always knew you had a great body but I never knew how great."

"Thank you, sir," she said, slowly pirouetting.

"Ey yi yi, now that's a backside."

"Ey yi yi," said Patty Jane, her eyes widening at Clyde Chuka's erection, "now that's a salute."

They slipped to the floor as easily as a dropped towel.

After midnight, Clyde Chuka walked Patty Jane home. Their arms were linked. Snow still fell, and sparkled under the streetlights.

"What's all this mean?" asked Patty Jane.

Clyde Chuka smiled. "What would you like it to mean?"

"Well, are we lovers now?"

"I wouldn't mind that."

"What about your pilot light theory? Your idea that everyone has only one true love?"

"My pilot light theory?" He sniffed and wiped his nose with the back of his gloved thumb. "Patty Jane, you believed that bullshit?"

Patty Jane's arm tightened around his. "Yes," she said, her voice soft and sad.

"Me too," said Clyde Chuka, squeezing her back. "Fortunately, I also believe in exceptions."

"How long have you believed in this exception?"

"For a long time."

Patty Jane felt both a laugh and cry well up. "Why didn't you say something? Do something?"

"I was waiting for you to make the first move. It was part of my love strategy."

"You talk as if it were a game."

Clyde Chuka pulled Patty Jane to him and under the falling snow, kissed her fiercely on the mouth. "It was a game . . ." he said, "a game I really wanted to win."

Seventeen

B<small>Y THAT SPRING</small>, Nora finally got up the courage to ask her grandmother something she'd been wondering for a long while. They were taking a drive after church — part of a ritual which they enjoyed immensely. Nora had gone through the ranks of Sunday school with Ione helping her memorize Bible verses at home and explaining the meaning of parables.

Patty Jane joined them in church on holidays but she was not a regular member. "I don't feel comfortable," she tried to explain to her daughter. "I always get the feeling that even though God isn't judging me, the minister and congregation are."

For Ione and Nora, Sundays were special. They enjoyed the flurry in the bathroom, the spritzing of cologne, the curling of hair and the adjusting of slip straps. Unlike her mother, Nora paid careful attention in church, listening to Pastor Nelson as if she might be quizzed later.

Nora and Ione often stopped for lunch after church, most often at the Canteen or, in the summer, at the Airloha Drive-In, where they ordered StratoBurger baskets and the famous Hot'N-Tots, cinnamon-flavored Cokes.

But on this Sunday, bright and green and smelling of new blossoms, they decided to drive along the Mississippi until they had an inclination to stop. Nora rested her elbow out the open window, a gesture she thought very adult.

"Grandma," she said finally, "do you think Mom and Clyde Chuka will get married?" When there was no response, Nora said, "Grandma?"

"I used to drive these streets looking for your father," said Ione. "Fourteen years later I still find myself on the lookout."

"You don't think you'll ever find him." Nora's voice was bitter.

Ione shrugged, her chest inches from the steering wheel.

"Once a mother thinks her child is lost for good, well, then I suppose he is dead."

"You still didn't answer my question."

"About Patty Jane and Clyde Chuka?" Ione squinted her blue eyes against the sunlight. "Well, she's not even divorced from your father, you know. Not that that couldn't be taken care of easily enough. She certainly has the ground."

"Grounds," Nora silently corrected her.

"So, yes, I hope your mother and Clyde Chuka get married. It would be a different ending, but a happy one."

And then Ione, who believed driving with her hands at the ten and two o'clock positions was the reason for her spotless safety record, took her right hand off the steering wheel to squeeze her granddaughter's hand.

That same morning Harriet woke up with a furious headache and a mouth that seemed vacuumed dry. She had spent the night in a motel on the fringes of downtown St. Paul, her room paid for by a kind soul who had found her sitting next to an alley trash dumpster, vomiting up Ripple. Harriet was conscious of being moved by someone or something blue, but she accepted it in the matter-of-fact way of a person who's been drunk a long time.

Sunlight shone through the thin, geometrically patterned curtains and Harriet tried to will her pain away while figuring out where she was. When she wasn't successful at doing either, she rolled slowly off the bed. In the bathroom, she splashed cold water on her face, ignoring the mirror's reflection. She had learned it was better not to look. One rational thought pierced the heavy fabric of her headache and she remembered the figure in blue. A cop? A mailman? A cop or a mailman had brought her here?

The riddle was solved by what lay on the writing desk next to the bolted-down TV: a pink-and-white striped cotton dress, folded neatly, a pair of white flats her size, a thermos, the day's edition of the *St. Paul Pioneer Press*, a bottle of cough syrup and a note. When she unfolded it, a ten-dollar bill fluttered to the floor. The note read:

> I let myself in this morning but decided not to wake you up. Hope the clothes fit and the syrup helps your cough. Use your imagination in spending this money. For food, maybe a movie! Not booze! I'm a police officer who found you and felt something for you as I had a problem with booze myself. I'm in AA now and haven't had a drink for six years. Come to a meeting at St. Joseph's Church on St. Clair Avenue. Any Monday, Wednesday or Friday night and I'll be there. You're too pretty to live in the gutter.
>
> Your friend,
> Reese Brown.

"Thanks, Reese," thought Harriet, picking up the ten-dollar bill, debating if she should go for a good bottle of J&B or a lot of Ripple. Maybe a couple bottles of wine and a carton of cigarettes. A whole cigarette, not a butt found on the street, would be a great luxury.

She sat down at the desk and poured coffee from the thermos.

"Well, isn't this nice," she said, putting her feet up and unfolding the paper. Above a photograph of Richard Nixon, she noticed the date of the newspaper: June 23, 1968. Her headache pounded as the weight of the date settled her mind: It should have been her fourteenth wedding anniversary.

She put her head in her arms. And as she wept, she called the names of those she loved best and had lost: "Oh Avel, oh, Patty Jane."

Eighteen

A WOMAN WEARING a collection of scarves around her neck wrote out a check in the amount of eight hundred dollars to Clyde Chuka for his sculpture, *Planetscarium*.

It was Clyde Chuka's first big show and from the "sold" signs adorning the sculptures, it looked like the art triumph of the summer.

"It speaks to me," the buyer said to her husband.

"A globe with an ax through it? What does it say?" he asked. "Ouch?"

Patty Jane smiled. Ione had expressed the same sentiments.

"I understand my own crafts — needlepoint and crochet and rosemaling," she had whispered to Patty Jane. "I understand Degas's ballet girls. But this," she shrugged her shoulders, "this I don't understand."

"I felt the same way," Patty Jane whispered back, not wanting her confession to be overheard. "I felt like an ignoramus when Clyde Chuka and I went to museums and people talked about 'energy' and 'angst.' But then Clyde told me there are no right answers to art. You see what you see."

When Ione and Nora and a contingent of House of Curl regulars left, Patty Jane milled through the uptown gallery, eavesdropping on the conversations.

"Now this," she heard from a man wearing a flouncy shirt and a curling mustache, "this is freedom finding its escape, hope pushing through a crack in the sidewalk, faith blowing its holy horn." The man had been standing in front of what looked like a car fender that had been crumpled in an accident.

The real art though, if you asked Patty Jane, was Clyde Chuka. He was wearing a buckskin shirt, its beading in the shape of a moon and a star. Merry Chuka had made it and Patty Jane wanted to compliment her on it in person, and, more importantly, ask if she'd seen Harriet anywhere, but Clyde Chuka said he wouldn't bet money on his mother showing up.

The room, an annex off a warehouse, was filled with the smell of a sweet tobacco. A young woman wearing a skirt the size of a wide belt held out a thin grey cigarette to Patty Jane.

"No thanks," said Patty Jane. She had tried marijuana once — fearful with each puff that J. Edgar Hoover would burst in the door.

It was after midnight when the gallery party ended and the bartender carried out a box of empty wine bottles.

"Are you hungry?" asked Clyde Chuka, rubbing his palm, sore from so many handshakes.

"Not really," said Patty Jane. "I sort of went wild with those little cheese cubes." She shook her head and burped softly. "I could use some Pepto-Bismol."

"Let's take a walk to the lake, then."

The night was balmy and quiet, the street's commerce ended hours earlier. The couple walked west toward Lake Calhoun and Patty Jane recited the story Clyde already knew; the story of Harriet and Avel's meeting and how Avel's car was loaned out and never returned.

"Avel once told me he had lost a car and his heart on the same day," Patty Jane said.

Harriet had assumed that the man who had put her up for the night in a decent motel room, the man who had left her some pretty clothes and a ten-spot, was a one-time-only benefactor. She certainly hadn't thought he would become, in two months of a hot and windy summer, the second love of her life.

He had found her again, the day she left the motel room, newly showered, the pink-and-white shirtdress hanging shapelessly from her thin, knobby shoulders. Reese was no Dick Tracy; his logic was simple. After the 11:00 A.M. check-out time, he knew she would be in a bar or liquor store near the motel. He found her roaming the aisles of Mr. Fran's Liquor.

He stepped out from behind a cardboard cutout of a blond woman holding a bottle of vodka. "I'm Reese Brown."

"Reese Brown," he said again, following her. "I set you up in that motel?"

"Thanks," said Harriet, her eyes darting up and down the aisle lined with quarts and jugs of her favorites — Annie Green Springs and Boone's Farm.

"I left you the ten bucks that you're about to spend on rot gut."

"Like I said, thanks a lot." Her eyes focused on a "manager's special" — four bottles of Carioca for $8.49.

"I was hoping you'd spend it on food or something. I'll bet you can't weigh more than ninety pounds."

As she gathered up bottles in her thin arms, Reese stifled an urge to put her over his shoulder. When he was a young, hot-tempered man, his wife had told him, "Reese, you can't manhandle every situation," and he had taken that advice to heart. Now, he tempered most impulses with steady, even thought. He shrugged elaborately, the palms of his big hands lifting toward the ceiling. He followed her to the cash register and while the cashier rang up Harriet's purchase, Reese wrote another note to Harriet. It said, "For help, call me," and he signed his name and his phone number. He folded the note and put it into her dress pocket.

She offered him a wide and erratic smile. By the time she told the cashier to throw in a couple packs of Old Gold, he was gone, the canvas shade banging against the door.

Reese Brown had been a policeman on the St. Paul force for twenty-two years, exactly half his life. He had fulfilled his boyhood dream, loving the simple tasks of driving an old and addled woman home when she wandered off, of answering a frantic babysitter's call and showing her, with his heavy-duty flashlight, that the noise on the roof was not an intruder but a branch from a cottonwood tree brushing against the eaves. These were his specialties. And when he had to deal with a world whose light was offset with darkness, with people who wanted to hurt each other, he tried to help.

He was a giant of a man — 6'5", built solid — and full of gentleness except for a small trickle of violence that ran through him like lava. It was a violence fueled by injustice; as a kid he had watched his father slap his mother around. He had been suspended from the varsity basketball team when he knocked some teeth out of a chippy forward giving too many cheap shots.

It was his round-cheeked wife who helped him reroute this fury into something manageable. "Talk to me, Reese, just talk to me," she had said to him one bitter New Year's Eve when he had shot and killed a holdup man who had fired at him and his partner.

He did, and so it was all the more shocking, the brevity of the note she left him and their two children: "I fell for someone else."

He began to drink in the evenings after the kids had gone to bed, then after the divorce papers arrived from Las Vegas, drank in the mornings too. For almost three years he was able to save up his drunks for early morning or late night hours, but once, on duty, he slipped into a gas station toilet and drank from a thermos of vodka. His partner found him there, singing *I'm Sorry* into the mirror.

Reese stood quietly, while the vein of anger he thought was dead rose within him and he smashed his fist against the cheekbone of Officer Keith Eggert. The two concocted a story for Eggert's wound (there were some rock-throwing thug they'd run across in Frogtown) and the Captain believed them. Eggert asked only one thing of Reese and that was to get help. He gave Reese the address of a church where people who drank went for meetings.

Reese referred always to Eggert as "the man whose cheekbone I had to break to save my life."

Harriet wandered in a lunch hour crowd in downtown St. Paul, panhandling. "Spare change?" she asked defiantly, extending a dirty, shaking hand. The street light turned green and Harriet wavered on the sidewalk. A school bus came lumbering by and there, framed in the window, was her niece. Seeing Nora's pale, blond hair and clean Scandinavian profile immediately sobered Harriet. And then Nora turned to look out the window and saw her. Like clouds moving from sun to storm, Nora's expression changed from happiness to horror.

Once a classmate of Nora's having her hair done for the Snow Ball asked who the woman was playing the Beatles on the harp.

"My aunt," Nora had said proudly.

"You're lucky," said the girl wistfully. "All my aunts wear muumuus and think Pat Boone is the King of Rock and Roll."

In a school paper, Nora had written she wanted to be a musician like her Aunt Harriet, and she had recently started playing the trumpet.

Now Nora stared at Harriet like Saint Peter regarding a gate crasher. Harriet twirled in a cyclone of despair and ran from the cries coming from the bus window that Nora had struggled to open:

"Aunt Harriet! Aunt Harriet!"

She ran until she collapsed, on the grassy banks of the State Capitol. A maintenance crew was repairing the sprinkler system as Harriet pressed herself into the manicured grass.

A few people approached her to help, some timorously asking, "Ma'am?" but she was unreachable and they backed away, scared and embarrassed. She sat up just as a Samaritan directed a policeman to her. She saw that the palms of her hands were crosshatched with grass imprints. She stood up, blinking away dizziness.

"You all right, Ma'am?" asked the policeman.

"No," said Harriet and she breathed raggedly, "but you can't arrest me for feeling bad, can you?" She had meant it as a joke — it had been so long since she told a joke — but it sounded like an accusation and the old cop winced.

Reese Brown was studying a hangnail while listening to Doug tell the group about waking up drunk and AWOL on a boat off the coast of Nam. About twenty-five people sat in folding chairs, filling the small room in the basement of St. Joseph's (normally used for prayer meetings and Bible study) with cigarette smoke.

". . . So I was looking at a court martial and probably a big case of the clap considering the Saigon hookers I'd spent the weekend with," Doug was saying, "but all I cared about was 'Where's my next drink and how am I gonna get it?'"

The assembly murmured in recognition. It was stuffy and hot in the small windowless room and Reese was restless, tapping his big feet and pulling at a forelock of reddish blond hair. All he seemed able to concentrate on were his hangnails and his after-meeting plans. He was going to put a couple bottles of Fresca in the freezer and drink them ice cold while standing shirtless in his backyard, watering the lawn. He might even turn on the sprinkler and stand under it.

There was a hesitation and Reese lifted his head, wondering what profound insight had shut up the whole room. He saw that people's attention was not on the speaker at the front but on someone standing in the doorway in the back. He squinted — his prescription needed to be changed — and it took him a moment to realize the person in the doorway was the woman he had put up in a motel room a couple weeks ago.

She looked bad. She wore the clothes that he had given her but they were torn and greasy. Her hair was matted and eczema crawled up the side of her face. Fear darkened her eyes as she stood on the threshold.

Reese's rubber-tipped chair leg squeaked as he rose and Harriet, seeing him, felt relief fill her.

"A friend of mine," Reese said. There were a chorus of hellos. Reese took her hand and she smiled, a scared and brave smile, and Reese saw pretty white teeth under the grime.

Harriet said nothing as the meeting progressed. She listened to testimonials with a hard concentration, still holding Reese's hand. He hustled her out of the room when the meeting ended, and they walked toward Reese's house in silence, underneath an awning of green elm leaves.

"This is it," he said, nodding toward the small, neat house. In an odd way, he felt as if bringing this unknown woman to his house had been rehearsed and they would both know what to do. He took her into the hallway and she finally released his hand. He opened the linen closet and took out a pile of towels and washcloths.

"Here you are . . ."

"Harriet," she said — her first word to him.

He pushed open the bathroom door. "Nothing like a hot shower to make you feel better, Harriet."

Listening to the stream of the shower water, "Lord," he prayed "let her let me help her." He sat on the edge of his daughter's narrow bed, studying the posters she hadn't taken to college — Paul Revere and the Raiders, the Desiderata, Fess Parker as Daniel Boone. He began to get a little nervous, thinking maybe Harriet had slipped in the shower or passed out.

"Harriet? Harriet, are you all right?" he asked, rapping on the bathroom door.

There was no answer but Reese heard the groan of the pipes signalling the water being turned off.

"I'll be in the kitchen," he said loudly. "There's a robe for you on the doorknob."

A pot of coffee was brewing and he was absently doodling on the face of Ho Chi Minh in *Time* magazine when Harriet came in. Reese carefully clicked the point of his ballpoint pen and set it on the folded oblong of newspaper.

She sat down at the table, holding the pink quilted lapels of the robe together, and Reese poured her a cup of coffee, pushing it wordlessly toward her. He offered her a cigarette and took one himself. She didn't bend her head coquettishly or touch his hand when he lit her cigarette.

"My name is Harriet Dobbin," she said, blowing a stream of smoke toward the ceiling, "and I've been drunk for almost a year now."

Reese settled into his chair.

"I left my family. I prostituted myself. I lied, I stole; there wasn't anything I wouldn't do to get a drink."

She paused and took a sip of coffee.

"It's good," she said, "although I'd like it better with a shot of whiskey." She laughed bitterly. "As much as I hate to think about whiskey, I'm thinking about whiskey."

Resse nodded. "I understand."

Harriet's nostrils fluttered. "I saw my godchild today. My niece, Nora. She used to be a fan of mine, and then she saw me today. She was on a school bus."

As the night darkened, Reese listened carefully to her fitful story, nodding his head, holding her hand when she needed it, lighting her cigarettes. He looked big and solid and impassive, but inside triumph was flitting around his heart like a hummingbird. This woman was so lovely and she was coming into his life.

Labor Day was not so much a holiday for Harriet as it was an anniversary. For thirty days, she had not had a drink more potent than Mountain Dew. She was exhausted physically from the daily battle to say "no"; still, in her head and heart, she was beginning to feel possibility again. Like a teenager before a third driving test, she thought.

She looked at the lump next to her, buried in twists of sheet, its form rising in steady, sleeping breaths: Reese Brown. Early morning sunlight crept through the blinds and fell against the bed in narrow stripes. Harriet held her arms up and stretched, luxuriating in a clear head and the man she loved beside her.

She patted the night stand for her cigarettes. Reese was a smoker, too. "It's the next thing we're going to give up," he had said and Harriet rejoiced at his use of the plural. But he was a deep sleeper and lighting up wouldn't disturb him. She had become the kind of smoker who, with the first inhale of the day, sucked up the take-charge taste into her brain. The first puff was like a summons to open for business, to begin the daily job of staying away from the old demon, alcohol. With the cigarette in one hand, welcoming the acrid smell, Harriet rested her other softly on Reese's shoulder.

Nineteen

Patty Jane stood behind Inky Kolstat. Their eyes, reflected in the mirror before them, were locked in combat.

"Your coloring's all wrong for red hair," said Patty Jane, pulling at strands of Inky's white cloud. "Let me give you a brunette rinse."

"Patty Jane, am I the one paying for this or did you change your policy?" She shook her head defiantly. "Besides, red's the rage in Hollywood."

"Says who?" asked Bev, standing behind the next chair, combing out Myrna Johnson's set.

Inky rolled her eyes. "Says Ann Margret. Says Shirley Mac-Claine."

"Says Howdy-Doody", said Bev, thinking that Inky's monthly lecture series, "Legends of Hollywood," was doing so well that she was riding a high horse.

"Line seven for Patty Jane. Line seven for Patty Jane," said Nora, seated at the small appointments desk. Nora liked to announce incoming calls that way, even though there was only one line.

"Give me that," said Patty Jane, taking the receiver.

Nora looked at her mother with approval. She had just dyed her hair back to its natural color, a shiny chestnut that held light in its waves. She wore a cotton poor-boy sweater and a short print skirt. Nora was proud her mother didn't walk around in a housecoat with her slip hanging out. Now, if only she'd dump those horrible clodhoppers.

Suddenly the color drained out of Patty Jane's face. "What?" she whispered into the phone.

Clyde Chuka looked up. He was across the room filing Gudrun Mueller's yellow nails but the urgency of Patty Jane's whisper carried.

"Yes," she was saying. "Here? Yes . . . of course . . . please." She hung up the phone and covered her face with her hands.

"Mom?" said Nora.

The buzz of the people in the shop stopped and the room filled with a worried and unnatural silence.

Finally Patty Jane dropped her hands. "Harriet's coming over," she said and then her voice rose in speed and pitch. "My sister's coming home!"

Pandemonium broke out as women sprang from under dryer hoods and out of swivel chairs. Customers and employees hugged each other and crushed around Patty Jane.

"Was that her on the phone?"

"No, he said he was a friend of hers."

"A boyfriend?"

"I don't know."

"Did he say she's all right?"

"Yes . . . I think so."

"When will she be here?"

"Soon, he said."

"Please," she said, wiping tears away, "I'd really like to meet her alone." She looked at Clyde Chuka and Nora. "I mean alone with my family."

"No problem at all," said Dixie.

"But I'm not even dry yet," said Alva Bundt's cousin, who was visiting from Mankato.

"This would make a great movie," said Inky Kolstat.

"I'll finish you up," said Dixie to Alva's cousin. She surveyed the women in various stages of styling. "We can have everyone out of here in fifteen minutes."

"Sure we can," said Bev Beal. "Pauline, get over here and I'll comb you out."

Hair dryers were pushed to "High," curlers flew and scissors snipped, sounding almost musical. Dixie was right, the shop was cleared in fifteen minutes and everyone, with the exception of Alva Bundt's cousin, was happy enough with the results.

"Well," she said, patting her damp hair, "I guess this is what I get for being disloyal to Deena's Snip 'N Clip."

Nora swept up locks of hair from the floor and Clyde Chuka put away the Lazy Susans full of curlers and hair pins.

When the shop had cleared, Patty Jane stood in front of a mirror, nervously combing her hair.

"How do I look, Clyde? Oh my God, do you think she hates me? I mean I should have looked for her harder in St. Paul after Nora saw her." The comb stopped. "What if it's some big un-funny joke?" She put down the comb and then picked it up again. "Did you say I looked all right, Clyde?"

"You look fine, Patty Jane," said Clyde Chuka. "Everything will be fine."

They were sitting in the living room, Patty Jane nervously running her thumbnail across her lip, when they heard the back door open.

Nora took her mother's hand. "Come on, Mom, it'll be okay."

Patty Jane was a deadweight. "My legs won't move."

"We're in here!" shouted Nora, panic brightening her words.

"So you are," said Ione, coming through the dining room, carrying a bouquet of red and gold mums.

"Marvelous day," she said, "the air is so clean you want to swallow every breath. I bought apples from the road stand, the most delicious —." She stopped, her smile fading. "What is it?"

Nora fell back in her chair. "Oh Grandma, we thought you were Aunt Harriet."

"Harriet?" Ione searched Patty Jane's face.

Patty Jane nodded dumbly. "We got a call. She's coming home."

The doorbell rang. Patty Jane rose, surrounded by the cocoon of her loved ones. The cocoon moved silently toward the front door and onto the ribbed plastic runner that led to the small entryway.

As Patty Jane fumbled with the doorknob, four hands reached out to help her.

"Sorry, I forgot my key," said Harriet as the door opened.

"It wasn't locked," said Patty Jane.

Patty Jane and Harriet stood on the door's threshold, their heads buried in each other's shoulders, arms clamped around each other. The sisters seemed to exist in another dimension, meeting in an odd light of love and joy and pain and hurt. Clyde Chuka cleared his throat and the noise brought them back to where and who they were.

"You were gone for such a long time!" whispered Patty Jane.

"I wanted to come back every day," said Harriet. "But I was so ashamed. I couldn't come back 'til I was sober."

Patty Jane breathed in the familiar smell, of her sister: cigarette smoke and Halo shampoo.

"Mom," said Nora finally, wedging into the sisters, "my turn. Aunt Harriet, I was so scared when I saw you."

"I know," said Harriet, smoothing Nora's fine pale hair, "I was too." Then, remembering the man who had brought her back home, she released Nora. "Everyone," she said, drawing Reese into the entryway, "Reese Brown. He saved my life."

As they moved inside to where the partition leading to the

salon was open, Harriet straightened and cried, "Hello, my love!" dropping Reese's hand. A rich laugh gathered deep in her stomach as she stepped, her arms outstretched, toward her harp. It stood in the corner near Clyde Chuka's manicure table, dusted secretly each night by Patty Jane and in the morning by Ione.

Harriet tilted the harp onto her shoulder and began to play. Reese Brown said, "Sometimes in her sleep, her hands would move like that."

"Wait'll you hear her sing," whispered Ione.

Patty Jane concentrated on Harriet's face, not her playing. There was a trace of eczema on her temple and dark smudges under her eyes. And her hair — "I could give her a nice rinse," Patty Jane thought blissfully, "or maybe a couple of blond streaks."

Twenty

IONE CALLED a conference one rare evening when the four females dined alone. Clyde Chuka was working on a new piece and hadn't been in the shop for two days. Reese was giving a 4-H group a tour through the precinct station.

Inky Kolstat's lecture, "Gable and Cooper, Last of the Real Men," was beginning at seven and a double batch of butterscotch brownies was baking in the oven in anticipation of a full house. Still, there was time to sit down at the kitchen table and have, as Ione said, "a head-to-heart."

"That's heart-to-heart," said Harriet.

"Well, whatever it is, hurry up, because I'm expecting a very important phone call," said Nora.

In the ninth grade, Nora was pursued by a legion of gangly, boys who discussed her with longing as they clustered near Marty's Malts, passing a single Marlboro between them.

"This won't take long," said Ione. She refilled the mugs of coffee and sat down, her lips pursed. She had memorized a speech and plunged into it with no prelude.

"Min barn — my child — the love between a man and a woman is a rare and precious thing. Those who find it are lucky indeed."

Patty Jane and Harriet looked at each other, moving their shoulders in a slight shrug.

"Your mother and your aunt are lucky women. They love and are loved and their love makes them want to spend much time with their menfolk, including time at night."

Nora watched her grandmother's cheeks bloom pink. She sensed Ione's drift, and enjoyed watching her try to paddle through it.

Ione carefully stirred her coffee, even though she drank it black. She cleared her throat. "Now, you know that I am a God-fearing woman and the Ten Commandments are rules I try to live by. Your mother and aunt do too, in their fashion." Her spoon clanked against the rim of her cup. "But if you will notice, there is no commandment about not sharing your bed as well as your heart with your beloved." She looked to the women around the table and smiled triumphantly. "There."

The room was buttoned up in silence as Nora, Patty Jane and Harriet communicated with their eyes, asking, "What is she talking about?"

Harriet lit a cigarette and Nora brushed her forehead with her fingers, feeling for pimples. Patty Jane finished her coffee and decided it was up to her to elaborate on Ione's sermon. She and her daughter had had their birds-and-bees talk years ago.

"Nora, are you bothered that we have a sex life?"

"Sex life," sputtered Ione. "Uff-da mayda."

Nora rolled her eyes. Adults could be so squirrely.

"I never meant to offend you, pumpkin," said Harriet. "I mean, Reese and I'll stay at his house all the time if you like."

"Uff-da mayda," said Ione again, furiously brushing invisible crumbs off her placemat.

"Mom," said Nora. "Harriet." Her voice was weary with teenaged wisdom. "I think it's really cool you guys are in love. And I know you, um, make love when you're in love. What's the big deal? Hey, I'm fourteen and a half years old." She smiled, her eyes at half-mast. She was pleased with herself.

"Well," said Harriet. She cleared her throat. "Well, Reese *is* my fiancé after all."

Three voices asked the same question: "What did you say?"

Color came into Harriet's face and she rolled the edges of her placemat. "Well, surely all of you knew we were headed in that direction." She traced an appliqué on the tablecloth with her fingernail. "No official date . . . but soon."

"Mom?" asked Nora and there was a hint of hope in her voice.

Patty Jane shrugged. "Sorry, it's not going to be a double."

Harriet made an official announcement to the women of the House of Curl on Saturday, the busiest day of the week at the shop, and when everyone had congratulated her, Harriet called for a Dance Break and a dozen women and Clyde Chuka swung their hips. Ione had to get Alva Bundt a glass of water, so furiously had she done the pony, and tips fell out of Bev Beal's smock pocket when Karen Spaeth dipped her backwards in a tango.

Then, Harriet joined Reese at the podium when he announced their engagement at Thursday night's AA meeting and the standing ovation that greeted the announcement was a minute long.

"A toast!" said Reese's sponsor and he went to the big coffee urn and began filling the styrofoam cups.

"To Reese and Harriet — a long and prosperous and alcohol-free life," he said and the room was full of white steaming cups raised in salute.

Despite the cloud of smoke formed by the cigarettes of the chainsmokers, Harriet felt a holiness in the meeting room; they were in a church of course, albeit in its small basement. She had memorized the Twelve Steps, her Book of Psalms. To her, the people here were fellow parishioners, gathered together to help themselves and each other, a cornerstone for what Ione termed "basic Christianity."

Harriet was now able to forgive her parents. She remembered her father telling her on a rainy summer afternoon, "There are a million reasons to drink, Harriet, and you only need one." Now, she understood how alcohol could grip like a steel jaw and not let go.

She brought Patty Jane to the meeting, wanting her to understand the people and process that had ushered her back to sanity. Throughout, Patty Jane cast surreptitious glances around the room, curious about the people Harriet had spoken of with such reverence. To herself, Patty Jane admitted she was surprised by their normal appearances; she had expected a roomful of rheumy-eyed men in dirty overcoats and women who looked like Hennepin Avenue hookers.

When Harriet spoke, Patty Jane sat as still as a broken clock, even though springs, wheels and cogs were unwinding and turning and shifting inside her. Harriet looked so frail, standing there behind the podium, yet Patty Jane doubted if there was anyone stronger in the room.

"Monday was fine — I worked at the House of Curl all day and helped Ione make some cream puffs, which, by the way, were so good I had three." She turned her head and coughed into her hand. "Then Reese picked me up and we saw a movie and everything was great. Last night though, I was in the shower and all of a sudden I had this . . . huge . . . desire for a vodka martini — it's what I first drank when I started drinking — and I couldn't think of anything else; it was like there was a big neon sign in my head, flashing: Vodka Martini, Vodka Martini, Vodka Martini. Reese and I talked for a long time and I had about four glasses of lemonade — straight, no vodka — but it was hard."

The skin on Patty Jane's arms devolved into something reptilian as goosebumps rose from her wrist to the hem of her short-sleeved sweater. "Holy shit," she thought, "it's still a struggle." Harriet appeared so happy in her sobriety that Patty Jane had the impression it was easy to maintain.

"It's a day-to-day thing," said Reese, in the car on the ride home. "I've been sober for nine years and yet there are still times when I think I'll go crazy if I can't have a bourbon and sour."

Patty Jane looked out the passenger window and into the lit windows of houses on Snelling Avenue.

"I guess I was hoping that the urge was gone for good."

"I wish," said Harriet, cozy between her fiancé and her sister. "But we just take things — "

"One second at a time," finished Reese, and he and Harriet chuckled softly. Patty Jane turned away from the lives behind all the lit-up windows to face the ones next to her.

"Think how different things would have been if Anna and Elmo had gone to AA."

"I have," said Harriet. She pulled the lighter out of the dashboard and studied its glowing tip before lighting two cigarettes. She passed one to Reese. "But remember, Mom and Dad never thought they had a problem. And if my life has taken me to where I am now, then I wouldn't change a thing." Her mouth pursed and she blew smoke rings at the rearview mirror. "Well, maybe just a dozen really rotten years."

"Yeah," agreed Patty Jane. "Maybe a dozen really rotten years."

Reese turned on the car radio. "No offense, girls," he said, holding his cigarette between his teeth, "but you're starting to depress me."

"Get used to it, Reese," said Patty Jane and she leaned over and swatted him playfully on the knee. "It's the Dobbin terrain — all hills and valleys."

Twenty-One

WHEN EVELYN BRIGHT canceled her Monday night Music Appreciation class, Harriet offered to teach it. She played a Sibelius album and talked about mood and theme and how a cello section could sound like thunder coming over the hills, but then she found herself lifting the needle off the record and telling the assembled group that it was a lot easier to like music — to like anything — if first you liked yourself.

Four of the five women assembled seemed to be interested in Harriet's lecture about taking responsibility for your own actions, but Gudrun Mueller, who bought tickets to the symphony when she could scrape enough money together, rose and said, "Entschuldigen Sie, Bitte, but are we not going to listen to the rest of the Sibelius?"

Sheepishly, Harriet made a mental note to confine her sermons to people who wanted them.

She spoke to Clyde Chuka of her frustration. There were people who needed help but weren't getting it. "Your mother, for example. I'd love to take her to an AA meeting with me."

They were on their break in the dining room. Rain had been

falling from a slate sky all day and there had been little business. Patty Jane had gone to a parent-teacher conference and Harriet and Clyde Chuka had played Rook and pinochle and Hang Man. Now they were on their third break in two hours.

"The greatest medicine man of the Sioux Nation couldn't cure my mother's taste for booze," said Clyde Chuka, helping himself to a lemon coconut bar.

A coughing fit interrupted Harriet's next sentence and she spit phlegm into a napkin.

"That's a wicked cough," said Clyde Chuka.

"I know," said Harriet, her eyes watery. "Bronchitis." She wadded up the napkin and put it in her pants pocket.

"Look at this rain," said Clyde Chuka. "I should pack up my cuticle-remover and get out of here. None of my appointments will come out in this."

"Inky Kolstat came out. Dixie's giving her a wash and set right now."

"That woman's death wouldn't stop her from keeping a hair appointment."

Clyde Chuka pushed aside the plate of lemon coconut bars. "Let's close up shop, Harriet. Get our raincoats on, do some singing in the rain."

They shared a big black umbrella Avel had given Harriet years ago. The umbrella's arc was so wide and encompassing it was as if they moved under a ribbed tent.

Lightning flashed in the afternoon sky, spidery, illuminated lines that hopped above the rooftops. They walked along Minnehaha Avenue, dodging the waves of water the wheels of passing cars churned up. Squishing over a slick carpet of yellow and red leaves, they tried to avoid the bigger puddles.

Despite their discomfort, there was a sense of adventure in being part of Mother Nature's tantrums. They passed a barber, who stood at his shop window in a white, high-necked smock, smoking a cigar and shaking his head. A desperate cat shrieked at the front door of a house and when the door finally opened, the cat gave a shrill meow as if to say "How could you?" before streaking in.

They walked about a mile when Harriet said, "I've got two inches of water swimming around in my boots." She gestured across the street. "There's the Come Right Inn. Let's stop there for a minute."

"Harriet —"

"Not for a drink. Well, coffee maybe. And maybe your mother'll be there. Maybe I can talk to her."

"Why do I get the feeling that this was your destination all along?"

Inside the Come Right Inn, there was that sense of gaiety in having found shelter from the storm. But Harriet shuddered. "This is where it all started," she thought. She looked around the dark room, and sure enough, there was Merry Chuka near the jukebox, swaying her fanny to Aretha Franklin.

"There's your mom," she whispered. "And she's feeling no pain."

Merry did a funny backwards stroll, rolling her hands as if stirring the air.

"Two coffees," said Clyde Chuka to the bartender, and wearily sat down on a barstool to watch his mother bugaloo.

"Hello," said Harriet to Augie. The bartender grunted back and Harriet could see he hadn't taken personality lessons since the last time.

When the music stopped, Merry shut her eyes and froze, holding the pose.

"What the hell, Augie," she said. "I put in a quarter." She slapped the machine on the side.

"Knock it off, Merry, you got your three songs already," said the bartender. He turned to Harriet and Clyde Chuka and rolled his eyes. "Some people."

"Some people are other people's mothers," said Clyde

Chuka. Leaning back on his barstool, Clyde Chuka pleated his tongue and whistled loudly.

From the jukebox, Merry snapped her head up. "Clyde?" She ran toward the bar, listing like a ship with a hole in its keel. She jumped on the barstool next to Harriet and fell off into Harriet's arms.

"Oh me, on my," the older woman said. She righted herself and ordered a round of drinks, "for my son and his girl."

"Coffee's fine for us," Clyde Chuka told the bartender. He put his arms around her round plump shoulders. "Ma, I don't drink, remember? Neither does Harriet. And she's not my girl. Patty Jane — her sister — she's my girl."

Merry tilted her head back, resting it on the pillow of Clyde Chuka's arm. "Sorry," she said to Harriet. "I need glasses." She paused and her eyes were buried in round cheeks pushed up by her big smile. "I need plenty glasses. Full ones."

"Mrs. Chuka," Harriet began "do you remember me? I sat in that booth over there getting drunk with you and Mervin . . . about a year and a half ago."

A pall came over Merry's face. "Melvin. That's his name. But he's gone. Dead as a doornail. D-E-D, dead."

"Ma!" said Clyde Chuka. "You never told me that. Melvin's dead? What happened?"

Merry sighed. "He went up to the Rez — the one he was raised on near Leech Lake. His sister's kid was getting married. He got plastered at the wedding feast and wandered off. They found him floating in two feet of water."

"Christ, I'm sorry," said Clyde Chuka.

Merry stuck out her lower lip and shrugged. "Not the first man I lost. Not the best, either." She finished her beer and banged the bottom of the glass on the bar. "Whatsamatter, Augie, tap run dry?"

"Mrs. Chuka," Harriet began again, "Melvin didn't have to die. Neither do you."

"Not too much foam now," said Merry, carefully watching Augie fill her glass. She turned to Harriet. "Listen, kiddo, everybody's got to go sometime." She drank hungrily from the glass and a foam mustache appeared on her upper lip.

"But why let booze kill you? Let Mother Nature take its course."

Merry snorted. "Mother Nature can take her course and I'll take mine." She burped loudly and wiped her mouth on the back of her hand. "Clyde, who is this person anyways and why is she bugging me?"

"AA," said Harriet, her voice an urgent whisper. "AA can help you. Here." She wrote the address of St. Joseph's church on a cocktail napkin and gave it to Merry, who crumpled it up into a ball and threw it across the room.

"Hey," said Augie, "no littering."

"Get my place back no matter how long I'm gone," said Merry, tapping her barstool. "I gotta visit the little girl's room."

At that moment, a women's voice screeched from the back of the bar. "Well, you don't expect me to spoon-feed you, do you?"

"Gee," said Harriet, as the voice ranted on. "That sounds like the crazy woman who used to come into the shop."

Augie listened with Clyde Chuka to Harriet's story.

"One day she just started flipping out. She's screaming, 'You in your fancy uniforms! I'm the doctor! I wear the white coat!' You helped Patty Jane throw her out once, Clyde, remember? The day you were hired." Harriet sipped at her coffee and grimaced. It was bitter. "She hasn't been in for years, but I'd recognize that voice anywhere."

As if on cue, the woman opened her mouth and brayed.

"That's it," whispered Harriet.

There was a thump, like a frozen roast dropped on a table, and Merry Chuka's voice. "Will you get out of my way, you lunatic?"

"It would be my mother who picks a fist fight with a crazy."

216

Clyde Chuka took a dollar out of his wallet and set it on the bar, calling, "Come on, Ma, I'll take you home."

"I'm just waiting for an apology from this clumsy bitch is all," yelled Merry from the back of the bar.

"Clumsy bitch!" screeched the woman. "You're the one who barreled into *me*, you old squaw!"

"Oh yeah? I'll show you barreling, white bitch." Merry took a drunken step backwards.

"Ma," hollered Clyde. Zipping his jacket, he trotted over.

"Take this!" cawed the woman, flicking back her long, grey hair, as she pushed Merry against the wall. Above them, a plastic bear holding a can of Hamms trembled.

"Ma!" Clyde said, grabbing Merry. The woman straightened herself and, eyes glittering like black diamonds, pointed at Merry.

"Fool. Next time I'll kill you." She turned and went back to her booth. She grabbed her companion's arm and pulled him up the narrow aisle toward the door.

"Nice couple," thought Harriet. "She picks fights and he's drunk."

Clyde Chuka sat his mother down on a black plastic chair against the wall and Harriet was surprised to see Merry's chubby hands covering her face, her braids hanging, slightly shaking. Nerves in Harriet's back twitched and she was a schoolgirl again, defending the four-eyed kid against the playground bully. She followed the pair, her rubber boots squeaking on the wood floor. "Hey, you," said Harriet to the woman's back. "What's the matter with you, anyway!"

The woman ignored her and pushed the door open. Rain gushed in.

Harriet was prepared for the woman's anger, but she was not prepared for the man who turned to face her. Wreathed in a mixture of grey daylight and neon barlight, his face was oily and pallid, its features sunken in age and sickness. Harriet saw hair dyed a flat black, but below it the sad, still powerfully blue eyes of her brother-in-law, Thor Rolvaag.

The door slammed, shutting out Thor's backward glance. Harriet stood immobile, until she felt underneath her raincoat a trickle run down her legs.

Reese was at the station house, banging the side of a defective vending machine which refused to give up a pack of Juicy Fruit, when a narcotics detective told him he had a call. Clyde Chuka's voice was strained. He asked Reese to please come down to the Come Right Inn. "It's not that, Reese," he said quickly. "Harriet's fine. I mean she hasn't been drinking. We just need you here, right away." He cleared his dry throat. "And could you bring some of Harriet's clothes, some pants and underwear, a pair of socks?"

As Reese Brown barreled into the Come Right Inn, Augie flinched and ducked behind the bar.

"Relax," laughed a customer. "All he's armed with is a paper bag."

"Jesus God, my mind imagined a million things," Reese said, as he dropped to his knees in front of Harriet. "I can only thank God there's no smell of alcohol on you."

"I saw Thor, Reese," said Harriet.

"Thor? Patty Jane's . . ."

"He was like a ghost," Harriet continued. — "No, a ghost would have looked better." She looked down at the paper bag. "I peed in my pants, Reese. I was so scared I peed in my pants."

"I don't know how we're going to tell Patty Jane," said Clyde Chuka. "Or Ione — and man, what about Nora?"

"Who was Thor with?" asked Reese. "Why didn't you stop him?"

"I didn't see him. Harriet did. Just as he was leaving with some crazy woman my mother got in a fight with." Clyde Chuka rolled his eyes. "My mother was here, too, but she ran out once I explained to her who Thor was — is. She said 'White man's ghosts are the spooks of the spirit world.' " He rubbed the back of his neck. "When I figured out what Harriet was talking about, I ran outside, but the street was empty."

Reese walked to the bar and took a small notebook from his pocket. "The man in here before, you know his name?"

Augie shook his head.

"What about the woman he was with?"

"Crazy bitch. But at least she always pays her bar tab, which is more than I can say for a lot of 'em."

"She got a name?"

"Yeah. Temple."

The bartender wiped his hands on a grey wet towel. "Temple Curry. She's a doctor. Or she was. She showed me her license once. Brought it right here to the bar."

"Thanks," said Reese. His finger sped down the narrow columns of a nearby phone book. He wrote an address down and called to Clyde Chuka and Harriet, who had just exited from "GALS," "Let's go get Thor."

Twenty-Two

Reese PULLED UP to a stately colonial house on West River Road with a wide lawn that faced the Mississippi River and St. Paul.

"Holy cow," said Harriet weakly. "This is it?"

Reese checked the address written in his notebook. He nodded.

Clyde Chuka whistled softly. "So she's crazy *and* rich."

The late afternoon was darkening into evening. The rain had stopped but the air was still damp and the sky was mottled with dark clouds.

Walking up the brick steps, Harriet thought it must be twice the size of the House of Curl and Reese's house combined. From the windows, green canvas awnings snapped in the night breeze.

They stood for a moment in front of the oak door before Reese pushed the doorbell. Muffled chimes rang somewhere inside.

The door opened slightly and then began to close, but

Reese, his foot already in place, pushed it open with a hefty shoulder.

"Police!" he yelled, and he, Harriet and Clyde Chuka tumbled off the steps of an expensive and well-maintained house and into a garbage dump.

A smell of rotting food and dirty cat litter made Harriet want to retch. Everywhere she looked, loose newspapers and oily paper bags stuffed with magazines rose in piles. A crooked path wended its way between the towers, from the foyer into the living room, and it was on this path that Temple Curry ran from them.

"Get out of my house!" She jumped up on a grimy silk couch, kicking aside a pile of tools. "Show me your search warrant!"

Reese approached her slowly, his arms spread, palms up, Harriet and Clyde Chuka clustering behind him. "I'm not arresting anyone," he said. "We've just come to see Thor."

"He doesn't want to see you!" The pitch of Temple Curry's voice careened like an over-the-hill opera singer. She paced up and down the couch, losing her balance from time to time. "Thor is mine and he's happy!" She picked up a wrench and pointed it at Harriet. "He doesn't want your sister so get out of here!"

A chill seized Harriet. What did this mad woman know?

"Put down the wrench," said Reese. "We're not going to hurt you."

The woman brayed and threw the wrench at the fireplace.

"Thank you," said Reese evenly, "Now, where is Thor?"

The woman folded herself onto the couch. "I am Dr. Temple Curry," she said, patting her hair and puckering her lips. "Remember that." Her head dropped back and she began to giggle.

Reese huddled with Harriet and Clyde Chuka.

"One of us should stay with . . ." Reese nodded in the direction of Temple Curry. "And since I'm armed, it should be me."

"Let's try calling him," said Clyde Chuka and raising his voice, he cried, "Thor!"

"Thor!" called Harriet.

"He's not a dog. He doesn't obey commands," said Temple Curry, and giggled again.

Harriet reached for Clyde Chuka's hand. "I guess we'd better look."

"Be careful," said Reese.

They followed the path into the dining room. So many bulbs were broken or burned out in the chandelier that only a dim light flickered. The room was decorated as chaotically as the living room. The newspaper drive continued; dozens of piles tottered against two walls. A massive oak table was piled with board games, more papers, a bicycle wheel, a crate of rotted peaches. Two cat boxes narrowed the path underneath an archway and one of them was being used by a fat, three-legged Siamese. The stench rose up and took on texture, and Harriet and Clyde Chuka held their noses, as they passed the fat cat twitching its tail.

"Thor?" called Harriet, again.

The kitchen was a health inspector's nightmare. The wall above the stove wore a skin of yellow grease. Blackened pans were scattered around like shells on a beach. Encrusted plates and cups formed lopsided pyramids in the sink. The counters were covered with open boxes of cereal, potato chips, tins of do-nuts and jelly rolls, and a cat — this one tiger-striped — poked its way through the city of boxes, licking the icing off a donut.

Clyde Chuka motioned to a heavy wooden door. "I'll bet this leads to the basement." He opened the door and peered down a steep flight of steps lined with cans. "Let's take a look."

"Not the basement," said Harriet. "That's *too* scary."

They hesitated at the top of the stairs until they heard faint humming and a pecking sound, like a woodpecker tapping at a tree.

"Go," Harriet whispered, nudging Clyde Chuka in the back with the knuckles of her other hand. The pecking and humming grew louder as they descended the stairs. The humming was a simple melody, a child's song of three notes. At the foot of the stairs, a bare light bulb burned. A few feet from the steps stood another barricade of boxes and crates and barrels. It took Harriet and Clyde Chuka a moment to find the path dug out of it. They passed a door with a sign reading, "The Doctor is In."

The high-pitched humming grew louder and suddenly they arrived in a village of birdhouses. Hundreds of birdhouses. On pedestals, on wooden poles, on the floor, hanging from the wall. Intricately built and painted bird houses. The one closest to Harriet was an apartment complex; twenty windows for a commune of birds. There were bungalows built in a U shape, with tiny painted pine trees nestled around them. A section of pastel adobes nestled close to one another, and Victorian birdhouses with cupolas and turrets and lattice porches competed for space with log cabins made from woven cane.

The Geppetto of birdhouses sat at a workbench, his once-wide shoulders hunched and sloped, his arms thin and white under his short sleeves. He held a nail and in a staccato movement, hammered it into the eave of a roof. His three-note tune continued as Harriet and Clyde Chuka stood watching him.

Finally, Harriet swallowed the lump in her throat and said, "Thor?"

He dipped his head and turned to them, the right side of his mouth turned up into a smile.

"Thor. I'm Harriet. Your sister-in-law? You were married to my sister, Patty Jane."

Harriet's head bobbed, nodding encouragement, but Thor set his hammer down and stared at her, his hands folded in the lap of his khaki pants.

"Thor," said Clyde Chuka softly. "My name is Clyde Chuka.

I know Patty Jane, too." His voice cracked. "We've come to take you home."

"Home?" said Thor, his voice as high and light as a boy's. "Home?" He stood obediently, shaking the wood curls off his lap. Harriet reached out her hand and he took it, his own as warm and moist as bread dough.

He touched each birdhouse he passed, like a father patting his children's heads.

Thor sat quietly on a heap of clothes as they discussed what they should do.

"Well, I don't know," Harriet said. "Should we call before we go over there? Or do we just show up with him?"

Clyde Chuka watched the fat Siamese cat prowl the length of the window seat. It was easier to watch the cat than look at Thor.

"I think we should call," said Reese. "Forewarned is fore-armed."

Harriet bit her lip. "I agree, I guess." She turned to Temple Curry. "You have a phone?"

"I'm no barbarian," she said and her voice, for the first time, softened. "It's behind that steamer trunk."

Patty Jane picked up the phone on the third ring.

"Patty Jane?"

"Oh, hi, Harriet. Hey, Dixie left me a note about you guys playing hookey today. Guess I'll have to dock your salary."

"Patty Jane."

Worry flared in Patty Jane's reponse. "Honey, are you all right?"

"Patty Jane, is Ione home?"

"Yes — do you want to talk to her?"

Harriet swallowed. "Yes. Put her on the upstairs phone and tell Nora to listen in, too."

"Harriet, is it Clyde Chuka?"

"No. Just get everyone on the line."

Harriet cleared her throat. "Okay. I'm with Reese and Clyde Chuka and we'll be home in a couple minutes. Now this is going to be very hard to understand, but we're bringing someone with us." Harriet squeezed her eyes shut. "It's Thor. We found Thor."

The collective gasp on the other end of the line filled Harriet's ears. "He's not the same," she said. "We'll be home soon. I'm sorry."

"I'd say the jig's up, Thor," said Temple Curry. "Fourteen and a half years, baby, not a bad run." She hoisted herself over the arm of the couch and crawled over boxes to Thor. She held his head between her hands and kissed him. "Okay," she said finally. "Let's go."

"Wait a second," said Harriet, "you're not coming with us."

"Listen, you," said Temple Curry, "if you think I'd miss this, think again. I'm the only one who knows what Thor can't tell you. And what's your plan anyway? You're going to bring Thor back into the family fold?" She looked at Clyde Chuka, a sneer pulling her lip. "Well, the family's changed, hasn't it? Is Patty Jane going to renew her wedding vows now?" Her lips spread into a smile. "What do you think, Cochise?"

"I deserve my confessional," she said to Reese. "A few words before my execution."

"Min sonn! Minn sonn kommer hjem! Minn sonn kommer hjem!" Ione was a broken record, pacing the kitchen floor. Nora sat at the table, hiccuping. She had thought her father was a finished story. Patty Jane spent the waiting time in the bathroom.

The three women froze at the slam of car doors, then footsteps.

"Mommy!" said Nora.

"Buck up," said Patty Jane and, with her head high and her back straight, she walked to the door.

Harriet was holding the screen door open. Clyde Chuka was saying, "Come on, one more step, that's it," and suddenly they were in the kitchen; Harriet, Clyde Chuka and between them, a stooped man, his face both old and young, his black hair wet from the rain.

Harriet almost laughed when Patty Jane asked, "What the hell happened to you?" her first words to her husband in fifteen years. Ione rushed to her son, overcome that she was holding her Thor again until she realized he wasn't hugging her in return. She stepped back, looking into his face.

"Harriet! Clyde Chuka! What's the matter with him? What's the matter with my son?"

Reese stood in the threshold and held up his arm, which was handcuffed to another's. "Here's the person who can answer your questions, Ione."

He led Temple Curry, who was smiling and fluttering her fingers like a guest of honor greeting well-wishers, into the dining room. "Might as well get comfortable," he said. "This could be a long night."

"You've been here before, haven't you?" asked Patty Jane when Reese uncuffed Temple Curry. The doctor nodded. Patty Jane turned to Harriet. "We kicked her out of the House of Curl, remember?"

Ione led Thor to the couch and gently pushed him onto it. She looked at Temple Curry, squinting her eyes. She nodded, remembering. "She was acting crazy."

"That's my specialty," said the woman with the flowing grey hair. "Allow me to introduce myself," she said, standing behind the coffee table, facing her audience. The rest of the group was quiet, holding their breath like children called into the principal's office.

"I am Dr. Temple Curry. Temple," she said to Nora, who quickly broke eye contact, "is my first name. Curry is my last.

One might think of a Bombay restaurant with religious over-tones!" She laughed.

The phone rang but no one rose to answer it.

"Shall I began again?" asked Temple Curry, and for over an hour, with few interruptions, she told her story. She had told it to herself dozens of times, in anticipation of the day she would finally make it public.

"That house that some of you barged into earlier," she began, twisting a button on her cuff, "has been in my family for fifty years. My father Jerod was a doctor *and* a lawyer, so you can see my stock is blue chip." A whooping laugh escaped her. "Of course, practicing medicine does not insure one's physical *or* mental health, does it?

"I was one lonesome cowgirl growing up — no sisters, no brothers, no friends. My parents did, however, encourage my studies, and in 1945 I became a doctor — an oral surgeon. By then my father had died and my mother, afraid to be alone, en-couraged me to open my office in the house."

Temple Curry couldn't have hoped for a more rapt audience; there was absolute silence from the others in the room. She dragged the wing chair to the coffee table and sat down, putting her feet on the table. Her feet were muddy — she had already tracked on the rug — but not even Ione scolded her. Temple drew her shirt cuff across her nose.

"You see, my mother was hard to take care of — she seemed to have entered an early senility. She used to lie for hours un-derneath the piano bench . . . Anyway," she took a deep breath, "you can't blame me for letting off a little of this tension through my work. Once I pulled the wrong molar on this fussy schoolteacher. Then I began to do root canals on perfectly sound teeth. When I extracted the upper and lower molars of a patient, leaving the impacted wisdom teeth intact, I knew something was amiss. I had fine legal assistance from my father's firm, but eventually my license to practice was taken away.

"And that's why I know I'm not crazy, because I am completely aware that I'm off-the-wall."

She nodded at Thor, whose chin was tucked into the V-neck of his sweater. Asleep, he snored.

"Past eight and he's out like a lamb."

"What did you do to him?" asked Ione. Her voice was soft but behind it loomed a threat.

The woman flicked the ends of her wild salt-and-pepper hair.

"I'm getting to that," she said irritably, as to a heckler in the crowd.

"In one year I lost my practice and my mother — heart attack, just like that. But then one winter morning, the Norske King Thor was sent to me by the gods."

Tension skittered around the room and Temple Curry sat poised for a moment, relishing her hold over them.

"I had taken to sledding on the hills of my and my neighbors' homes . . . at dawn, when I had the snow and the cold all to myself. I had a wonderful toboggan; it had been my father's and it was one of the few things I did that gave me true pleasure. Then one day I looked up from a nice fast ride and I saw a man across the boulevard, skipping and running and hopping. Methinks, now there's my kind of fellow. A sprite. A sprite dancing and jumping by dawn's early light. Then, splat. I saw him sail up into the air and smash into a tree, head first. I practically fell over when I saw this beautiful creature lying on the ice, looking like Sleeping Beauty's older brother.

"Of course I surmised this was God talking to me personally. I rolled him onto the toboggan and pulled him home."

"He was unconscious?" whispered Patty Jane.

"Oh, for almost two days."

"And you didn't go for help?" It seemed she had been ejected from her chair, so forceful was her lunge toward Temple Curry. All she wanted was to squeeze the pulse out of this awful woman's neck, but Clyde Chuka and Reese scrambled around the couch and grabbed her.

"Remember," said Temple Curry, her voice dripping with condescension, "I am a doctor. I knew I was going to have to find a way to feed him — let alone hydrate him — when he blinked open those heavenly blue eyes. He drank a quart of water and had a bowl of chicken noodle soup that evening and then he fell asleep. For months he didn't speak a word, he just ate, slept, and whimpered once in a while."

"Fandon!" said Ione and although no one knew what the direct translation was, they all got the drift. Temple Curry ignored her.

"I learned enough about him through his wallet: his driver's license, a picture signed 'to Thor from your loving wife, Patty Jane,' blah, blah, blah. He even had a list of names under two headings: Boy and Girl."

"He did?" said Patty Jane, softly. She looked at Nora. "Those were names for you, sweetheart."

Temple Curry banged the heels of her muddy shoes on the coffee table, calling for attention. "Damaged goods or not, I felt destiny had made me a very special delivery. I knew my gain was someone else's loss. I staked out that apartment of yours and then followed your move to your present abode cum beauty parlor."

"So you're the one who sent the notes from Thor and the money?" Patty Jane's voice had the flat amazement of someone who'd just witnessed a horrible accident.

"Bingo." Temple Curry stretched elaborately, and wiggled her fingers toward the ceiling. "We spent the rest of that winter and spring in hibernation but when summer came I thought my man and I deserved a little vacation time. Did you ever notice the notes had out-of-town postmarks?"

She leaned forward and took a handful of nuts from a glass dish on the coffee table. "They're always so chintzy with the cashews," she said, inspecting her take. "There's about ten filberts to every cashew."

"Why did you even bother to write at all?" asked Harriet, "and why send money?"

"I am not heartless," said Temple Curry. "I was more than willing to send a little cash to Thor's first wife to tide her over."

"Thor's *first* wife?" Patty Jane, Ione and Harriet asked as a chorus.

"Now wait just one second," said Patty Jane. Clyde Chuka strengthened his grip on her shoulders. "You're telling me you and Thor *got married*?"

"That's exactly what I'm telling you."

"You couldn't have married Thor," said Ione as a huge anger lifted her off the couch. "He was already married!" She slapped Temple Curry across the face.

"We didn't need a license. The union between Thor and me went beyond something okayed by a state bureaucracy or religious dogma." Temple Curry rubbed her cheek and stared with hate at Ione.

"But you *slept* with him?" said Patty Jane.

Temple Curry sneered. "Please. Don't abase yourself." She looked at each face in the room and when her gaze fell on the sleeping Thor, Patty Jane saw the woman's features soften.

Then Temple Curry laughed, the same braying laugh Harriet and Clyde Chuka had heard in the Come Right Inn, the same laugh, Ione realized, she had heard years ago when she was with Harriet in Del's Dairy and the crazy woman had pushed her groceries off the counter and onto the floor. When Temple Curry stopped laughing, the coldness returned to her eyes.

"I might sue you for assaulting me," she said to Ione. "Now where was I?" She looked at Patty Jane and beat a rhythm on her thighs with her hands. "Oh, yes. I was about to tell you how much I enjoyed being a customer in your salon de beauté — while Thor was out in the car, asleep in the back seat! That tickled me, especially as that was the day you so highhandedly ousted me!"

Patty Jane groaned.

"Now, as I recall, our first trip was taken that summer — Patty Jane, you got your first note then — but when the Mighty Bites cereal box thing started, I figured I had to lie low. Thor, my little cardboard celebrity, was content to stay in the house. Then he began constructing things with whatever he could get his hands on — salt shakers, boxes, toothpicks. I finally let him loose in my father's basement woodshop and . . ." She looked to Clyde Chuka and Harriet. "You've seen the results.

"After a couple years passed I finally dared venture out locally with Thor. I dyed his hair — black becomes him, don't you think? And we began to share a somewhat normal life. As normal as two abnormal people can have, right, honey bun?" She blew a kiss to the snoring Thor. "That's my story," she said, standing up to take a bow. "Abridged but essentially complete."

Harriet blew fat smoke rings at the ceiling. Ione's face was streaky with tears. Clyde Chuka massaged Patty Jane's shoulders. Thor snored, and Nora, who had been perfectly still throughout the doctor's soliloquy, suddenly bolted up — but it was too late. She leaned over the coffee table and threw up into the glass platter of mixed nuts.

Twenty-Three

"It's pure speculation," said the doctor, wiping his glasses on a corner of his white coat. "Certainly, with immediate treatment and therapy, Mr. Rolvaag might have regained many — perhaps even all — of his cognitive faculties and then again, maybe not. Head traumas are difficult to predict."

Ione snapped and unsnapped the clip of her purse, while Patty Jane fidgeted. They were listening to a lecture they had already heard.

Dr. Lumley was the third doctor Thor had been taken to that week. It wasn't as if Patty Jane was expecting a miracle: an injection of this or that and he'd be able to carry on an adult conversation — she only wanted to hear something concrete: yes, 42.8 percent of rational thought is eradicated when contusions to the head occur — some simple diagnosis that would stop the "if onlys" that batted in her head like moths against a screen.

"Thank you for your time," said Patty Jane, pulling Thor up by the hand. Thor looked at her quizzically.

"Sorry," Dr. Lumley said.

"Aren't we all," agreed Patty Jane, guiding Thor toward the door.

It had been a subdued household the morning after Thor's return. People spoke in hushed tones and moved quietly, as if they had gathered for a funeral, which in a way, Patty Jane pointed out to Clyde Chuka, they had.

The first night, Patty Jane and Clyde Chuka had stayed up late, adding logs to the fire, keeping watch over Thor. He slept so deeply that more than once Patty Jane touched his neck, feeling for his pulse.

"What are we going to do, Clyde?" she asked. They sat on the floor with their backs against the coffee table, alternately watching the fire and Thor.

Clyde Chuka shook his head.

"Of all the world's shit," said Patty Jane, and she put her head to her knees and cried.

Clyde Chuka held her and cried, too. At that moment, life seemed too full of pain and loss and old and new loves. Just as the occupants of the House of Curl seemed to have fit the puzzle together, they were asked to make room for a piece that belonged to a different game.

"It's so strange," said Patty Jane finally, "for the longest time, I wanted to find Thor — learn why he left me, what he was doing. But then his being gone became more real than his being here. I sort of shut the door on Thor." A trace of a smile played on her lips. "I never thought it would be reopened and this," she nodded toward the curled-up, sleeping man on the couch, "this would be behind it."

"What if he had come back the way he was?" Clyde Chuka struggled to ask the question.

"Oh, Clyde," said Patty Jane, holding his face with her hands. "If he had never left, I might have grown old with him . . . or we might have divorced. I don't know. We were so young then. When I think back, I barely knew him."

"So you would have turned off your pilot light?"

Patty Jane smoothed the lines etched into Clyde's forehead. "I would have told him I'd switched to electric."

When Reese checked in on Temple Curry the next day, he found her dead. In bed with seven cats — all in various stages of rigor mortis — she had apparently fed them and herself overdoses of sleeping pills. Reese took the envelope marked "Thor" that lay on a soiled satin pillowcase and called the morgue. The envelope contained a one-page letter stating that Thor Rolvaag and/or his guardians had inherited Temple Curry's estate and that a copy of the letter was on file at her attorney's office.

In a P.S. to Patty Jane, she wrote, "I would like to apologize but I can't. I taught him how to use the toilet, how to hold a knife and fork. I kept him supplied in wood and tools. I KEPT UP HIS TEETH, FOR GOD'S SAKE! Still, you get him in the end."

Patty Jane stripped the dye from Thor's hair and bleached it back to its original pale blond. When she was finished, she pushed him around in the swivel chair to face the mirror and he touched his hair and smiled.

"That's right, Thor, that's the real you," said Patty Jane.

There were minor victories, moments of hope, when it seemed as if Thor might be brought back in small chunks. For his first breakfast, Ione had made rommegrot, a Norwegian porridge heavy with butter and cream, and when she served it to him with the simple order "spise" — "eat" — he looked up at her and said, "Jeg vil spise."

Ione's hands flew to her chest and she stepped backward.

"Forstår du? — you understand me?"

"Ja, jeg forstår deg. Har du kaffe?"

"He understands me!" shouted Ione. "He wants some coffee!"

The doctors had been impressed by Thor's recall of a language learned as a child, but as Dr. Lumley advised, "Things like this happen sometimes. It doesn't naturally follow that his full emotional or mental recall will return." And it was true. In Norwegian Ione would tell him that she was his mother; she would point at Nora and Patty Jane and explain, and even though Thor repeated, "Mutti? Datter? Min Fru?" he had no concept of what the words meant.

Patty Jane brought him into the shop and introduced him to clients and staff. She wanted him to be as much a part of the household as possible. Ione brought him to church and the whole congregation applauded when Pastor Nelson announced the return of a prodigal son.

In Patty Jane's basement, Clyde Chuka set up a workbench for Thor behind the furnace. Temple Curry's attorney accompanied them to West River Road to pick up Thor's tools and as many of his birdhouses as they could fit into the trunk of the DeSoto. The lawyer apologized profusely.

"Really, had I known the circumstances, I would have turned her in immediately. I knew she was missing a marble or two, but I had no idea at all she was harboring a missing person."

Patty Jane and Ione came along to see the house which was now theirs. "As a gesture of goodwill," the attorney said, "I'll hire cleaners to toss out the garbage and save the valuables." He looked around at the towers of papers, boxes and pyramids of garbage bags. "If they can find any."

In silent, painful wonderment, Patty Jane and Ione explored the basement. Clutching each other, they stood next to a conclave of birdhouses that could have been a miniature block of Victorians in San Francisco.

"So he became an architect after all," whispered Patty Jane. "A builder of birdhouses."

Ione shook her head. "Not birdhouses, Patty Jane. Remember?"

Patty Jane recalled that autumn evening so many years ago when she had shown Ione the model house Thor had built for her.

"Love nests?" she said. "You think Thor was building love nests?"

"Building *you* love nests," said Ione.

Patty Jane whispered, "Oh, Ione, that's way too much for me."

Nora had gotten advice from everyone (How many soft knocks had there been on her bedroom door, how many voices asking, "Nora, open up, can we talk?"). Time, they all agreed, was the tonic that would make everything better, but what was she supposed to do until that time had passed?

She brought her best friend, Lori Mellstrom, home one afternoon and hustled her to her bedroom.

"Nora, is that you?" asked Ione, as the two girls reached the top of the stairs.

"Yeah, Grandma. Lori's with me."

"There's fresh coffee cake in the kitchen."

"Takk," said Nora, shutting her bedroom door.

Lori fell backwards on Nora's unmade bed. "God, Nora, what's the big rush?"

Nora didn't answer. She rummaged through her 45s and finally put on "The Last Train to Clarksville", even though both girls thought they were outgrowing The Monkees.

The girls lay on Nora's bed, their hands folded over their chests, staring at the ceiling. Nora had made a giant daisy out of shiny yellow contact paper and its petals spread from the ceiling light fixture.

"Miles Coombs said 'Hi' to me in the hall today," said Lori.

"I bet you could get him," said Nora. "I heard he's going to ask Brenda for his ring back."

For a moment, Nora allowed herself the luxury of thinking

about boys, but then she sat up and sighed wearily, hugging a pillow to her chest.

"Lori, promise you won't tell anyone if I tell you a secret?"

"Course not!" said Lori, scrambling to sit against the headboard. "What?"

Nora studied her fingernails. Clyde Chuka had given her a manicure but she had peeled away most of the frosted white polish.

"My dad's here," she said, so quickly that Lori shook her head, not understanding. "My dad is here in this house."

"What?"

The arm of the record player lifted and it clicked off.

"Aunt Harriet and Clyde Chuka found him a week ago. He was living with this crazy woman and he's really weird — it's like he's sort of retarded — he doesn't even know who I am!"

The last few words came riding out on a crest of a sob and Lori put her arm around her friend.

"I hate him, Lor — I hate him! He's like this little kid in this grownup body!" She wiped her nose with the back of her hand. "I feel sick just sitting near him! He's creepy looking — white like a ghost and skinny and bent over and I've heard all my life how I look like him and I can see it even though he mostly looks like some troll — I see myself in him and it freaks me out! I always imagined I'd find him on a canoe trip through the Boundary Waters. He'd be this guide, see, and I'd get caught in some white water and he would save me. It was going to be so cool! And now he drools when he eats."

Patty Jane noticed her daughter's red and swollen eyes when she came downstairs holding her best friend's hand. She watched as Nora brought Lori over to the arm chair where Thor sat and said, "Dad, this is my best friend, Lori Mellstrom. Lori, this is my dad."

Nora's plan had been to see her friend to the backdoor, to make Lori repeat her promise not to tell anyone what she had been told, but as they walked down the stairs and she saw Patty Jane pulling an afghan around Thor's shoulders, an immediate decision flamed in her mind: until I can handle things, I'll pretend I can handle things.

The simplicity of the plan astonished her; she felt the same exuberance as when she figured out an algebra problem. She repeated the new formula to herself: Until I can handle things, I'll pretend I can handle things.

Twenty-Four

ON THE MORNING of her sister's wedding day, Patty Jane woke to a pale winter light creeping beneath the window shade. She had barely slept, yet she awoke delighted to plunge into the day.

There had been a stag party of sorts the night before at Clyde Chuka's. Patty Jane and Harriet had crashed it, pounding on the door and shouting in gruff voices, "Party Patrol." They interrupted nothing more sinister than a poker game.

"Honey, I'm afraid I'm losing our honeymoon getaway money," said Reese.

"Win it back," said Harriet sweetly, kissing the top of his head. "Or don't come home."

Clyde Chuka had invited Thor but Nora said no, she'd take care of him; it wasn't as if Thor would feel left out or anything.

Patty Jane regarded her daughter with a mixture of pride and awe and because she couldn't help it, a small measure of cynicism. She watched as Nora served Thor his supper, tucking his napkin under his chin, cutting his meat, refilling his glass with the milk he couldn't seem to get enough of. Ione called her a

239

blessing and Harriet said, "We could all learn from her," but Patty Jane couldn't help thinking there was something forced about Nora's Devoted Daughter routine.

"What do you mean?" asked Nora, inspecting a pimple on her chin, in her mother's car mirror. Patty Jane was driving her to school.

"What's with this turnaround with your father?"

"What turnaround?"

Patty Jane sighed, tapping her fingers on the steering wheel. "Nora, you could barely look at Thor when we first got him back. And now . . . now you can't do enough for him."

Nora looked out her window, rubbing the condensation with her finger. "Hey, there's Greg Kraus. Drop me off here, okay?"

Before slamming the door, she ducked her head back in the car and said, "He's my dad."

"That doesn't really answer my question," said Patty Jane, watching her daughter run to her latest boyfriend.

Nora's vow to pretend to handle things until she really could handle them had a surprising benefit; she was starting to feel affection, real affection, for her father.

"He's pretty out-of-it," she confided to Lori, "and he's weird . . . but he's mine."

When the door had been shut on the last guest at the stag party, Patty Jane pushed Clyde Chuka against the door and kissed him hard. It was the first night she had stayed with him since Thor's return.

Certainly, nobody had expected her to give up her new love for one that only existed in memory, but she found herself putting Clyde Chuka off. She finally realized that it was not a warring sense of loyalty and confusion that kept her from Clyde Chuka's bed but exhaustion: her brain and heart were tired from the enormity of her new responsibilities.

Now, the morning after, Patty Jane turned on the radio and

made a pot of coffee, humming to The Lovin' Spoonful. She cleaned leisurely, tossing beer cans into a brown grocery bag and emptying ashtrays.

For the stag party, Clyde Chuka had moved his art pieces into a corner. Patty Jane studied one that stood on a pedestal of balled-up wire. A figure made of a fender, pieces of mirror and wire hangers rose up, taking the form of a woman or an animal — Patty Jane wasn't sure which. She circled it slowly, like a curious dog.

"Like it?"

Patty Jane jumped. Clyde Chuka was leaning against the door frame, his arms crossed, nude.

Patty Jane wiggled her eyebrows at him. "Do I ever."

He walked toward her and Patty Jane stepped back, watching him, her hand to her chin. "Hmmmm," she said, "fairly good lines, although this seems less a piece of uniformity than . . . struggle."

"Did you say struggle?" He was almost to her but Patty Jane stepped backward, keeping a foot of distance between them.

"No, I take that back." She let her eyes wander slowly down his chest to his groin. "Not struggle. Defeat."

Clyde Chuka's mouth split into a grin. "Defeat, you say. This tower of power looks defeated?"

"Ooh, that's what it is. Funny how subjective art can be."

They reached out for each other, waltzing backward to the couch.

The first snow of the winter of 1968 was falling as Patty Jane, matron of honor, led the small procession up the aisle of Ione's church. She wore a sky blue velvet dress. Clyde Chuka, watching her from his usher's vantage point at the front of the church, thought she looked a dazzling mixture of princess and prom queen.

Patty Jane wobbled a bit as she walked. She wore a pair of

high-heeled pumps dyed to match her dress. Harriet had insisted her sister retire her clodhoppers for the day.

Before the organist had begun the wedding march, Patty Jane had smoothed Nora's hair and straightened Thor's lapels; she had admired Harriet's bouquet — an array of casablanca lilies, stephanotis, and tea roses — remembering the garden flowers they had stolen for her wedding; there had been nervous chatter and quick makeup checks and a reminder to Nora not to walk too fast. It was only now, as she stood at the front of the church, that Patty Jane allowed herself to step out of the proceedings and simply watch. Clyde Chuka, his hair woven into a tight braid, looked as handsome as a man in a rented tux could look. Ione sat in the front row, smart in her beige suit, flanked by her son and her granddaughter. Thor was still thin and stooped, but from his daily walks with Patty Jane and Clyde Chuka, he now had more color and the deep blue crescents under his eyes were fading. His smile was strong and white; as Temple Curry had said, she had maintained his teeth.

Looking at Nora, Patty Jane felt a burst of mother love. Her daughter wore a dusky rose taffeta dress Ione had sewn. As she came down the aisle, Inky Kolstat snapped her picture, remarking loudly, "She's like a teenage Tuesday Weld."

The organist held a mighty chord before launching into "Trumpet Voluntary." Harriet came up the aisle wearing the dress she had picked out for her wedding with Avel. Under the gauzy net of her veil, her hair hung down her back in loose waves. She held the bouquet as well as a lily she had taken from Avel's grave. ("I know he'd celebrate our marriage," Harriet had told Reese. "This way he can at least send flowers.")

Reese held Harriet's hand, running his thumb along her palm. He was taller than Harriet by nearly a foot and more than twice her weight, and yet it was her sure, steady grip that was holding him up, that kept him from passing out from humility and happiness.

Harriet pressed her shoulder into his, feeling safe in its solidness. She thought that some of her worst days — the days when her mourning for Avel was so mind-destroying; the days when she was living in the streets and selling herself for a bottle — those days were not as bad as this day was good.

Pastor Nelson finished a prayer for unity and Evelyn Bright, rustling in a dress of a hundred chiffon pleats, walked from the front pew to the harp by the baptismal font. She sat down, rubbed her hands together, and began to play *"Greensleeves,"* her face pink with intensity. She had bought the wedding couple monogrammed pillowcases, but this song was her gift to Harriet.

Nora tapped her feet and fidgeted and scratched until her grandmother shot her a disapproving look. She was a co-conspirator in what was coming next and it was hard to suppress her excitement. According to the program, after the harp solo, the vows were to be taken, but Nora knew there was an unannounced act coming.

Evelyn Bright finished the song with a plink at the end of her glissando and there was a reverent moment of silence, the equivalent of applause in the church.

Nora saw the pastor's slight nod, his signal, and watched as Harriet let go of Reese's hand, patted it and turned around. Harriet walked to the left side of the church, the train of her gown sweeping the carpet. As the congregation began to murmur, she went to the podium and bent slightly, all the while smiling widely at Nora. There was a round of shoulder shrugs in the wedding party.

Harriet lifted the tent of netting that covered her face, looked at Reese and then, from inside the podium, removed her trumpet. She fingered the keys briefly, wet her lips, and put it to her mouth. She played the song she finally felt capable of playing, the song Louis Armstrong had made his hymn, "What a Wonderful World."

For the past month she had been picking Nora up from

school (explaining to Patty Jane that she didn't get to see enough of her niece these days) and they drove to the Vet's Hospital parking lot to practice their trumpets. Nora was astonished at her aunt's remembered technique and skill — she hadn't played since Avel died — but Harriet said, no, her breath control stunk, she might never get her lip back, and didn't Nora hear how her notes flattened at the end?

Aunt and niece had spent happy hours in the DeSoto under darkening late autumn skies, practicing scales and duets. Occasionally people would sit on the trunks of their cars, listening for a few moments before visiting the hospital.

Patty Jane was ready to throw her bouquet to the rafters when she heard Harriet's first few bars. She was so thrilled she didn't notice her own daughter slip out of the pew until she was next to her aunt, taking out her own hidden trumpet. Nora accompanied Harriet as her aunt put her trumpet down and sang her favorite verse:

> I see skies of blue and clouds of white,
> The bright blessed day, the dark sacred night . . .
> And I think to myself,
> What a wonderful world.

After the sung verse, Nora took the harmony, playing to the left side of the church while Harriet blew the melody to the right. Nora held the last note while Harriet climbed up and down a dizzying scale. Then they pulled their mouthpieces away from their lips at the same time. The congregation couldn't help it; they burst into an applause that shook the lilies in the plant stands. Harriet kissed her niece and Nora carried the trumpets back to the pew where Thor, in a gesture he had learned from a television commercial, made a circle out of his thumb and forefinger.

"Wowie," he said. "Wowie, Nora."

Twenty-Five

"You won't need that, Ione," said Patty Jane.

"Yeah, Grandma," said Nora, taking a cardigan from her, "you've already packed three sweaters."

"I just like to be prepared," said Ione. She stood in the middle of the bedroom, hands on her hips. On her bed lay the green suitcases that for years had held nothing more than hope and dust. She had dreamed of lugging them into Paris hotels and cruise ship suites and tents pitched in the Kalahari, but now the prospect of actually packing them was daunting.

Norman and Ruth Fitch, a retired couple from her church, were going to tour the United States by camper and had offered Ione the chance to ride shotgun.

"You've talked about traveling for years," said Ruth, who was Ione's closest friend in the Naomi Circle, "now we're giving you the chance."

"Won't I be in the way?" asked Ione.

"If you are, we'll send you home," said Ruth.

"By Parcel Post," added her husband.

When Ione told Patty Jane of her plans, her daughter-in-law applauded, "Oh, Ione, it's what you've always wanted to do."

"Well," said Ione, looking at her son sleeping on the wing chair, an afghan draped over him. "I think I will cancel. I have Thor to think of now."

Patty Jane let out an exasperated puff of breath. "Ione, don't insult me. I'll be here. Nora'll be here — Hellonia, we'll all be here. Just because you're his mother doesn't mean you're the only capable one."

Ione flushed. "Uff-da, Patty Jane, I don't mean that." She shook her head, trying to cool the warmth on her cheeks. "I . . . I just don't want to burden anyone to fill up my own desire."

Patty Jane placed her coffee cup none too gently on its saucer. "Ione, I'm not in the mood for any Norske guilt right now. Think of yourself for a change!"

Ione and the Fitches made up an extensive list of *must sees*: antebellum mansions of the South, the Grand Canyon, Pennsylvania Amish Country (Ione could understand how a group of people could live without electricity and modern transportation, but zippers?), the coast of Maine. Their arrival back in Minneapolis wasn't scheduled.

Ione surveyed the mounds of clothing.

"So you don't think I'll need all this?"

Impulsively, Patty Jane hugged her. "Ione," she said, feeling the woman's strong back under her hands. "You've emptied all your drawers and your whole closet."

"My stars," said Ione, her voice a soft, girlish whisper, "my dreams have come true and I'm scared I won't know what to do with them."

But she did. She regaled the House of Curl with technicolor postcards: Mesas at Sunset, Nebraska Cornfields at Sunset, Hollywood Boulevard at Sunset, Sunset at Yellowstone. Nora charted the progress of the traveling seniors with pushpins she jabbed into a map hung above the appointments desk. The pins followed a wavy line to the West Coast and then gradually fanned out as Ione and the Fitches began traveling eastward.

"My," said Crabby Bultram, surveying the map as her pincurls dried, "that woman is going to wear herself out."

"San Francisco," said Paige Larkin dreamily, looking at the map, "Spence and I spent a weekend at the Top of the Mark. Talk about romantic."

"Los Angeles," whispered Inky Kolstat, "I hope she doesn't forget my matchbooks from the Brown Derby."

The mailman had just delivered another postcard (Sunset over the Alamo) and Patty Jane read it aloud.

" 'I'm eating chili full of beef and peppers. Last night Ruth and I got out the sleeping bags and slept under a big western sky. We're thinking of becoming Cow Girls."

"My ex lives in Texas," said Alva Bundt, being combed out. "He's drilling for oil but from the size of my last child support check, he hasn't struck yet."

"I sure wouldn't mind doing some traveling," said Bev. She spritzed the mirror in front of her vanity with window cleaner and rubbed the mist in with the cuff of her smock. "Ten below today, did you hear?"

Patty Jane arched her eyebrows. She had already reprimanded Bev earlier about not cleaning her combs and brushes. Remembering how defensive Bev had become, she decided not to lecture her about using a cloth to clean glass versus one's own uniform. Bev's son Ricky was in bootcamp and her mind was on his leaving for Viet Nam.

Patty Jane checked the appointments book. A new customer was coming in for a frosting at eleven. She had a half hour of free time.

"Harriet, let's take a break." She looked up from the book. "Harriet."

Harriet, who had been dozing behind her harp, opened her

eyes and leaned forward, bringing down the front legs of her chair. "Huh?"

"I was going to ask you to join me on break but I guess you were already taking one."

Harriet yawned. "Put the coffee on. I need it."

To the percussion of Thor's hammering downstairs, Patty Jane started the coffee and scavenged through the kitchen cupboards, looking for something to put on a dessert plate. In Ione's absence, her homemade desserts had been replaced by store-bought cellophane-wrapped cookies and packaged cakes with indefinite shelf lives.

"Harriet, are you all right?" asked Patty Jane. She scrutinized her sister carefully.

"I'm tired, that's all," said Harriet, lighting a cigarette.

"Maybe you need a check-up."

Harriet exhaled smoke, trying to restrain a smile.

"What?" asked Patty Jane. "What's going on?"

"Sex. Sex, sex, sex. I'm a newlywed, Patty Jane, and I'm suffering from the effects of too much sex." She sipped her coffee. "That or the end result of sex."

A grin traveled to the fullest corners of Patty Jane's face. "How far along are you?"

Harriet shrugged. "A couple of weeks? I can't tell. You know how irregular my periods are. I think I had a grand total of five last year."

Patty Jane narrowed her eyes, studying the bones under her sister's open collar. "I didn't think there was any left to lose, but it looks like you've lost some weight."

"Just like you did, remember?"

Patty Jane nodded, smiling. "At first, yeah. Thor said, 'No one can be pregnant and lose weight at the same time.'" She tilted her head slightly, listening to the hammering. Thor had made two dozen more birdhouses in the five months he'd been with them. "Are you throwing up at all?"

Harriet shook her head. "Just when I think of labor."

Patty Jane stretched her arms across the table and took Harriet's hands in her own. "What does Reese think?"

Suddenly shy, Harriet pulled her hands out from Patty Jane's and wiped a drop of coffee off her cup. "I haven't told him yet. I've sort of been waiting for confirmation."

"Then go to a doctor."

Harriet laughed. "This from the woman who didn't see a doctor until she was in her seventh month?"

"Times have changed. Besides, I knew everything was fine."

An eclipse of worry passed across Harriet's face. "And you don't think everything is for me?"

"I was twenty-one, Harriet. You're thirty-five. You should be monitored, that's all."

Harriet struck a match but shook it out. "I'm trying to cut down on these things."

Over dinner of gummy elbow macaroni and hamburger, Clyde Chuka asked, "Nora, what gives with your mom and Harriet? They're giggling like maniacs."

Nora speared a piece of limp macaroni with her fork. "You don't think this stuff is funny?"

Thor, who ate Patty Jane's slap-dash cooking with the same relish as Ione's professional meals, looked up from his plate, smiling. While the complex machines that propel a funny story or sail a one-liner had broken down in him, he enjoyed the sound of laughter and responded to it.

"Oh, Dad," said Nora, "don't encourage them." She took his plate and her own and rinsed them at the kitchen sink.

She had turned fifteen the week before and felt immeasurably more mature than the giggling older women. She put the kettle on for her father; after dinner, Thor liked hot water with lemon.

"Nora, honey, don't be mad." Patty Jane wiped tears from her eyes.

"I'm not *mad*, Mother," said Nora, cutting a wedge of lemon.

"I am," said Clyde Chuka, feigning gruffness. "Didn't anyone teach you two manners?"

"No!" screeched Patty Jane and Harriet simultaneously.

Nora set the cup of hot lemon water in front of Thor. She excused herself then, citing math homework. Patty Jane looked at Harriet and Harriet nodded, understanding the question in her sister's eyes.

"Party time in Nora's room," said Patty Jane, rising. "Men do the dishes."

Nora groaned as her mother and aunt followed her up to her bedroom. She had planned on doing *some* math, but more importantly, Greg Kraus was going to call her at seven-thirty and she didn't need an audience. Patty Jane had given her a birthday present she had long coveted — her own Princess phone.

"I'm going to have a cousin?" asked Nora. "I mean a real one?" She sat on her bed, leaning against the headboard. Patty Jane and Harriet sprawled across it on their stomachs, their legs swaying lazily in the air.

"I'm not absolutely sure but I'm pretty positive," said Harriet. "Just don't tell anyone yet."

"What about Uncle Reese?"

Harriet smiled. "Nora, when he hears this news, the man will blow a gasket. He sits in Dale and Bonnie's rooms when he misses them. He'd love another kid." Her voice softened. "My instinct is pretty reliable, but I want to be 100 percent positive before I tell him."

"Well, they can test you, you know." Nora counseled her aunt.

Patty Jane smiled at her daughter. "We called this afternoon. Harriet goes in to kill the rabbit Thursday."

Nora couldn't help but admire how pretty and young her mother looked, lying there like one of her friends, legs crossed at the ankle and waving in the air.

"You're goofy, Ma," she said, pushing her feet against her mother's side.

"I'm goofy?" Patty Jane rolled over, grabbing Nora's feet. "What about your crazy aunt here?"

"I hate to break this up," Clyde Chuka said, opening the door, "but Myrna's in the kitchen, setting up for her cooking class."

"So?" said Patty Jane.

"Tonight's topic is 'Exciting Entrées', said Clyde Chuka, his face taking on an expression of exaggerated concern, "Don't you think you'd better sit in, Patty Jane?"

"Forty-two states," said Ione, looking at the map that lay like a paper blanket over her lap. "I can't believe that we've seen forty-two states."

"We'll see four more new ones on the way home," said Norman Fitch. "That'll bring our grand total up to forty-six."

"We can add, dear," said Ruth.

Ione smiled. She had spent nearly five months on the road with the Fitches and they were still friends. They were sitting on the fold-up plastic woven chairs next to the camper, admiring the rocky Maine beach in the fading light. The coffee pot, charred black, perked over the fire; earlier they had grilled cobs of corn and three lobsters bought from a fisherman. It had been the best meal Ione had ever eaten.

It was late May, and the air was tinged with the deep green smell of forest pine and salt from the Atlantic waters. Ione carefully folded up the map, worn from so much use. She planned to frame it and hang it in a place of honor.

"Thanks to you both," she said softly. "Thank you for taking me along."

"There she goes again," said Ruth, "thanking us when we should be thanking her." Ruth dumped the used coffee grounds into the fire. "You know Norm and I can't travel by ourselves anymore. Our nerves can't take it."

"In fact," said Norman, "Ruth and I were talking just the other night. We'd like you to referee all our trips."

Even though homesickness sometimes plagued her like a low-grade fever, Ione prayed their offer was serious.

"Grandma's on her way home!" announced Nora, reading the back of a postcard (Sunset over Bangor).

"I hope she remembered my matchbooks," said Inky Kolstat.

It was a Saturday morning and the House of Curl was a hive of young women all hoping to be Prom Queen. Prom Night was hours away and girls from Roosevelt High and Minnehaha Academy paged through *Seventeen* and *Mademoiselle* and *Vogue*, looking at the models' hairdos, wondering if the French Twist worn by Jean Shrimpton or Lauren Hutton's geometric cut could be re-created on them. Several of the regulars agreed to postpone their standing appointments and played Scrabble in the dining room while Patty Jane and Dixie and Bev tried to keep order in what Clyde Chuka called the "feminine war zone."

Harriet had retired to her old bedroom to take a nap, claiming no one could hear her harp above the chatter anyway. Nora sat at the appointments desk, looking through the rest of the mail while sneaking looks at the senior girls. She would be a sophomore that fall.

"When did she say she was coming back?" asked Clyde Chuka. He was manicuring the nails of a girl who told him she had never touched an Indian before.

"She doesn't say," said Nora, picking up the ringing phone. "Patty Jane's House of Curl . . . one moment please." She held her palm over the mouthpiece. "Mom, do you have time for a shampoo and style this afternoon?"

"Another Prom Queen?" asked Patty Jane, waving away a cloud of hairspray.

Nora nodded.

"Sure," said Patty Jane, sighing. "But make it after three."

Flushed from overwork, Patty Jane was nevertheless enjoying the morning's madness. She had spent her own first prom in the emergency ward, waiting for doctors to sew up her father, who had fallen against an end table. In honor of Patty Jane's prom, he had raised more than one glass and then collapsed, his forehead meeting the edge of the table. Anna had been sleeping, so Patty Jane, who had just gotten her driver's license, knew she must drive her father to the hospital. She had draped her father's arm around her shoulder and hoisted him up. Blood from his forehead dribbled down the bodice of her pale yellow prom dress: a splattered red appliqué.

"Too late," she said, "my dress is ruined."

In the hospital waiting room, feeling martyred, she had watched people in various stages of distress stagger by.

"Somebody shoot you?" asked a small boy whose broken arm had been freshly cast.

Patty Jane shook her head and folded her gloved arms across her chest, trying to hide the blood.

Elmo had cried on the way home. "I ruined your prom, baby."

"It's not the first thing you ruined, Dad."

"Oh, baby," he said, crying harder, burying his head in his hands.

"Aw, Dad," Patty Jane said finally, hating her father for making her always feel she had to lighten the blame, "I'm just a junior. I can go next year."

"Is this what you had in mind?" asked Patty Jane, twirling the girl's chair in front of the mirror. It was a hairdo of four-inch high loops on the top of her head, corraled by a pink satin ribbon.

"Perfect," said the girl, smiling at her confident reflection, "it's absolutely perfect for a Prom Queen."

At the end of the day, twenty-one potential Prom Queens

had been processed at the House of Curl. Patty Jane collapsed on the couch. The scent of lilacs climbed through the open windows and she closed her eyes and inhaled the delicate sachet, a happy change from hairspray, setting gels, and overheated curling irons. Thor was curled up, asleep, on the opposite side of the couch and Patty Jane petted his stockinged foot affectionately.

"Thor, honey, your mom's coming home soon."

He didn't stir; Patty Jane had learned the only difference between Thor's sleep and that of a normal comatose was that Thor would wake up for dinner.

"Gee, Mom," said Nora, handing her mother a bottle of Tab, "Could you believe those girls? Hair, makeup, boys. Hair, makeup, boys. That's all I heard them talk about all day."

"Seems to me you've had certain opinions on those subjects."

Nora sat down and put her feet up on the coffee table.

"Yeah, well, I've got opinions about a lot of things. Like the war, for instance. How many of these girls worrying about being a Prom Queen do you see out protesting? None, I'll bet. Their hair would get all messy." Bev's son, Ricky — Nora's first crush — had been killed the second week of his tour of duty, stirring Nora's conscience to join demonstrations at the "U." She raised her voice with the college students in their recitations of "What do we want? Peace! When do we want it? Now!" She had also begun a Senate letter-writing campaign in civics class and embroidered peace signs into her jeans.

"Where is Clyde?" asked Patty Jane as Nora turned on the news.

"He ran up to Charlie's for some hamburgers. He said he wasn't in the mood for a Patty Jane Surprise."

"Hey, I can't wait for Ione to be back in the kitchen, either," Patty Jane said defensively.

"You said — and this is quoting you, Mom — 'With Ione

gone, it'll be the perfect opportunity for me to learn how to cook again.'"

"*Again*," laughed Patty Jane. "As if I ever really knew how." She stretched, watching a TV commercial in which a blond with a Swedish accent urged the audience to "Take it all off." "And where's that lazy bum, Harriet? She's been holed up in her room all day."

Harriet was sleeping, her bedsheets tangled around her legs.

"Harriet? Wake up, honey. Reese'll be here soon."

Nora, following her mother into the room, bumped into a wastebasket. "Mom!"

Patty Jane leaned toward her daughter, craning her neck to see inside the wastebasket. It was filled with wadded bloody tissues.

"Did she have a bloody nose?" asked Nora.

Patty Jane shrugged and turned to Harriet, shaking her hard. "Harriet, honey, wake up. Wake up!"

Harriet mumbled and began a yawn, but it was interrupted by a fit of coughing. There was something frantic in her eyes and she pointed to the box of Kleenex on the night stand.

She pulled out several tissues and held them to her mouth, her face purpling with the cough.

When the attack faded, Harriet sat very still, the tissues still pressed to her mouth.

"Let me see those," said Patty Jane, prying open her sister's hand. They were splotchy with brown sputum and blood and Patty Jane stared at them, sickened.

"Harriet," what's going on?"

Nora stood, whitefaced, and the Dixie cup of water she had gotten for her aunt trembled.

Harriet rubbed her face in her hands, wiping away fatigue. "Nothing," she said finally, and the voice that escaped through her throat was raspy. "I had a coughing spell, that's all."

Patty Jane picked up the wastebasket and shook it. "I'd say you had quite a few."

Harriet drank the water Nora gave her. "What?" The innocence in her voice was as sincere as an airport gift.

"How long have you been coughing up blood?"

Harriet shook her head.

"What does Reese think?"

"It's not something I choose to share with my husband, Patty Jane. 'Oh, look at all this gook on my Kleenex, honey.' "

"We're going to the doctor on Monday," said Patty Jane.

"Yeah," said Nora, her face brightening, "and then we can see how the baby's doing!"

"Yeah," said Harriet finally. "I suppose it's time."

Ione laid her hand on the horn, announcing the camper's arrival into the driveway. She had driven the last leg of their journey, leaving Des Moines at noon, and yet her fatigue vanished completely once they entered the Minneapolis city limits. She raced out of the cab, calling back to the Fitches to please remember the presents, threw open the back door and posed on the threshold like a vaudevillian who had just finished her act. But there was no after-supper gathering around the table. She ran through the dining room, the living room; she checked the bathroom and Patty Jane's room and then took the stairs two at a time, but each room she entered on the second floor was empty.

"No one's home," she said to Norman Fitch, who had trundled in behind her, arms filled with the gifts.

"You mind if Ruth and I take off then? We're kind of anxious to get to the old homestead."

"Remember," said Ruth, "this is just the beginning."

Nora was the first to see the opened back door.

"Grandma's home!"

Patty Jane bit her lip and looked at Clyde Chuka.

"Now remember," he said, "let's give her some time to enjoy her homecoming. Let her tell a few stories, show some pictures. She'll know soon enough." He turned the ignition off and they sat in the darkened car interior for a moment.

"Okay, Nora?" asked Patty Jane.

"Okay," said Nora, petulant. "You don't have to tell me twice." She roused her father, dozing in the back seat. "Come on Dad, your mom's home."

Patty Jane led the quiet group through the gentle night air, practicing a few smiles, hoping for a moment that Ione was tired and had gone to bed. But Ione was there to steer them to the kitchen table.

"Presents for everyone." She took Thor by the arm. "Hvordan har du det?"

He answered in Norwegian that he was fine and Patty Jane smiled, for Thor sounded like a child, his Norwegian clear and lilting. What a miracle that his mother's language was one of the few things that remained in a mind which had erased so much. But then she noticed a strange look on Ione's face and her hand clutching the collar of her blouse.

"Ione?" she said.

Ione shushed her viciously, staring at her son as he continued in the sweet and singing language of Norway. When he finished, he smiled and shifted his attention to the pan of fudge on the counter.

Ione looked at her son, scooping up fudge with his finger. Her eyes locked on her daughter-in-law's and Patty Jane felt the challenge in them.

"Thor tells me Harriet is sick." Her voice quivered. "He says she's going to die."

A great weariness fell upon Patty Jane as she nodded assent to the words Ione had just spoken.

"It's cancer, Ione. It's in her lungs, moving fast."

Ione stood up and Nora was struck by how her grandmother looked like a sad, old child. Ione sniffed and wiped her tears with the back of her fingers, suddenly businesslike.

"Will you take me to Reese's, Patty Jane?" she asked. "I'd like to bring Harriet the music box I bought her."

It was eleven-thirty and most of the houses on Reese's street were dark. A light summer breeze blew the smells of dewy grass and flowering bushes into their screened windows. No lights shone in Reese and Harriet's house, either, but they were both up, on lawn chairs in their backyard. On a wrought iron table, several candles flickered in their webbed glass enclosures. Reese was shirtless, and a band of sweat ran parallel to the waistband of his shorts. Harriet was shivering under a blanket. After the diagnosis, she had gamely announced, "No more cigarettes," and while she hadn't stopped cold turkey ("How can I quit now when I'm so nervous about this?" she had asked Patty Jane as she lit up in the car on the way home from the doctor's), she was limiting her intake to less than half a pack a day. She reassured Reese and Patty Jane that she was going to beat it, but in that place of absolute knowledge, buried deep behind arteries and muscle, she knew that death had begun its march. Still, she argued with herself, she had been wrong before.

Her main concern now, reclining on the patio furniture they had bought just the week before, was not to worry her husband, to control her hurricane cough, and to resist the urge to sleep around the clock.

"Someone's in the driveway," said Reese, setting his glass on the table. He opened the gate and by the light of the street lamp, he saw Ione knocking gently at the door.

"Hey, Ione," he called. "We're back here."

Harriet pushed her blanket down but Ione, walking briskly toward her, said, "Now, don't get up for me."

Harriet smiled. "So when did the Gypsy Woman get back?"

Ione swallowed hard, wanting to cry out, "Your hair! Your beautiful hair!" There was hardly anything left of Harriet's waist-length chestnut hair, only a few stubborn tufts that poked out of her scalp like weeds out of a cracked sidewalk.

"We . . . just got in this evening," she said. "I brought you some presents."

"For you, Reese," she said. Reese opened a small silver box and drew out a pinch of dirt.

"The dirt's from Gettysburg," explained Ione. And the snuff box, the clerk told me, belonged to a Rebel soldier from Savannah."

"What am I missing?" asked Harriet.

"Ione and I have become students of the Civil War," said Reese.

"What?" Harriet looked to Patty Jane, but she only shrugged back an answer. "When did this happen?"

"When we saw *Jezebel* on TV," said Reese. "You gals were at one of Inky's things and we were sitting around learning about the fall of the Confederacy."

"And that Bette Davis," said Ione shaking her head. "Uff-da mayda."

"Well, thanks, Ione," said Reese, fingering the initials engraved on the lid. "Now I've got a Civil War collection, well, the start of one."

Harriet smiled at her husband. "And I thought your only hobby was watering the lawn." The last word of her sentence was lost by an eruption of coughs.

When Harriet leaned back, gasping for air, the night air resounded with silence. Her breathing returned to normal, and she was able to ask Ione, "Now what do you have for me? If it's anything for my hair, I'll kill you."

The nausea had been an easier side-effect of the chemotherapy than losing handfuls of her long hair. Patty Jane had cut it short so that the loss wouldn't be so startling, but soon enough there was no way to disguise Harriet's baldness. Tonight, not expecting company, she had neglected to put her scarf on.

Ione set the present in Harriet's lap and Harriet unwrapped it carefully, lifting each piece of tape like a bandage from a child's knee.

"A music box!"

"We got it in Vermont. It's an antique. At least that's what the shop owner told me. It looks old though, don't you think? Of course, you can never tell when you're getting ribbed off in one of those places." Ione clamped her mouth shut to stop her nervous chatter.

Harriet opened the lid. The lilting notes of "The Harmonious Blacksmith" colored the air.

"Handel," said Harriet. Her eyes shone. "Thank you. You've heard all about me, I take it."

Ione nodded glumly.

"Squealer," said Harriet, narrowing her eyes at her sister.

Patty Jane smiled bitterly. "We thought she was pregnant."

Harriet shook her head. Shadows played on her face from the candles and Ione saw Harriet's eczema had returned fullforce.

"I wanted to be. Boy, did I want to be." Reese's hand found hers. "I mean, to have Reese's child. And then to be pregnant . . . well, it would have explained a lot of how I felt."

"We'll help you in every way we can," said Ione.

"I know," said Harriet.

Down the block, a dog barked. Harriet lifted the music lid and they sat quietly, listening to the sounds of Handel.

Twenty-Six

THE SUMMER OF 1969 was rainy and emerald green exploded throughout the Twin Cities. Lawns grew in fast motion. Minnehaha Falls roared down into a churning creek. Sunday afternoon picnickers, encouraged by a blue morning sky, often found themselves gathering up by briquets and cake pans as rain pelted the park.

Reese and Harriet had moved into Harriet's room above the House of Curl, traveling back to St. Paul twice a week for lawn care, general maintenance and, Harriet joked, conjugual visits.

Having Harriet close was a source of relief to Patty Jane. She took her cue from Harriet, who seemed determined to delight in every day, to spend her hours like lottery winnings.

Harriet still played her harp in the shop for short intervals and she occasionally announced Dance Breaks. Patty Jane had planned to cancel the summer's classes, but Harriet insisted they go on — "Shoot, I've been waiting all year for Inky's 'Annual Hollywood Extravaganza Slide Show.' "

On her "Independence Day Is Discount Permanents Day" circulars, Patty Jane added the P.S.: "We always need your business but right now we especially need your friendship. Come by often."

Daily the shop was crowded: Myrna Johnson had her hair trimmed Monday but returned on Wednesday to show off her new waffle iron; Paige Larkin came in every morning, passing around her new blond baby; Inky brought in scrapbooks from her days as an Orpheum usher. Gloom was buried beneath jokes and gossip and the fellowship of women united to make things easier for the sisters.

One evening, after Reese and Harriet had gone to a movie, Patty Jane made a telephone call, only allowing the voice on the other end a "Hello?" before unleashing her invective.

"Evelyn Bright, if you're not ashamed of yourself, I am."

There was a pause on the line and a tremulous, "Patty Jane?"

"Don't you think Harriet notices your absence? Of course she does. How dare you stay away when she needs you the most?"

"Patty Jane — "

"If you're not here tomorrow morning, I don't want to see you in here again."

"Patty Jane, I love Harriet, you know that, but I just can't stand to see her sick, I just can't." Patty Jane hung up.

Evelyn Bright was at the shop the next morning when it opened.

"I'm here!" she cried out, her arms outstretched. She drank cup after cup of sugary coffee and watched for Harriet anxiously, occasionally participating in Dixie's and Karen Spaeth's debate on whether one could absorb knowledge by sleeping with a book under the pillow.

"Nonsense," said Karen, "what does the ear do? Scan the pages and then translate the information to the mind?"

Dixie slid a rattail comb up and down Karen's hair. "All's I know is this: my daughter sleeps with her geometry book every night and she brought home a B+ on her semester final. She spritzed Adorn into the crown of Karen's head — excessively, Evelyn Bright thought. "All's I'm saying is Debbie's no mathematician so how do you explain the B+?"

"Maybe she cheated," said Evelyn.

Karen laughed but Dixie's smile was sour.

Evelyn was thankful she was holding Paige Larkin's baby when Harriet finally entered the House of Curl. Evelyn lifted the baby in front of her, his fat legs kicking, until she could rearrange her features into an expression other than shock.

"Evelyn, you old dog," said Harriet, grinning. "I thought you had ditched me for some other musical prodigy."

The smile Evelyn had strained to hold suddenly collapsed and she burst into tears. As Harriet hugged her, Evelyn bowed her head in shame. Instead of comforting her friend, her friend was comforting her.

"I'm so sorry," she said finally, dabbing at her eyes with a scented bandana exactly like the one Harriet was wearing. "I was just so scared to see you."

"I don't blame you," said Harriet. "I'm scared to see myself." She began to cough, racking coughs that bent her over. Evelyn's renewed tears broke the silent agreement between the women in the shop to keep cheer afloat. As they all responded in the same way, swabbing their eyes and blowing their noses, a new customer opened the door to the House of Curl. Immediately, she did an about-face and walked out, thinking, "Someone must have gotten a *really* bad perm."

"What do you think," asked Harriet, striking a pose. "Cleopatra?" She set a blond wig on her head. "Yvette Mimieux?"

Patty Jane nodded. "Not too bad. But I still like the dark one. It makes you look gamine — like Audrey Hepburn or Leslie Caron."

"I like 'gamine,'" said Harriet. She put the short wig back on, fluffing its curls with her fingers. Looking into the mirror, she sucked in her already sunken cheeks. "I'll take it."

She and Patty Jane had spent nearly an hour in the hat and wig department of Power's, trying to find something not too ridiculous to cover her bald head. By silent agreement, the sisters tried to make the outing fun, firing jokes like sharpshooters even as they were about to surrender.

Surrender, according to the doctor they had just visited, was a strategy they should consider.

"We could start on a new course of treatment," he had said, looking not into, but just above Harriet's eyes. "But I think it would only make you sicker." Patty Jane had always appreciated Dr. Hurley's honesty, but now she wanted him to lie, lie through his teeth.

"So what do I do?" asked Harriet, tying and retying the ends of her scarf.

The doctor lifted his hands, palms upward.

"I'd get my affairs in order," the doctor said.

The saleslady rang up the wig.

"It looks real cute on you," she said, handing Harriet the sales slip.

Harriet fingered the stiff curls. "It sure is hot."

"All wigs are," said the saleslady. "You'll get used to it."

As the doors closed on the elevator to the Tearoom, Harriet suddenly and forcefully cried out, "Well, doctors can be wrong, you know!"

Five other women turned their heads to look at Harriet and then, in unison, moved them back.

"That's right," said Patty Jane. "You know," she said, her voice light, "I'll bet this one doesn't know what he's talking about."

Harriet flashed a frantic smile. "I'll bet he got his medical license by mail order."

The five other women on the elevator stared at the floor indicators.

"I heard he wanted to be a proctologist," said Patty Jane, "but he couldn't tell his you-know-what from his elbow."

"Oh my," said one of the shoppers.

Harriet shook her head, tsking. "You don't say. I heard he wanted to be a brain surgeon but they decided a man shouldn't operate on something he doesn't have himself."

"He's the dumbest doctor on the planet Earth," said Patty Jane.

Harriet nodded. "Did you see him try to take my temperature with the stethoscope?"

The elevator door opened and the other shoppers quickly hustled out. "Let's go home," said Patty Jane. "Didn't Ione say something about making some apple pie?"

The group assembled for Paige Larkin's "Making the Most of Your Money" seminar had already devoured one of the apple pies.

"Sure, it's easy for her to make the most of my money," Bev Beal whispered to Dixie. "Her great aunt just left her ten grand."

"Plus her husband's in insurance," whispered Dixie back.

It wasn't a class the two hairstylists would normally attend, but neither had an appointment and Ione's desserts made any class bearable.

"Will you two be quiet?" asked Alva Bundt. Encouraged by Clyde Chuka, she had begun to market her folk art and rosemaling and fantasized about opening a small business.

Karen Spaeth was asking why, as a single woman, it was so hard to get credit, when Gudrun Mueller raised her hand and asked if anyone minded if they talked about Harriet.

"What's Harriet go to do with financial independence?" asked Alva.

"Nothing," said the German woman quietly. "I just think it would help to talk about her."

"I agree," said Crabby. "Who's going to teach 'Music Appreciation?' What about our choral group?"

Her jowls dimpled as she bowed her head. "I'll miss her more than I can say. I'll miss the music she brought into my life."

"You see?" said Gudrun. "I think talking can only help us."

"I wasn't all that confident in my singing but she let me take the solo part in 'That Old Black Magic,'" sniffed Crabby. She said my voice reminded her of Rosemary Clooney's!"

"That's it for me," said Bev Beal. She stood up, brushing pie crumbs off her smock. "I'm not going to hold a wake for someone who isn't even dead."

Crabby blew her nose. "She said I had rhythm! Nobody in my whole life ever told me I had rhythm!"

Twenty-Seven

REESE TOOK A leave of absence from the police force and increased the male population at the House of Curl. He sat by Harriet on the small chair at the appointments desk and listened to her play the harp. He passed her tissues when the coughing got bad. Answering the salon's telephone had become Reese's duty, as Nora had her first out-of-the-shop job, wearing a white paper hat and a bleached apron to fill orders for Strato-Burgers at the Airloha Drive-In.

"Patty Jane's House of Curl," Reese announced in his deep voice, "hold the line, please."

Now that there was general acknowledgment of Harriet's illness, she felt as if a knapsack of bricks had dropped off her shoulders. No pretending that she was suffering from nothing more serious than a rough cold. Still, she struggled with panic, fighting the blackness.

"Reese," she begged, "don't let me go."

"I won't," Reese said, praying he was telling the truth.

Late one night, Patty Jane was shaken out of a deep sleep.

"What?" she cried, realizing that the grip on her shoulder couldn't be Clyde Chuka. He was working late in his studio.

"Patty Jane," whispered Harriet, crawling into bed with her sister. "It's me."

"What time is it?" said Patty Jane. "Are you all right?"

"No!"

Patty Jane held her sister's narrow knobby body, shivering in its sweat-dampened nightgown.

"What's the matter, honey?"

Harriet gasped for breath. "I'm so scared, Patty Jane. I'm so afraid I think I'm going crazy."

"Oh, honey. Scared isn't crazy."

"What will happen to me?" asked Harriet. "What if there *is* an eternity? I don't want to be me through all eternity!" The absurd truth of Harriet's words was enough to make a tiny prick in Patty Jane's grief and she let herself laugh.

"What's so funny?" Outrage stiffened Harriet's voice.

"Oh, honey. 'I don't want to be me through all eternity.' " Patty Jane mimicked her. "At least you could play the harp with the rest of the angels . . . or sing in the Celestial Choir. What would *I* do forever?"

Harriet's laugh was faint, but it was a laugh. "Maybe the angels need perms."

Patty Jane lifted the back of Harriet's nightgown up and down, hoping to fan it dry. "But Harriet, if God can invent such a thing as eternity, then God could also invent a way that we could handle it."

"You think?"

Patty Jane held Harriet, finally feeling her body relax. "Hey, I'm your big sister. I *know*."

Nora was spending as little time as possible at the House of Curl. She volunteered to take other girls' shifts at the drive-in, claiming she was saving up to buy a car.

"You can't get your license until you're sixteen," Patty Jane reminded her.

"It's not that far away," said Nora.

She came home smelling of hamburgers and fried onions and the heavy perfume the drive-in owner used to deodorize her kitchen. She took many long baths, working her way steadily through boxes of Ione's tropical bath salts. When she wasn't working or with her friends downtown or at Lake Nokomis, Nora was in the basement with Thor and his birdhouses, helping him paint a roof or glue a shutter or file a rectangular front door for a blue jay. She felt Thor's basement workshop was the only tranquil place in the house, and her father the only person she didn't need to pretend to.

"It's not fair," said Nora, "Why does it have to be Harriet? What did she ever do to anyone?"

Thor looked up from his lathe and shrugged. His eyes were kind but his brows lifted in puzzlement.

"She smokes — big deal — lots of people smoke."

"I don't smoke," said Thor in his slow, child's voice.

Nora wandered the path between two rows of birdhouses.

"Hey, Dad, this one's new, isn't it?" She walked around a robin highrise, running her fingers along its edge. "Cool." She let herself be distracted for a moment, counting the balconies.

Then suddenly she stumbled over to the work bench and cried in the arms of the simple man who was her father.

As the days passed, each day taking more of her strength, Harriet thought about Nora.

"I can't stand her avoiding me," she told Reese.

"She's scared, Harriet."

"Duh," she said, using one of Nora's more obnoxious expressions. "But that doesn't make me miss her any less."

Reese turned onto the Parkway. The windshield wipers waved rain away in wide arcs. Harriet had wanted to take a drive in the rain, nothing relaxed her more than sitting close to Reese, the radio tuned to a station that played 40s music, feeling snug as the car plowed through puddles.

"I'm getting hungry," said Reese as Glenn Miller led his orchestra through "Moonlight Serenade."

"You're always hungry," said Harriet, touching the crook of his arm. "Got anything in mind?"

Reese turned left. "How about a nice juicy StratoBurger?"

The Airloha was perched on the edge of 34th Avenue, across the street from the Page airport hangar. A wooden palm tree rose behind the squat white building, its paint chipped and sun blistered. A half-dozen speakers lined the circular driveway. Reese put the car into idle and he and Harriet read the ten-foot-high wooden menu.

"Welcome to the Airloha!" its heading said, "home of the Famous StratoBurger Basket!"

Reese rolled down his window halfway. Cool air breezed into the front seat.

"May I take your order, please?" came Nora's voice, scratchy over the speaker.

"Your mother says you don't like to take orders," said Reese.

Over the top of the car ahead, Harriet and Reese saw Nora look out at them.

"Uncle Reese . . . Aunt Harriet . . . hi!"

"When do you get off, honey?" said Harriet.

Nora studied her wrist. "Ummm . . . soon, I guess."

"Good, we'll wait for you."

"But . . ."

Reese leaned toward the speaker. "And we'll take two Strato-Burgers, everything on both — and a Coke and . . ." he looked to Harriet.

"And a Hot 'N Tot," said Harriet.

Nora slid their food out on a tray. "I'll be off in ten minutes," she said, avoiding eye contact.

They parked on the other side of the lot, near some benches and birch trees. Harriet's eyes watered from the Hot 'N Tot — a Coke heavily laced with cinnamon syrup — and she pretended to enjoy her hamburger and fries.

Reese had quit smoking completely a week after Harriet's diagnosis, and Harriet now found herself unable to smoke in front of him or anyone else without feeling their scorn and her guilt. She longed for a cigarette at this moment.

"Whew, it's wet out there," said Nora, climbing into the back seat. Rain matted her white shirt to her shoulders. "So how come you guys are here?"

"That's my get-to-the-point Nora," thought Harriet. She rested her arm along the edge of the seat.

"I've missed you."

"Missed me?" Nora flushed and looked out the window. "Why would you miss me? I haven't gone anywhere."

Harriet said, "Nora, I know you've been avoiding me and I don't blame you — it's a pretty scary thing. But I need some time with you before — "

"Before you die?" Nora's words hung in the air like a storm cloud.

"Reese, are you done, honey? Because if you are, why don't we just drive for a while."

They drove past Bossen Field, its baseball diamonds studded with puddles, and around to the far south side of Lake Nokomis. No one spoke.

Finally, Harriet took a deep breath. "You're mad at me, aren't you?" She could feel Nora's shrug in the back seat. "I didn't choose to get sick, you know."

"They found out a long time ago smoking was bad for you!" Nora's voice was loud.

"A couple years ago. I already had a nice habit going by then." Harriet twirled her wedding band. "Besides, nobody knows for sure if cigarettes caused my cancer."

There was an edge to Nora's reply. "Right. Maybe it was the matches."

Reese drove along the slick lake road. Harriet looked at him, needing some direction, but his fingers fanned out from the steering wheel, a gesture that meant, "Don't ask me."

She tried a different tack. "If I don't beat this, I want you to have my harp." She glanced at the rearview mirror to see Nora's reaction. "The trumpet too, of course; it's so much better than the old school one of yours — but take the harp, too. I think you'd be a quick study."

Nora sat motionless, but her teeth were furiously chewing the insides of her mouth.

"And take care of Patty Jane, because I know it's going to be rough on her — "

"Aunt Harriet!" Nora lunged forward, clinging to the thin arm Harriet had draped across the seat. "Don't die. Please don't die!"

Reese pulled over into the parking lot by the Big Beach, which claimed its title by comparison with the narrow blade of sand called the Little Beach.

"Come up here, girl," said Harriet, and Nora climbed into the front seat, between Reese and Harriet. They put their arms around her.

"Why you?" asked Nora. "Why you and not someone like Crabby Bultram or my homeroom teacher?"

"Nora," said Harriet, half-smiling, "haven't you learned yet how hard life is to figure out?"

"Why does something terrible happen to everyone I love?"

"Something terrible usually happens to everyone," said Harriet.

Nora snorted. "But *comparatively*," she drew out all the syllables of the word, "comparatively speaking, our family seems to have had a lot more terrible things than most people."

Harriet sat back, genuinely surprised. "No, we haven't."

"Oh sure!" said Nora, her voice weighted with sarcasm. "Grandma's husband gets hit by a streetcar, my other grandparents were drunks — no offense. Mom's husband disappears and when he comes back he's lost about two thirds of his brain. Avel — no offense again, Reese — Avel was killed and you turn into an alcoholic. I'm not a jerk, Aunt Harriet. I know our history."

Reese nodded. "When she puts it that way, Harriet, I see her point."

"As your mom would say, Nora, 'What am I doing here in Camp Shitamuck?'" Harriet took Nora's hand. "Hey, Reese, look at this. Nora's growing her nails." She lifted Nora's hand and, clutching it in her own, set it on her lap. "Nora, I'm going to say something that might sound sappy but listen anyway. There might be a test. Our family has had some rough times — some real rough times, but you know what? The good times would still tip the scale. And do you know why? Good old love, sweet love."

There was a long silence in the car and when Nora spoke, her voice quavered. "You're right. It did sound pretty sappy."

"Sappiness has its place," said Harriet. "Now, I could go on and on about how at times I look at you, thrilled by your loveliness. Bowled over because you turned out like . . . like a Beethoven symphony — full of challenges and unexpected turns. I could go on about my husband" — she tilted her head and looked at Reese — "and how the safest place in the world for me is in his arms — I could go on and on but I can't because it's hard to catch my breath." She gasped for air and smiled. "And like Patty Jane says, when I get to Heaven, I won't need harp lessons."

Nora flared her nostrils, tasting the salt of mucus and tears. "You'll be giving them, Aunt Harriet."

T wenty-Eight

PATTY JANE WOKE EARLY on the morning of August 20. "Clyde," she whispered.

"Harriet?"

Patty Jane nodded. "I'm going to make some coffee."

"Do you want me to come?"

She pulled the tangled sheet over his dark body. "Give me a couple minutes, okay?"

When she turned on the kitchen light, she saw that dawn was blanketed by a dark, rainy sky. "Good," she thought, "Harriet will like that." Earlier in the week, when the sun had broken through the storm and shone mightily, Harriet had said it depressed her to be sick in cheerful weather.

For a month Reese had carried Harriet up and down the stairs. Her intent had been to spend time in the House of Curl, but she would get only as far as the living room and say to Reese, "That couch over there looks pretty good."

She had refused to go to a hospital. Her last goals were to keep tubes and medication out of her body, to see Evelyn

Bright's student quartet compete in the State Fair Talent Contest, and to die at home.

"Well, she's going to get most of her wishes," thought Patty Jane as she poured a cup of coffee. The Fair wouldn't open for two days.

The first swallow burned in her chest. The grass is getting long, she thought. She'd have to get Nora to mow it. She remembered Harriet and herself as kids, taking turns pushing a rusty handmower across a yard full of crabgrass and dandelions. Sometimes, to move the mower, it would take both of them, shoulder to shoulder pushing the wooden handle, their faces red and sweaty.

They would sing rounds or make up jokes or play "When I." One would begin a sentence, "When I grow up . . ." and the other would finish it, ". . . I'll make sure there are no ration coupons and people can eat as much butter as they like."

One afternoon they pushed the mower around in muggy heat as their mother slept it off on the porch couch. Patty Jane had said loudly, sarcastically, "When I'm a mother . . ." and Harriet had stopped pushing on the mower, brushing her hair behind her ear. She stared at Anna, whose leg dangled off the couch, and said, ". . . I hope things'll be easier for me."

Patty Jane had sneered, wanting to wave away Harriet's answer like a mosquito, but she was immediately humbled by the look in Harriet's eyes. It was love, tender and fragile as the morning glories that climbed the trellis under which Anna snored. When their mother awoke that afternoon, both girls served her lunch — a grilled cheese sandwich and a pear — and Anna had laughed and said she felt like a guest at the Ritz.

"Patty Jane?"

"Ione. I'm up earlier than you for a change."

"It's Harriet, isn't it."

Patty Jane sat down heavily. "You feel it, too?"

Ione rubbed her arm. "Something. Something about today just . . . feels different."

By the time the second pot of coffee was perking, Clyde Chuka and Nora joined them.

"I think I'll call in sick today," said Nora.

"I think that's a good idea," said Patty Jane. She watched as her daughter stirred milk into her coffee. When had she passed the Kool Aid stage?

Ione sliced some cinnamon bread and Clyde Chuka toasted it and they sat eating until Reese came down. He was dressed in his police uniform.

"Reese . . . you're going to work today?" asked Patty Jane.

Reese smoothed his thinning red hair with a big hand. "Harriet wanted me to dress like I was the first day we met." His voice cracked. "The day I carried her to a motel and she couldn't tell if I was a cop or a mailman." He stood tall, holding the back of the kitchen chair where Harriet usually sat. "She's pretty . . . ah . . . she thinks it's time to say good-bye."

"Already?" said Patty Jane.

They followed Reese upstairs in a silent line. "Everyone's here, Harriet," said Reese, touching her cheek.

Propped up against the pillows, Harriet opened her eyes. She wore a white cotton nightgown and her bald head and neck seemed to emerge as if from a cloud.

"Hi," she whispered. Although her face was as pale as the bed linen, Clyde Chuka thought to himself, "Death is going to celebrate today, taking someone as beautiful as Harriet."

The open window let in gusts of cool, damp air.

"It smells so fresh in here." Harriet tried to breathe deeply. "I never thought I'd have a deathbed scene," she said slowly. "I always thought I'd go quick — hit by lightning or something. But this is good. I'm glad you're all here."

She shut her eyes again and Patty Jane put her hand on an arm that felt as thin and inert as a rubber tube.

"I love you all," said Harriet and her announcement made them all surge forward. "But that's not telling you anything you don't already know."

Harriet felt uncomfortably hot, a heat from within that was moving through each vein, each nerve.

"My Ione," Harriet whispered, reaching for the older woman's cheek, "the traveling gourmet."

Nora took Ione's place, and Harriet felt the girl's tears.

"Practice your trumpet, Wonder Girl." she said. "I'll be listening."

Patty Jane crawled under the covers with Harriet. "Does this mean you're not going to the Fair?" asked Patty Jane.

"Sorry," whispered Harriet. "Eat a corn dog for me, okay?"

Patty Jane nodded. "Way to go. Way to go and leave me."

"You're not mad?"

"Yes. But I'll get over it."

"You think Mom and Dad will be there?"

"Yeah," said Patty Jane. "They'll be there. The best of them will be there."

"Did I ever say thank you?"

Patty Jane swallowed hard. "For what, honey?"

"For walking me to school. For painting my toenails when I had the mumps."

Harriet felt weariness tugging at her like a tide, and she shut her eyes and let go. She heard "The Harmonious Blacksmith" and she was drawn into a sunny fall day. She was standing on a street corner, wearing a dress that exposed a smidgen more of her leg than was proper. A car came slowly toward her, a beautiful oyster-colored Packard whose chrome threw off light like a prism. When it stopped in front of her, she got in the passenger door. "Avel!" she said aloud to the small man behind the wheel.

Harriet opened her eyes. "Don't worry, Reese. We'll save a place in the front seat for you."

Her eyes fluttered shut as Avel floored the accelerator.

Rain still drummed on the roof and Patty Jane thought how musical it sounded. She looked at the bedroom ceiling, half expecting a heavenly choir, but it offered nothing more than its textured plaster and frosted glass fixture.

There was a new presence in the room, however. At the door stood Thor, bleary-eyed, his blond hair mussed, holding Harriet's music box. He stood straight as a sentry, until the music trickled its last notes and then he said simply, "Goodbye, Harriet."

Patty Jane wore three-inch heels to Harriet's service.

"Those are some gams," said Clyde Chuka, whistling low.

"Well, I feel stupid as hell," she said, tottering up a grassy bank to the gravesite, "but Harriet always loved it when I got out of my Hush Puppies."

The sun shone and a breeze hinting of the September close by pulled at the women's hair and the men's pant legs. Patty Jane heard the words of the preacher but what spoke loudest to her was the great gathering of people who stood in a crescent around her.

"Look at this, Harriet," whispered Patty Jane. She spoke not to the pale grey coffin covered in sprays of waxy flowers, but to the green and blue of land and sky, to the trees still heavy with leaves and birds, to the clouds unraveling like bolts of cotton.

Later, she walked to the cars with the House of Curl group.

"I learned The Jerk during one of her Dance Breaks," said Alva Bundt to Evelyn Bright.

"She reminded me of Cyd Charisse," said Inky Kolstat. "Except with long hair."

"She and I communed once with my brother's spirit," said Esme Ames.

Crabby Bultram wiped her wide face with a hanky. "She said I had rhythm!"

Patty Jane only half-listened to these reminiscences; she was concentrating on later plans. She was going to walk around the neighborhood and see and hear Harriet in its landmarks, in the streets and houses and lakes they had known together. She planned to walk a long time and then with gratitude and sorrow, go home. Home was always the place she went to when she had to start over.

Epilogue

Epilogue

Reese said grief is a lot like sobriety; you get through it one day at a time. We were all worried, especially my mother, that Reese would find solace in his old friend the bottle, but he stayed on the wagon as if he were bolted in. For years, he came to supper every Wednesday and Friday night. We were able to laugh about it later but at the time it was unnerving: Reese was stoic and calm during the main course, but invariably sobbing by dessert. This was a pattern that lasted for months until once, as Ione was serving a banana cream pie topped with meringue a quarter foot high, he rubbed his hands together and said, "Umm. Maybe I'll skip the tears tonight."

Now it's twenty-five years after Aunt Harriet's death. There is nothing left of the pale and stooped black-haired man Temple Curry brought home to us. My father, Thor Rolvaag, covers a daily walking route that takes him around Lake Nokomis twice. He knows his phone number by heart in case he gets lost. He has great energy and it's a thing to admire even as it's sad to think how little of it moves to his brain.

Still, there are surprises. We discovered that like the

Norwegian language, Thor had full recall of hockey. The first time he got back on the ice — after a few falls and sprawls — he was zipping across the rink like an NHL all-star. I could see that he was a natural, and I stood with my mom on the warming house ramp and watched him.

"In his youth," said Patty Jane, so quietly I could barely hear her, "your dad was a prince."

He skates in pick-up games down at Lake Hiawatha and sometimes I'll go watch him sneak the puck away from men decades younger, stickhandling it before he slips it past a surprised goalie.

Emotionally, Thor has crossed a new frontier. He loves to hug and tells me at least twice a day, "Nora, jeg elsker deg." He laughs when I tell him that I love him back. His brain may be short circuited, but his heart isn't.

My father has also prospered. His career took off when Paige Larkin, attending one of Inky's Hollywood seminars in the basement, saw Thor's workshop and bought five birdhouses for her backyard. She brought in some of her wealthy friends who used words like "quaint" and "American Folk Art" while loading birdhouses into their station wagons. All the houses he made as the prisoner of Temple Curry — six hundred thirty was my mother's count — have long since been sold and he works diligently filling new orders. We display the birdhouses in the part of the house that used to be the beauty parlor, now that it's been stripped of hairdryers and vanities and shampoo sinks.

When I was a junior at Stanford, my mother decided to quit working in the beauty salon. She was busy running House of Curl classes and traveling with Clyde Chuka, but her big reason for hanging up her curling iron was Harry. It was just too hard, she said, to try to unroll a perm and breastfeed at the same time.

Harry's my little brother — named after our aunt — and the biggest surprise of Patty Jane's forty-second year.

"I thought I was having hot flashes," she told me over the phone. "Ha! Some hot flash."

"Tell her the due date," said Clyde Chuka in the background.

Patty Jane giggled. "He's due on our anniversary."

"But Mom," I said, cupping the receiver so the freshman at the phone next to mine wouldn't hear, "you and Clyde Chuka aren't even married."

Patty Jane laughed again. "I mean the anniversary of the first time we had sex."

"Mom!"

The freshman looked up and I smiled wanly.

Home for summer vacation, I fell in love with Harry Freeman Chuka as soon as I held his chubby body, as soon as he grabbed my earring and tried to rid me of my ear lobe. Harry brought a wonderful sense of renewal into the house. His birth seemed to not only close our chapter of grief, but to open a brand-new book. Clyde Chuka was pixilated with fatherhood. My mother's figure got a little rounder, a walking advertisement for motherhood.

Merry Chuka hand-sewed and beaded a deerskin tunic for her grandson but she never saw him wear it, dying months before his birth.

Ione assumed the role of Harry's grandparent. Once when she was bragging about him, Alva Bundt pointed out that, technically speaking, she wasn't really Harry's grandmother at all, and Ione, clipping her words like a gardener at a rosebush, replied, "You can go snuff your technicalities."

My Grandma replaced her green suitcases for sturdier luggage long ago; she and the Fitches spend the winter months traveling. These past years, they have settled in a trailer park in Arizona, but they have been to Scandinavia, taken a Caribbean cruise, and toured Asia.

Everyone in my family has passports that have their share of stamps. Clyde Chuka's work is now a hot commodity in the art world. He's had shows in New York and London and Tokyo. He's been invited to Moscow for his third exhibition there. His piece, *Revenge of Mount Rushmore* (an eight-foot replica of the Statue of Liberty whose torso has been carved into a totem pole), toured the republics, attracting great crowds. In Russian newspapers, he is referred to as "Mr. America."

Still, when he is home, he likes to spend a few hours each week giving manicures. He says he gets his best ideas holding women's hands. His manicurist's table, as well as all the other beauty equipment that was once in our home shop, has been transferred to the basement of the house we inherited from Temple Curry. What was once Thor Rolvaag's prison is now "Patty Jane's House of Curl, Etc."

Where once Thor's birdhouses collected dust, vanities and swivel chairs dominate. Bev Beal and Dixie Anderson reign as senior stylists. Dixie has recruited her daughter Karen (the one I once locked in the fruit cellar) into the beauty business. Classes occupy the main floor of the House of Curl, Etc., ranging from Phrenology to Understanding NASDAQ.

And here I am, practicing law out of Temple Curry's old dentist's office. I've lined the walls with books and taken out all of her equipment except the porcelain spittoon, which I encourage clients to use.

I remember hours of childhood spent eavesdropping on my mother's and Aunt Harriet's late-night conversations. I remember sitting happily under a turned-off hair dryer in the House of Curl, privy to the discussion of women. I have always liked to listen to people's stories; now, as an attorney, I get a chance to change endings of the stories they tell me.

The legal affairs of Clyde Chuka and Patty Jane are filed in a maple cabinet Thor made. Clyde Chuka is building an art school/workplace on the Prairie Island Indian Reservation, so

I've been busy working on its start-up details. He pays me a ridiculously high hourly rate with the simple rationale: "Why not?" I also draw up paperwork for Patty Jane, whose business cards read "Consultant for Change." She gives lectures to women's groups throughout the Twin Cities.

After law school, I started practicing in L.A. Maybe it was listening to Inky Kolstat's Hollywood stories for so long. The motions for the return of the prodigal daughter began when my mother and I were having lunch in an outdoor health food restaurant on Sunset Boulevard.

"Don't tell me you eat like this all the time," said Patty Jane. With the tines of her fork, she flipped little curds of tofu around her plate.

"Mother, man — and woman — does not live by cheeseburgers alone."

"Why should they," asked Patty Jane, "when there's pecan pie and fudge and popcorn?"

She, Clyde Chuka and Harry were in Los Angeles for a Director's Guild dinner honoring Geoff Bell, the man whose short films shocked a House of Curl audience years ago. Since his "smut fest" screening, he has gone on to become a well-known director of action/adventure films.

"Geoff says you could be in the movies like *that*," said Patty Jane, snapping her fingers.

"Well, what about you?" I snapped my fingers back to her. "I'd think he'd have a part for a blowsy-looking woman in her mid-fifties."

"Blowsy?" This tickled my mother, who still wore a size eight. She chuckled as she flagged down a waiter. "Say," she asked him, "what have you got in the way of dessert?"

"Today's special is our very popular whole-wheat sugar-free carrot cake."

"I said dessert," said my mother, "not punishment."

After settling for a café mocha, Patty Jane stared at me, her head cocked. "Nora, what would you think about coming home and working for me?"

Droplets of peppermint tea sputtered from my mouth. "Ma, come on. There's got to be someone in Minneapolis who can tie bandanas and serve coffee."

Patty Jane smiled, unclipping an earring. She rubbed her earlobe. "I could use your legal services. You wouldn't believe the inquiries I've been getting from people interested in the kind of open school we run. I've been invited to talk to some people in Chicago about it."

"You have?"

"Yes. A lot of things are happening, Nora. And Clyde Chuka could use a good lawyer, too — you're so good at drawing up contracts and he's getting commissions galore."

"Ma," I said, "I've got a life here."

Patty Jane reached for my hand across the table. "I know you do, Wonder Girl. All I'm asking is for you to move it east a couple states."

I thought I had RSVPed a "No" to my mother's impractical invitation, but as the months passed in an undistinguishable blur of warm days and smoggy starless nights, I found myself doodling pictures of snowmen and pine trees on my legal pads. In Griffith Park, I searched for autumnal-looking leaves I could press. I began to go to an indoor ice rink, showing off as only a person who grew up on skates can.

By all accounts, I was living the good life. Out of law school, I had been hired by Jasperson, Oakes and Belzer, one of Los Angeles's most prestigious law firms.

But entertainment law grew less appealing each year. I represented television stars who craved publicity but sued publications who didn't understand their kind of publicity. I negotiated a settlement for an actor whose costar had punched him in the nose for butting in front of him in the lunch-wagon line, and I prepared the case for a dog trainer who claimed his poodle, star of the hit series, *Bones and Caviar*, hadn't gotten a fair share of merchandising profits.

The first winter back in Minnesota when the wind chill factor was twenty below zero for two weeks, I questioned my rationality, but once I remembered to dress in layers, I rediscovered winter fun. Skating on a frozen lake or tobogganing down Cedar Hill and then sitting in front of a fire with a mug of hot chocolate. The experience may not be Nirvana, but it's at least related.

I thought I'd move into an apartment building overlooking the river or one of the lakes, but after three years, I'm still in my childhood bedroom. I've taken down the rock posters and the contact paper daisy off the ceiling, but even with new sand-colored paint and levelor blinds, it is still my old room. My best friend, Lori Mellstrom (married and divorced, working mother of two), loves to flop on my bed; she says it reminds her of the days when the future seemed an exotic destination.

We're all still here at the original House of Curl and until I start a family of my own, I'm happy to be with this one. I like to share a pot of coffee and conversations with Patty Jane in the kitchen. I like to sit at the computer as my whiz-kid brother explains his intricate programs. I like to see Clyde Chuka come home from his studio, covered in plaster dust or paint.

And I like to be near Thor. I like to sit in his workshop, helping him paint birdhouse mailboxes or flagpoles. I like to walk with him to the Falls pavilion in the summer to get a cherry snowcone. Sometimes he sings a Norwegian song Ione taught him long ago.

My career isn't stellar and I don't make as much money as I did representing wronged movie stars. I get work from Ione's Naomi Circle sisters and I just filed a radio-jingle plagiarism suit on behalf of Evelyn Bright. I work *pro bono* for WAMM —

Women Against Military Madness — and I'm happy to report that my class, "Know Your Rights," is a pretty big draw at the House of Curl, Etc. Looking over last week's attendance records, I saw that only two classes attracted more than mine: Paige Larkin's "Human Sexuality" and Inky Kolstat's "The Death of Marilyn Monroe: FBI, CIA or KGB?"

It looked for a time as if Patty Jane were on the verge of a dynamic career, lecturing on the beauty salon as classroom. But, after spending a weekend in St. Louis, she decided that a traveling businesswoman was not something she wanted to be.

"Life's enough work as it is," she told me after I scolded her for declining an invitation to speak in New York. "What's so hot about being alone in airports and hotels and conference rooms with bad lighting? If someone wants to pay to hear me talk — when they could have heard it for free and gotten their hair shampooed to boot — hell, they can pay me. But they better be within driving distance of my home because my rule is to be in bed with Clyde Chuka every night, listening to Harry singing to the radio in the next room."

There are big doings, as Ione says, going on tonight. It's the thirty-fifth anniversary of the House of Curl's opening. Evelyn Bright has gotten a combo together — Harry will be on the drums and I will even sit in on a few songs. I still play the trumpet; it's a good antidote to law. Evelyn's brought in a keyboardist who teaches at the McKern School of Music, trying to do some matchmaking. She's had a minor success; the teacher and I are having coffee next week.

Thor built a raised platform where the honorees (the original House of Curl staff — Patty Jane, Ione, Dixie, Millie and Clyde Chuka) will sit. Harriet's harp will be positioned to the left of Patty Jane.

There will be testimonials and roasts, and then I will present my mother with a thirty-five-block quilt designed and sewn by

House of Curl denizens. The quality of craftsman[ship]
from "blue ribbon" to "thank you for entering." Ione's b[u]
course, is beautiful; it's a picture of a lantern on a table. A
triangle of yellow gauze that looks like light spilling against th[e]
table, upon close examination, is a heart. Tiny even stitches
outline each piece of fabric and at the bottom, in embroidered
calligraphy, it says, "Oh, the light we've shared."

Inky Kolstat made a silhouette of Patty Jane, but it looks
more like a profile of a water buffalo; and Dixie, who doesn't
sew at all, simply wrote in magic marker: "Thank you for being
my friend."

After the quilt presentation, I'm supposed to give my speech.
My speech. The essays I wrote for my bar exams were easier. I
have sat for hours, in my reclining dentist's chair, wondering
what I should say. I was going to talk about coming home to
Mama instead of a husband. But I ditched that idea because my
mother is sensitive about my lack of what she calls a "pilot
light." More than anything, she wants me to have a Clyde
Chuka or an Avel/Reese in my life.

"Mom," I said, "it's sexist to think a woman can't find fulfill-
ment without a man."

"Oh, Nora," said Patty Jane, "I just don't want you to be alone
in the big storms."

I thought about posing the question, "Who is Patty Jane?"
and listing some of the quirkier facts of my mother's bio: she's
only had one cavity in her life despite that sweet tooth; she
started shooting baskets when Clyde Chuka put up a hoop for
Harry and has won every game of Horse since; and she's never
divorced my father.

"It seemed it would have cut more ties than it needed to," she
explained. "Clyde Chuka and I don't need to be married in the
paper sense, so what's the big diff?"

Ione smiled. "She wants me to stay her official mother-in-
law."

h two legal pads but when I read through adn't said much. In the end, it was a letter e, that gave me the anchor for my words. ng for years on what she calls a "spiritual Fitches ran into her in Calcutta ten years latest letter that I will use in the speech to my mother tonight.

I will walk to the speaker's podium in the olive silk dress Ione has made for the occasion. I will hear the murmur of approval and probably Inky Kolstat saying, as she always does, "She sure had the wrong career in Hollywood!" I will look out at the faces of women who were lucky enough to find a place where they could not only talk, but be heard. I will look at the faces of those I love and think of the postscript written by Avel Ames' octogenarian sister from a tin-roofed shack in Nepal.

"Sometimes I laugh at myself, a silly old woman who seeks God in powerful incantations. But that laughter is bittersweet because I realize that if I had loved the people who tried to love me, I might have found God closer to home."

Then I will turn toward Aunt Harriet's harp, to Patty Jane, and I will recite the last part of that P.S.: "Gadzooks! What a big chunk of God is to be found by looking into the face of someone you love!"

I know we will cry then, but laughter will sneak in, just as tears have been known to crash our fun. And when we finish blowing our noses, we'll put on the coffee pot and have dessert, as we always do.

(Jennifer Borg)

About the Author

Lorna Landvik was raised in Minneapolis, attended the University of Minnesota, then moved to San Francisco and then to Los Angeles. There she worked as a stand-up comic at the Comedy Store and Comedy Improv and scouted bands for Atlantic Records. She has published fiction and nonfiction in magazines and newspapers. She now lives with her husband and two daughters in Minneapolis, where she works as an actress and writer.